TRIAL BY FIRE

What Reviewers Say About Carsen Taite's Work

Her Consigliere

"With this sexy lesbian romance take on the mobster genre, Taite brings savvy, confidence, and glamour to the forefront without leaning into violence. ...Taite's protagonists ooze competence and boldness, with strong female secondary characters. ...This is sure to please."—*Publishers Weekly*

"Such a great story! I was literally living for every moment in this. Both Royal and Siobhan were strong, powerful, authoritative women who I was absolutely captivated by. Their worlds and jobs were both edgy and exciting, providing that thrill of a little bit of danger along the way, especially when their emotions and affections for one another started to show. I adored them both and genuinely couldn't get enough of them. They were amazing!"—*LESBIreviewed*

Spirit of the Law

"I'm a big Taite fan, especially of her romantic intrigue books that are about some aspect of the law. She is one of the best writers out there when it comes to writing about courts and lawyers, so when you see a new book of hers in that category, you know you are in for a treat. And a treat is the perfect way to describe what reading Taite's books feel like, like eating a bowl of your favorite Ben and Jerry's ice cream."—*Lezreviewbooks*

Best Practice

"I had fun reading this story and watching the final law partner find her true love. If you like a delightful, romantic age-gap tale involving lawyers, you will like *Best Practice*. In fact, I believe you will like all three books in the Legal Affairs series."—*Rainbow Reflections*

Drawn

"This book held my attention from start to finish. I'm a huge Taite fan and I love it when she writes lesbian crime romance books. Because Taite knows so much about the law, it gives her books an authentic feel that I love. …Ms. Taite builds the relationship between the main characters with a strong bond and excellent chemistry. Both characters are opposites in many ways but their attraction is undeniable and sizzling."—*LezReviewBooks.com*

Still Not Over You

"*Still Not Over You* is a wonderful second-chance romance anthology that makes you believe in love again. And you would certainly be missing out if you have not read *My Forever Girl* because it truly is everything."—*SymRoute*

Out of Practice

"Taite combines legal and relationship drama to create this realistic and deeply enjoyable lesbian romance. …The reliably engaging Taite neatly balances romance and red-hot passion with a plausible legal story line, well-drawn characters, and pitch-perfect pacing that culminates in the requisite heartfelt happily-ever-after."
—*Publishers Weekly*

"*Out of Practice* is a perfect beach read because it's sexy and breezy. There's something effortless about Abby and Roxanne's relationship, even with its occasional challenges, and I loved that I never doubted that they were right for each other."—*Lesbian Review*

Leading the Witness

"…a very enjoyable lesbian crime investigation drama book with a romance on the side. 4.5 stars."—*LezReviewBooks.com*

"…this might be one of Taite's best books. The plotting is solid, the pacing is tight. …*Leading the Witness* is a thrill ride and it's well worth picking up."—*Lesbian Review*

Practice Makes Perfect

"Absolutely brilliant! …I was hooked reading this story. It was intense, thrilling in that way legal matters get to the nitty gritty and instill tension between parties, fast paced, and laced with angst. …Very slow burn romance, which not only excites me but makes me get so lost in the story."—*LESBIreviewed*

Pursuit of Happiness

"This was a quick, fun and sexy read. …It was enjoyable to read about a political landscape filled with out-and-proud LGBTQIA+ folks winning elections."—Katie Pierce, Librarian

"An out presidential candidate (Meredith Mitchell) who is not afraid to follow her heart during campaigning. That is truly utopia. A public defender (Stevie Palmer) who is leery about getting involved with the would-be president. The two women are very interesting characters. The author does an excellent job of keeping their jobs in focus while creating a wonderful romance around the campaign and intense media focus. …Taite has written a book that draws you in. It had us hooked from the first paragraph to the last."—*Best Lesfic Reviews*

Love's Verdict

"Carsen Taite excels at writing legal thrillers with lesbian main characters using her experience as a criminal defense attorney."
—*Lez Review Books*

Outside the Law

"[A] fabulous closing to the Lone Star Law Series. ...Tanner and Sydney's journey back to each other is sweet, sexy and sure to keep you entertained."—*Romantic Reader Blog*

"This is by far the best book of the series and Ms. Taite has saved the best for last. Each book features a romance and the main characters, Tanner Cohen and Sydney Braswell are well rounded, lovable and their chemistry is sizzling. ...The book found the perfect balance between romance and thriller with a surprising twist at the end. Very entertaining read. Overall, a very good end of this series. Recommended for both romance and thriller fans. 4.5 stars."
—*Lez Review Books*

A More Perfect Union

"[*A More Perfect Union*] is a fabulously written tightly woven political/military intrigue with a large helping of romance. I enjoyed every minute and was on the edge of my seat the whole time. This one is a great read! Carsen Taite never disappoints!"—*Romantic Reader Blog*

"Readers looking for a mix of intrigue and romance set against a political backdrop will want to pick up Taite's latest novel."
—*RT Book Review*

Sidebar

"As always a well written novel from Carsen Taite. The two main characters are well developed, likeable, and have sizzling chemistry."—Melina Bickard, Librarian, Waterloo Library (UK)

"Sidebar is a love story with a refreshing twist. It's a mystery and a bit of a thriller, with an ethical dilemma and some subterfuge thrown in for good measure. The combination gives us a fast-paced read, which includes courtroom and personal drama, an appealing love story, and a more than satisfying ending."—*Lambda Literary Review*

Letter of the Law

"If you like romantic suspense novels, stories that involve the law, or anything to do with ranching, you're not going to want to miss this one."—*Lesbian Review*

Without Justice

"This is a great read, fast paced, interesting and takes a slightly different tack from the normal crime/courtroom drama. …I really enjoyed immersing myself in this rapid fire adventure. Suspend your disbelief, take the plunge, it's definitely worth the effort."
—*Lesbian Reading Room*

"Carsen Taite tells a great story. She is consistent in giving her readers a good if not great legal drama with characters who are insightful, well thought out and have good chemistry. You know when you pick up one of her books you are getting your money's worth time and time again. Consistency with a great legal drama is all but guaranteed."—*Romantic Reader Blog*

Above the Law

"…readers who enjoyed the first installment will find this a worthy second act."—*Publishers Weekly*

Reasonable Doubt

"I liked everything. The story is perfectly paced and plotted, and the characters had me rooting for them. It has a damn good first kiss too."—*Lesbian Review*

Lay Down the Law

"This book is AMAZING!!! The setting, the scenery, the people, the plot, wow. ...I loved Peyton's tough-on-the-outside, crime fighting, intensely protective of those who are hers, badass self."—*Prism Book Alliance*

"I've enjoyed all of Carsen Taite's previous novels and this one was no different. The main characters were well-developed and intriguing, the supporting characters came across as very 'real' and the storyline was really gripping. The twists and turns had me so hooked I finished the book in one sitting."—Melina Bickard, Librarian, Waterloo Library (London)

Courtship

"Taite (*Switchblade*) keeps the stakes high as two beautiful and brilliant women fueled by professional ambitions face daunting emotional choices. ...As backroom politics, secrets, betrayals, and threats race to be resolved without political damage to the president, the cat-and-mouse relationship game between Addison and Julia has the reader rooting for them. Taite prolongs the fever-pitch tension to the final pages. This pleasant read with intelligent heroines, snappy dialogue, and political suspense will satisfy Taite's devoted fans and new readers alike."—*Publishers Weekly*

Switchblade

"I enjoyed the book and it was a fun read—mystery, action, humour, and a bit of romance. Who could ask for more? If you've read and enjoyed Taite's legal novels, you'll like this. If you've read and enjoyed the two other books in this series, this one will definitely satisfy your Luca fix and I highly recommend picking it up. Highly recommended."—*C-Spot Reviews*

Battle Axe

"This second book is satisfying, substantial, and slick. Plus, it has heart and love coupled with Luca's array of weapons and a bad-ass verbal repertoire. ...I cannot imagine anyone not having a great time riding shotgun through all of Luca's escapades. I recommend hopping on Luca's band wagon and having a blast."—*Rainbow Book Reviews*

Beyond Innocence

"As you would expect, sparks and legal writs fly. What I liked about this book were the shades of grey (no, not the smutty Shades of Grey)—both in the relationship as well as the cases." —*C-spot Reviews*

Nothing but the Truth

"Taite has written an excellent courtroom drama with two interesting women leading the cast of characters. Taite herself is a practicing defense attorney, and her courtroom scenes are clearly based on real knowledge. This should be another winner for Taite." —*Lambda Literary*

It Should be a Crime—*Lammy Finalist*

"Taite, a criminal defense attorney herself, has given her readers a behind the scenes look at what goes on during the days before a trial. Her descriptions of lawyer/client talks, investigations, police procedures, etc. are fascinating. Taite keeps the action moving, her characters clear, and never allows her story to get bogged down in paperwork. *It Should be a Crime* has a fast-moving plot and some extraordinarily hot sex."—*Just About Write*

By the Author

TRIAL BY FIRE

by

Carsen Taite

2021

TRIAL BY FIRE

© 2021 By Carsen Taite. All Rights Reserved.

ISBN 13: 978-1-63555-860-9

This Trade Paperback Original Is Published By
Bold Strokes Books, Inc.
P.O. Box 249
Valley Falls, NY 12185

First Edition: October 2021

Credits

Editor: Cindy Cresap
Production Design: Susan Ramundo
Cover Design By Tammy Seidick

Acknowledgments

The release of this book will mark eight years since I practiced law on a regular basis. I'm thankful for my career as a writer, but I have to admit I miss the hustle and bustle of the various county and federal courthouses in North Texas, particularly the Dallas County criminal courthouse. The Courting Danger romances are my way of revisiting the comradery, zealous advocacy, and familial feel in the large, diverse, and tight-knit community of adversaries struggling to find justice in a world that is often unjust.

Thanks, as always, to Rad and Sandy and the entire crew at Bold Strokes Books for giving my stories a home at the best publishing house in the biz. Huge thanks to my smart, funny, and very patient editor, Cindy Cresap. Tammy, thank you for the striking covers for this entire series.

Georgia—our daily check-ins keep me on track and motivated and I'm ever thankful for our friendship. Hugs to Ruth, Melissa, Kris, Elle, and Ali—I miss you all and can't wait until we can all gather in person again. Paula—our frequent talks keep me sane, and I owe you many dark beers and dirty martinis for brainstorming plot points and patiently reading every draft. You are the best friend a person could have and I'm grateful we're pals.

Thanks to my wife, Lainey, for always believing in my dreams even when they involve sacrificing our time together. I couldn't live this dream without you, and I wouldn't want to.

And to you, dear reader, thank you for taking a chance on my work and coming back for more. Every time you purchase one of my stories, you give me the gift of allowing me to make a living doing what I love. Thanks for taking this journey with me.

Dedication

To Lainey. I'd walk through fire with you, for you.

Chapter One

Tell me you'll be done at that hellhole in time to meet me for dinner. I made a reservation for seven thirty at that new place, across from the firm."

Wren stared at her cell phone. Was it too much to wish the woman she was dating wouldn't disparage her new job every time she opened her mouth? "It's not a hellhole," she whispered, avoiding the glare of the security guard who was barking orders at the man in line ahead of her. "And yes, seven thirty should work. I'll meet you there."

"Put everything in the bin. Even your phone." The guard was barking at her now.

"Diane, I've got to go. See you tonight." She clicked off the line before Diane could offer up further commentary, stowed her phone in her purse, and set it and her briefcase in one of the bins. The bin had barely made it through the scanner when the guard started issuing orders again.

"Step to the side."

Wren did as he commanded, but when he started plowing through the contents of her briefcase like it held a cache of weapons, she pulled out her bar card and held it out to him. "I work here. My name's Wren Bishop. This is my first day."

"Uh-huh," he grunted, pointing at her purse. "Are there any other electronic devices in here?"

He held out his gloved hand and she reluctantly handed him her purse, making a mental note to consolidate what she carried into the courthouse in the future, but hoping every day wouldn't require a forty-five-minute wait simply to get to her desk. When he was finally done, she asked him where she could find Judge Larabee's courtroom and received another grunt.

The elevator was crammed beyond capacity, and Wren spoke a silent prayer it wouldn't plummet to the ground and that the kid in the stroller next to her wouldn't get any of his Flamin' Hot Cheetos or cherry Dr Pepper on her new suit. When she emerged on the seventh floor, she found the courtroom she was looking for and eased open the door, dismayed to find the proceedings well under way.

"Shante Carver deserves justice."

The woman who spoke stood in the well of the courtroom and pointed at an easel holding a framed portrait of a beautiful Black woman dressed in an evening gown, and the content of her speech signaled she was the prosecutor in this case, Lennox Roy. Wren had followed the news all week, but nothing she'd read in the paper or heard on the radio had prepared her for Lennox's commanding trial presence. Lennox was tall, and fierce, and striking, and Wren stood in place, riveted by her presence. She had no idea how much time had passed when Lennox paused for the briefest of moments to stare in her direction. Feeling the burn of her glare, Wren winced slightly, and she carefully shut the door behind her, as quietly as possible. She settled into a seat in the last row of the gallery next to her new boss, Ford Rupley, and turned her focus back to the action.

"Whatever circumstances led her to be sleeping on the street, huddled in nothing more than a scrap of an old blanket, she was no different than the rest of us. Seeking warmth, seeking food, seeking shelter—she was a human being," Lennox said, while standing directly in front of the jury box. "A daughter, a sister, a friend. You've heard testimony about the circumstances that led up to her living on the street that cold January night, and while you may think you cannot imagine a life where you are not free to be your authentic self without fear of personal harm, I'm here to tell you that today it is your duty to do so. Whatever life experiences you have embraced, endured, or overcome, today you must put aside any personal bias and focus solely on the facts. Today, you do not sit in judgment of Shante. Your judgment shall be focused on the man who took her life."

She turned and pointed at the defendant, keeping her arm extended until every eye in the jury box was focused on him. "Randall Thomas kicked and beat and robbed Shante, a woman with only one or two possessions of value, not because she had done anything to him and not because he needed to steal in order to feed his family, but because he objected to who she was, that she was different than him. His defense consists of a single feeble excuse. He was offended to learn Shante's biology didn't match his expectations, and his attorney's insistence on using her dead name during the course of this entire trial is offensive and vile."

"Objection, Your Honor." The defense attorney, who Wren recognized as Gloria Leland, sprang to her feet. "The prosecutor knows better than to smear my client in this manner."

Her indignation was jarring, considering her client was universally viewed as a scumbag, but Wren wasn't entirely surprised. Gloria was a partner at Dunley Thornton, the firm she'd been working for the past four years, and Gloria had a reputation as an overly zealous advocate whose commanding presence brought in lots of money for the firm, which was why they kept her around even though the firm's focus was primarily civil litigation.

Lennox rolled her eyes in response to Gloria's outburst. "Withdrawn. I'm sure the jury is smart enough to sort out the truth." Without missing a beat, she picked up a stack of papers and waved them in the air. "The elements of the crime of murder are simple. A person commits the offense of murder if he intentionally or knowingly causes the death of an individual. Intentionally means he meant to cause the result. Knowingly means he was aware his actions were reasonably certain to cause death." She tossed the papers to the table and jabbed them forcefully with her finger. "Nothing. Absolutely nothing in the law says you can kill someone if you don't like them, if they are different than you, if you are…" She paused, and her next words were dripping with disdain. "If you are offended by the very existence of another person."

She strode back toward the jury box. "If you buy Ms. Leland's argument, be prepared for the consequences. Skin too dark? Woman versus man? From the wrong neighborhood? Nothing is off limits once you decide lives are only valued in terms of your own experience, your own perspective. That may be true in other parts of the world, but this is America, a land full of people with varied backgrounds and ancestry, and it's not okay to kill people because they are different. Send Mr. Thomas and anyone who would commit a similar atrocity a message—you are not above the law and your actions have consequences, not just for your victims, but for you. The State of Texas respectfully asks you to return a verdict of guilty."

Lennox strode back to counsel table, and a moment later, everyone in the courtroom rose when the judge dismissed the jury to begin their deliberations.

"That guy is toast," Ford said.

Wren looked over at the defendant huddled with his attorney. If the chief public defender in the county thought you were toast, you didn't have a chance despite having a high-powered attorney. Gloria commanded big bucks for her services. She usually represented rich corporations charged with white-collar crimes, and Wren wondered how much money Thomas's family had had to come up with to convince Gloria to get her hands dirty here at the state criminal courthouse on a murder case. "True. Gloria's good, but not that good."

"Do you think they paid her usual fee or is there some other connection that convinced her to take on this case?" Ford asked.

"Publicity. Most of Gloria's work is behind the scenes bullshit—deals worked out with the SEC and other agencies behind closed doors, so she doesn't get enough credit in the court of public opinion. Word is she plans to launch a run for senate next year, and taking this case will boost her name recognition."

"Wow. That's insane."

"Yes, but also brilliant. You know what they say—all publicity is good publicity," Wren replied.

"I guess you're right," Ford said. "Whether she wins or loses, she'll walk out of here a free woman with her name in the headlines.

A few weeks from now, no one will remember her notoriety was all about being on the wrong side of a hate crime."

Wren flinched at the sharp disdain that punctuated Ford's words. "Tell me how you really feel."

Ford laughed. "Look, I get it. The guy deserves a defense, but this one was pretty vile."

"Well, Professor, doesn't everyone deserve a strong defense? What would you have done if the PD's office had been appointed to represent him?"

"I would've tried the case if I couldn't work out a deal, but I damn sure would've tried to work it out first. If Thomas gets convicted, he's going away for a long time."

Wren started to ask him how he could be so sure when Lennox Roy appeared at her side. In the well of the courthouse, she'd been a force, but up close, she was even more formidable. Sharp features, stern countenance—many people might find the first impression off-putting but Wren saw the fiery passion in her eyes and knew her rhetoric wasn't simply a show. Lennox believed in this case with all her heart, and Wren was instantly drawn to her zeal. Lennox nodded at Ford in an "I know we work on different sides, but I have respect for you" kind of way, and then gestured toward her. "This one belong to you?" she asked, her question directed at Ford.

"Yes, she does. Lennox Roy, meet Wren Bishop. Wren's on loan and she started today. I thought she'd like to see her potential future competition deliver a closing argument."

"Nice to meet you." Wren stuck out her hand, pleased when Lennox clasped it with a strong grip. Her pleasure was short-lived.

"Nice to meet you too, but here's a pro-tip. I don't know how they do things across town at the fancy civil courthouse, but here we don't burst into a courtroom in the middle of proceedings, especially not during closing arguments." She spent a moment scanning Wren from head to toe. "Think of it like the theater. You wouldn't bust into the middle of *Hamilton,* would you?"

Wren grinned like the dig didn't bother her, while she tried to summon a great *Hamilton* reference in response, but before she could come up with something, someone across the room called out Lennox's name.

"I have to go," Lennox said. "I'm sure I'll see you around."

Wren watched her stride off, simultaneously intrigued and annoyed. She was used to getting the last word, but it was clear besting Lennox Roy was going to be a battle, and she was looking forward to it.

"She's not always that abrupt," Ford said. "But she is pretty intense."

"I get it. She's still deep in trial mode. Believe it or not, I have a tendency to get a little bitchy when I'm in the middle of a case too." She let her gaze linger on Lennox a second longer before turning back to Ford. "Fierce is a good thing."

Ford's curious expression made her wonder about her own and she quickly fixed her face into what she hoped was a neutral look. She'd never had a great poker face—it was something she'd been working on, and suppressing any sign she was fascinated by Lennox Roy would be a great way to sharpen her skills.

"She'll be a completely different person when she's not in the middle of a case," Ford said. "Seriously, everyone around here, no matter what side they're on, manages to put away their differences when we're not in the thick of it. It's like a big family—you have your arguments and your differences, but at the end of the day, we're all working toward the same goal. Speaking of the end of the day, Judge Aguilar has a fundraiser tonight at Sammy's and you should go. It'll be a good opportunity for you to meet a lot of people all at once in a casual environment. We'll go straight from here. Five thirty."

Wren thought about her dinner date with Diane and considered her options. Knowing Diane, dinner would be an extended opportunity for Diane to bitch about her new gig while regaling Wren about what a great day she'd had representing clients who could afford to pay. She kind of dreaded it, but she was big on keeping her commitments, no matter how casual. On the other hand, the fundraiser would be a great opportunity to witness Ford's promise about the big courthouse family. "I can come for a little while, and then I have somewhere I need to be."

"Great. Now, let's get you settled in."

Wren followed Ford up to the ninth floor where the public defender's office was located. He led her to the back of the suite to a tiny office that was crammed with a desk, a filing cabinet, and several chairs, all in cubicle gray. She was going to have to seriously reevaluate how she'd planned to decorate the place as most of the stuff she'd planned to bring from her office at Dunley Thornton wasn't going to fit in here, but she'd figure all that out later. Today, she was excited to get started with this new chapter of her life, and furnishings were the last thing on her mind.

"I know it's smaller than you're used to," Ford said.

"It's perfect," she said, not entirely convinced, but determined to make it so.

He pointed to a stack of files on her desk. "Those are yours. Your first appearance is in the morning. Nothing too big for the first day. A couple of pleas already worked out, an examining trial, and a few brand-new appointments you'll need to visit at the jail. I don't have any trials scheduled this week, so I'll be around if you need me, but the best way to get a handle on this stuff is to plunge right in." He pointed at his ear. "Call me if you need me."

He was gone in a flash, leaving Wren to examine the scattered surface of her desk and wonder what she'd gotten herself into. She pulled the stack of files close and hoped that coming here hadn't been a huge mistake.

"Hey, Lennox, you ready to head to Sammy's?"

Lennox looked up from the police report to see Johnny Rigley, her number two, standing in the doorway to her tiny office, located steps from the courtroom. "I think I'm going to skip."

"I thought you and Judge Aguilar are good friends."

"We are, which is why she won't care if I don't show up to schmooze with everyone else. I'll write the campaign a check—mission accomplished."

"Don't you want to celebrate the win today?"

She laughed. "It's like you don't even know me."

"I do know you, and that's why I know you could come out and have a drink with the rest of us and still be totally prepared for the punishment. Hell, you could stay out all night and still be going strong in the morning. Randall's going away for a long time—it's a slam dunk."

Lennox grimaced. The jury had come back after lunch with a guilty verdict—in record time—but the case wasn't over since they'd start the punishment phase of the trial in the morning. She'd prepared her arguments days ago, operating under the assumption the jury would convict, but trial prep wasn't the only reason she didn't want to go out with courthouse people tonight. "I don't celebrate wins, and nothing is a 'slam dunk.' It's okay to be glad a bad guy is going away, but that doesn't change the fact a woman suffered unspeakable cruelty and lost her life."

"Don't celebrate that part. Come lift a beer to the fact that Randall Thomas didn't get away with murder. That a jury put aside their own prejudice and listened to the facts. Come on, Lennox. Have one beer at a fundraiser for your best friend."

Johnny made a good case. Of course, he was likely motivated to since he knew if she didn't go out, he shouldn't either since he'd be expected to be right back at her side when court resumed in the morning. She knew the prosecutors under her command thought she was a hard-ass, and most of the time she didn't mind, but maybe Johnny was right. One beer wouldn't hurt, plus she'd be showing support for Nina. She could pop in, grab a drink, make the rounds, and be home by eight. She tucked the police report in her briefcase. "One beer. For each of us. I need you to be sharp in the morning too."

"Deal." He jangled a set of keys. "You want a ride?"

"Thanks, but I'll meet you there." The last thing she wanted to do was get stuck downtown when she had an early morning in court looming. She waited until he left her office to finish packing up the rest of the materials she wanted to review in preparation for sentencing. When she left her office, she found the courthouse deserted—not unusual for a Thursday afternoon, but she was grateful to be able to walk down the hall without running into someone she knew who'd ask her how the case was going or congratulate her on the guilty verdict.

When she reached Sammy's, she realized why the courthouse was empty. Throngs of attorneys and judges milled around, drinking beer and eating barbecue from the local favorite spot. A table by the door featured a sign-up list for Judge Aguilar's campaign newsletter and a large glass bowl already over half full of envelopes stuffed with cash or checks, campaign contributions for the upcoming election. Lennox dropped her check for a hundred dollars into the mix. It was the same amount she donated to every judge she supported for reelection; an attempt to be as fair as possible and not appear as though she was trying to curry special favors, but when it came to her best friend, Nina Aguilar, she would always go the extra mile by volunteering her time and lending an ear when Nina needed to dish about the campaign.

"You came," Johnny said as he walked toward her.

"I said I would," she said, bristling a little at his surprise.

"I figured you might ditch at the last minute."

She pointed at the beer in his hand. "I could definitely use one of those."

"They've got a bunch iced down on the patio. That's where Judge Aguilar is hanging out."

"Cool. I'll catch up with you later."

Lennox shouldered her way through the crowd. She kept her head down, but her attempt to make it to Nina without being noticed failed, and she reluctantly accepted many congratulations for the guilty verdict along the way. When she finally reached the patio, Nina was flanked by attorneys from one of the top criminal defense firms in town, two of their friends—Morgan Bradley and her wife, Parker Casey. The three of them waved her over, and Nina reached down into the iced cooler and handed her a beer.

"You made it."

"Why does everyone seem surprised I would turn down a free beer?"

Nina laughed. "Because it's not actually free since you've volunteered plenty of hours on the campaign and I'm sure you put an envelope in the jar."

Lennox tipped the bottle at her. "Good point."

"And we figured you'd be deep in prep for sentencing tomorrow," Parker said, immediately raising her hands. "Not to imply you don't deserve a little celebration for the guilty verdict today."

"Johnny shamed me into coming out, and I figured one beer wouldn't hurt. Besides, I've been prepping for punishment for a while now, and I didn't hear anything during the trial that changed my strategy. The defendant is an asshole, and he needs to go away for a long time. Period. End of story."

"Sounds solid," Morgan said. "Glad I'm not on the other side."

"It's simple and to the point." Lennox grinned. "But if you and Parker here were on the other side, I'd probably be home right now, making triple sure I was ready. I'm hoping the quick verdict is a sign the jury is fed up with this guy and his jackass attorney, but I'm not going to take any chances." She leaned in close to them. "Thanks for being the only people in this room not to prematurely congratulate me on the win."

"You act like we don't know you," Nina said. "Your superstition is warranted. It was a polarizing case, but it's probably a good sign the jury came back so quickly. My bet is you'll get whatever punishment you ask for, but I promise that's the last I'll say on the subject lest I jinx your mojo. Besides," she said, pointing at her chest. "Tonight is all about me."

"Yet, here you stand, hanging out with your friends instead of working the room." Lennox gestured to the crowd around them.

"I promise I've made the rounds twice already. There's only so many ways I can ask for money and votes. How many more months of this do we have to endure?" Nina grabbed her arm. "Hold up, there's a potential voter I haven't met. She's at ten o'clock. Be subtle."

In a distinctly unsubtle display, Lennox, Parker, and Morgan turned in the direction Nina referenced, and Lennox spotted the new public defender she'd met after closing arguments this morning. "Oh, her. She started at the PD's office today."

"You say that like it's a bad thing," Nina said. "She's pretty cute."

"She looks familiar," Morgan said. "I've seen her somewhere, but it wasn't at the courthouse."

"Not a face you'd soon forget," Nina added.

Lennox looked back at the new PD, fishing her memory for the unusual name. Wren, that was it. She was undeniably beautiful, fresh faced, pretty, and blond. "She looks...green. And she seems perky. I wonder where she came from. I meant to ask Ford, but he's been stuck talking to old Judge Henry since he got here. I doubt the poor guy even had a chance to grab a beer."

The trio nodded at her. "He's the worst," Parker said. "When I was a cop, a million years ago, he actually told the jury to pay close attention to the lady with the badge." She shuddered. "He called me 'Lady'—can you believe that?"

"Yep. He was a prosecutor's dream," Lennox said. "But totally not worth having a guy who smokes in his office and insists on having only female prosecutors assigned to his court. Why does he keep getting reelected?"

"Exactly why I need to stay in office," Nina said. "To balance out guys like Henry." She held up her right hand. "I hereby swear I will never smoke in my office or get handsy with the prosecutors in my court. Oh, and I'll be unbiased too. There, that should do it. Can we go now?"

They all laughed. "If only," Lennox said. "Go, work the room. Raise another grand and I'll buy you one of those free beers over there. In the meantime, I'm going to grab some barbecue before it's all gone. Morgan, Parker, you with me?"

"You're on your own," Morgan said. "We've got dinner plans. We're just here to show our support."

"More for me." Lennox strode to the cafeteria style line and picked up a tray. She rarely ate anything other than a Power Bar when she was in trial, and she couldn't remember if she'd had even that today. The smell of mesquite wood filled her nostrils and her stomach grumbled in response.

"What's good here?"

She turned at the sound of the voice, startled to see the new PD, Wren, standing directly behind her, craning her neck to see the food. "You must be from out of town."

"Come again?"

"Well, it appears you haven't been to Sammy's before which either means you're from out of town or you're not a real criminal lawyer." She smiled after delivering the assessment to prove she wasn't a complete asshole.

Wren laughed, seemingly unaffected by the slight. "Maybe I just don't eat out much. "

"Hmm." Lennox scanned Wren's well-manicured nails, her perfectly coiffed hair, and her designer suit, and visualized her doing business with high-powered clients at a fancy restaurant. "I'm guessing that's not true."

"Really? What else have you deduced simply by looking at me?"

She hesitated for a moment. She made a living out of studying people but discerning details and sharing them out loud were two different things. Then again, Wren had asked. "You've been in private practice for a few years, dabbled in some criminal law once, and now you're out to save the world with your newfound prowess. Am I close?"

"Barely warm. Private practice yes. All the rest is dubious."

"That's vague."

"It's only fair since you didn't answer the question."

Lennox squinted at her, trying to remember if there'd even been a question.

Wren pointed at the food. "I asked what's good to eat here?"

Lennox grinned. "Everything. And I mean everything. The meat, the sides, and if you have room for it, the dessert. Although if you have room for dessert, you're doing it wrong. I'm having the brisket, the squash casserole, and fried okra."

"Duly noted, and that all sounds amazing." Wren peered at the display of food. "I'm mostly in need of a snack. I have dinner plans later."

"Slider."

"Pardon?"

Lennox pointed to the rolls. "Small piece of brisket tucked inside a roll with some sauce and you're all set with the best snack ever."

Wren nodded. "Let me guess, in addition to your skills as a prosecutor, you're also a food aficionado?"

There was a slight lilt in Wren's voice. Was she flirting? Lennox immediately adjusted her tone from friendly to gruff to ward off any chance of reciprocation. "Aficionado sounds too fancy. I have a deep appreciation for barbecue and a few other very traditional foods, but I'm no foodie."

"You say that like it's a bad thing."

Lennox gave her order to Jake, the man working the counter. "Foodie sounds pretentious, and it makes me think of tiny little foods arranged on a plate to look like works of art instead of sustenance."

"Oh, so you don't like art?" Wren asked with an arched brow, which probably meant she was teasing, but Lennox wasn't quite ready to trust her instincts on that point with a woman she'd barely met.

"Why do I get the feeling you think I'm a neanderthal?"

"Why do I get the feeling you think I'm a food snob?" Wren pointed at the food behind the glass. She held her stomach and laughed again—a melodious and infectious refrain. "Trust me, if I didn't have plans already, I'd be scarfing all of this."

Jake handed Lennox her tray, saving her from having to come up with a quick retort. Good thing, because the day in court had robbed her of the ability to quip. But Wren's laugh was light and carefree, like she didn't have a care in the world, and for the briefest of moments, Lennox wanted to bask in Wren's glow. Could that kind of happy-go-lucky mood be contagious?

She shook her head, noting Wren's puzzled look, and sensing a series of questions wasn't far behind. All the more reason to take her food and get the hell away.

CHAPTER TWO

The first thing Wren thought when the waiter served the first course was what Lennox Bishop would think of the steak and blue cheese bruschetta with onion and roasted tomato jam. The plate was decorated with swirls of savory, decadent sauce, and she could almost hear Lennox whispering "pretentious." But surely even the surly prosecutor would be charmed by the careful attention to each amazing morsel.

"What are you thinking about?"

"What?" Wren wrenched her attention back to Diane. Her date.

"You were smiling. It's the bruschetta, isn't it? It's the best I've ever had."

Wren took the easy out. "It's divine." She lifted her wine glass. "And this is fantastic, but you're going to have to polish off the rest of the bottle on your own because I have an early hearing."

"But you just started today," Diane protested. "Shouldn't they give you some time to settle in before they throw you in the deep end?"

Wren took a minute to let Diane's question rock around in her head before responding, something she wound up doing a lot lately to keep from biting her head off at the condescending tone. They'd started officially dating a few months ago, and at first it had seemed like a perfect match. They were both in the litigation section of Dunley Thornton and had wound up working together on several major matters where they had to spend many late night hours scouring documents and preparing for hearings. It was only natural that all the together spilled over into their personal lives, and when they'd decided to make a dating relationship official it was more like a business transaction than anything else. Still, in the beginning they'd done the usual things new couples did. Stayed up all night talking and having sex without caring about showing up at the office dead-tired the next day. Surprising each other with little gifts and favors, and sexy lingerie. But the flirty fun of the new beginning had quickly faded into a dull routine where they ate out at fancy restaurants, and most of the time one or both of them were too tired to do anything after. Honestly, if they didn't work at the same firm and love great food, Wren didn't think they'd have anything in common. Now that they were no longer coworkers, she wasn't sure fancy dinners were enough of a bond to hold them together.

"It's not like I don't have any experience," Wren said, careful to keep her tone even. "I've handled criminal proceedings before, and I clerked for Judge Blair—he heard plenty of criminal cases in his court."

"But that was federal court where things are civil even when they're criminal. Dallas County is a free-for-all. Thank goodness you're only there temporarily."

Wren ignored Diane's fiftieth reference to the fact her stint at the PD's office wasn't a permanent gig. She was part of the lawyer-on-loan program Dunley Thornton had with the county. They loaned lawyers to the DA's and PD's offices on a temporary basis. The lawyers on loan got to hone their skills in a different environment that gave them a fresh perspective for their legal work, and the county benefitted from free legal work offered by some of the top attorneys in the area. "I'm sure stories of the chaos are overrated." She drank the last sip of wine in her glass. "I got to watch closing arguments in the Randall Thomas trial this morning. Gloria Leland represents the defendant."

"She's good."

"Yes, but I don't think anyone's good enough to convince a jury Thomas doesn't deserve to go to prison."

"Hmm," Diane said as she sipped her wine. "Didn't they charge that as a hate crime?"

"I think so, yes."

"Overreaching, if you ask me. Murder is murder."

"I guess it depends on your perspective. As a queer woman who could at any moment be targeted just because of who I am, I kind of like the idea of the law ensuring I have an extra layer of protection from harm."

"You really think a criminal is going to pause and think 'well, if I assault this particular person, I'm going to go away for longer, so I shouldn't do it'?" Diane asked.

"Maybe. We have similar protections in the law for police and elderly people and kids, why not queers?"

"That's what the range of punishment is for. And I hate when you use that word."

Wren sighed. They'd had this discussion before, and Diane always made it clear her sexuality didn't define her and she hated when lesbians embraced the word queer, which kind of made her want to say it even more even when it was completely out of context. "You don't have to use the term queer," she said, enjoying the grimace on Diane's face as she made a point of using the word again. "But it's how I choose to name myself." She made a show of looking over her shoulder and she lowered her voice. "Don't worry, I won't say it in front of any of the partners."

She smiled to indicate she was kidding, but Diane nodded solemnly like it was a promise she expected her to keep. "Anyway, it's not up to me, it's the law, and speaking of punishment, they start that phase in the morning. I'd like to catch a little of it before my hearing, so I should probably call it a night."

Diane took a big slug of her wine. "And here I was hoping you might come over. Tomorrow night, maybe?"

Her words slurred slightly, solidifying Wren's decision to go home alone. "Tomorrow is much more likely. I'll text you when I have a better idea of how the day is going." Instantly feeling guilty, Wren pulled out her platinum card. "Dinner's on me." Diane lamely protested, but Wren insisted. "It's the least I can do since I'm bagging on you early. You can get the next one."

The valet stand was hopping, and Diane insisted they bring Wren's car first, overemphasizing the fact she had to work. Once she was behind the wheel of her BMW M8, she let out a sigh of relief. Increasingly, dates with Diane felt like crossing a minefield full of explosive topics they didn't see eye to eye on, and it was wearing in a way that no amount of good food and wine could assuage.

When she reached her condo building, she took the elevator up to the top floor, wondering what Lennox was doing right now. Probably enjoying another plate of delicious barbecue and having a great time. Next opportunity she had to choose between staying at the party or going on a boring date, she was staying at the party.

She stowed her coat in the closet off the foyer and headed to the kitchen to make a cup of coffee. After rummaging through the cabinet for the last of her favorite blend, she made a note to up her regular online order. She'd spent plenty of late nights over the past four years at Dunley Thornton working to accumulate billable hours, but she had a feeling that was nothing compared to the workload she was about to encounter at the PD's office if the stack of files on her desk this morning was any indication. When the coffee finished brewing, she took a sip and contemplated substituting the expensive java for the coffee in the break room at the office because the stuff they made there came out of a warehouse style large bucket of barely tan grounds and wasn't fit for human consumption.

Fortified by caffeine, Wren set up her files at the large oak table in her dining room and spread out her notes for tomorrow's hearing. Xander Hernandez had been arrested for possession of marijuana after the cops pulled him over for failure to signal a turn, and the hearing tomorrow was to determine if the police had probable cause to arrest him. Even with her limited experience, she knew no one got pulled over for failing to signal a turn unless the cops figured they were also guilty of some other offense. They had asked Xander a bunch of questions before they determined that, based on his mannerisms when answering, he must be hiding something. The questioning had lasted just long enough for them to be able to call a canine unit, and true to form, the German shepherd alerted to the driver's side quarter panel of Xander's car, and a subsequent search revealed a hidden compartment with felony level amount of marijuana, which the cops rejoiced in as full support in favor of their decision to search the car in the first place.

Bootstrapping. That's what it was. They pulled him over for driving while Hispanic. She looked at the pictures included in the file. Big, flashy car with one of those nude lady cutouts hanging from the rearview mirror and an Our Lady of Guadalupe window decal, but nothing that screamed drugs on board. They hadn't turned on the in-car camera in time to catch the alleged failure to signal a lane change. Wren seriously doubted it had even happened, but a jury would have a hard time parsing the issue. They would see the big cache of pot and think, well, of course the cop was right that Xander was acting sketchy at the scene, because he was hauling a bunch of illegal drugs, and completely miss the point that cops don't have the right to search people's cars without probable cause to do so, and they couldn't hold someone at a traffic stop through bullshit efforts to stall until a dog could get there. "And don't get me started on the dogs," she muttered.

This case was a lot like ones she'd seen as a clerk for Judge Blair. Drug cases were the bread and butter of federal prosecutors and, despite Diane's implication that she lacked relevant experience, she'd been in the thick of plenty of suppression hearings on this very subject, having to research the law for the judge and often writing the opinions he would approve and sign. She spent another hour reviewing her notes and, finally satisfied she'd prepared as much as was possible, she decided to call it a night.

When she took her coffee cup back to the kitchen, she paused by the fridge, contemplating a snack. The food at dinner had been fantastic, but the portions were tiny, and she was now starving. She smiled at the thought of Lennox about to load up on a big plate of barbecue, telling her that if she made it to dessert, she was doing it wrong. She assembled the ingredients on the counter and made a half of a peanut butter and jelly sandwich and wished she'd followed Lennox's advice. If Lennox was nice to her the next time they talked, she'd tell her, but she didn't hold out much hope. People like Lennox Roy didn't warm up to other people very quickly, and Wren would probably be gone from the PD's office before she could get Lennox to crack a smile in some context other than teasing her about her lack of experience with courtroom decorum and barbeque.

❖

"Please tell me we can go now."

Lennox smiled at Nina who'd stepped away from a crowd of donors who wanted to get her to commit to supporting a new bail bond initiative. She pulled her keys out of her pocket and jangled them in the air. "Ready when you are."

"You're the bestest friend ever." Nina waved good-bye to Councilman Lionel Peters and grabbed Lennox's arm. "Car. Now. Before he follows us out of here."

Lennox led them out of the restaurant to her car which was parked in the dirt lot behind the building. Once they were settled in and headed out of the parking lot, she said, "You're a good actress. I was beginning to believe you were really into whatever story Lionel was telling you."

"Are you kidding? That guy doesn't need an audience to drone on forever, but when he has one there is no stopping him. He better have put the full dollar limit in the money jar tonight or next time I'll be ducking him the rest of the campaign."

"Speaking of next time, are you going to Morgan and Parker's cookout next weekend? I figured I could pick you up."

Nina play-punched her in the arm. "I'll be there, but I have to duck out early for another event, so you better meet me there. I know how you like to have your own set of wheels. I'd give anything to lay around all weekend and do absolutely nothing, but I have to attend every event, large or small, that has a glut of lawyers from now until the election." She leaned back in her seat and closed her eyes. "You know, if we keep showing up at these things together, people are going to start to talk, which would do wonders for my reputation considering you're a star right now, but it means you're never going to get a real date."

Lennox rolled her eyes. "Not looking for one."

"Ah, I get it. I'm your beard."

"Uh, no. You're my best friend and hanging out with you means I don't have to make small talk with a bunch of people who are showing up just to see and be seen. I hate election season."

"Me too."

"Kind of inconvenient when you're running for office."

"Tell me about it." Nina yawned. "All I want right now is a meal I can eat without having to detail my entire platform between bites. What are you hungry for?"

"Me?" Lennox shook her head. "I ate a huge plate of barbecue. I'm serving as your chauffeur only. I'll have a beer to keep you company, but the food choice is all yours."

"Burger, please. That place with the thin and crispy sweet potato fries. They have the most amazing aioli dipping sauce."

Nina's food fantasy conjured up the image of Wren, and Lennox wondered what fancy restaurant she was dining at right now. She wasn't sure why she even cared. More likely than not, Wren was on a date with someone who appreciated fancy dinners and precious food. Whatever. She'd met plenty of people like Wren over the years. They showed up to put in their time at the courthouse to add a little variety to their résumé and then went back to doing meaningless work for gobs of money in the big law machine. She gave the perky blonde two months tops before she was worn out from the pace and pressure of working in the trenches. Maybe not even that long.

Village Burger Bar in uptown was only moments away from Sammy's, but Lennox had to circle the block three times before she found a parking space. "You better really love these fries," she said after they ordered at the counter and found an open booth.

"And you better have meant it when you said you didn't want any, because I'm not sharing. And quit being grouchy. You're supposed to be in a good mood after your big win. No matter what the jury decides in punishment, you got a conviction, and considering who you were up against, I expected you to be a hell of a lot happier about it."

Nina was right. She should be happy, ecstatic even. She'd beaten Gloria Leland—a formidable foe. And her ex.

"I can't believe you ever dated her."

"That makes two of us." Not a day passed Lennox didn't think about what a big mistake that had been. Four years out and she still didn't understand how she'd mistaken Gloria for someone she could love.

"I'm so glad you crushed her in court."

Nina's fierce loyalty was oddly soothing, and she managed a smile. "It was a pretty great feeling."

"Maybe when you're done with punishment, you'll get some closure."

Lennox wanted to say there'd probably never be any closure where Gloria was concerned, but she knew Nina was trying to make her feel better. "Maybe."

"Then you can find a new girlfriend and stop having one-night stands with court coordinators and investigators."

No point denying it. Sex-only dates were all she was interested in, and the word girlfriend made her shudder. "Not interested."

"What about that new PD? She's cute. Didn't you say she's perky? You could use a little perky in your life."

"Not interested. Don't need any perk. Besides, she works for the *PD's office*, remember?"

Nina cocked her head to the side. "Right. I'm the one who said that."

"Public *defender*." Lennox drew out the last word, hoping Nina would catch on soon.

"What is wrong with you?" Nina squinted. "Oh wait, I get it. You think you can't go out with her because she's a defense attorney?"

Lennox threw her fist in the air. "Bingo. I was beginning to think you had one too many beers while you were glad-handing back at Sammy's."

"Rein it in, Roy. I heard the words, but they didn't compute. You didn't stop dating Gloria because she's a defense attorney. You stopped dating her because she was a shitty person. Big difference. Look at Morgan and Parker—they've defended some pretty crappy people over the years."

"But Parker was a cop." Lennox could hear how hollow her protest sounded, but she wasn't willing to cede the argument. She cast about for a more rational response. "And Morgan, well, she's probably the best criminal defense attorney I've ever met." She sighed. "I guess I just proved your point."

"You're really smart tonight."

A twenty-something appeared at their booth holding a tray with Nina's food. He set a platter down in front of her, and Lennox breathed in the scent of the sweet potato fries and immediately flashed to the look on Wren's face when she'd mentioned sliders. She might not be a foodie, but she knew good fries when she smelled them. She plucked a few from Nina's plate and ducked the hand that smacked hers away. Any hope the action would distract Nina from the conversation was dashed when Nina pulled her plate out of reach and jumped right back into it.

"Being single for so long has made you surly."

"Said the serial monogamist."

"At least I can commit."

"Over and over again. How's that working out for you?" Lennox regretted the words immediately. She was being defensive, and the look on Nina's face told her she'd pushed too hard. "I'm sorry. You're a brave soul. Braver than I could ever hope to be, putting yourself out there even when it doesn't work. You should never settle for less than you deserve."

Nina reached across the table and grabbed her hand. "And never should you, Roy. Never should you." A moment of not at all awkward silence passed, and then Nina released her hand and pushed the platter between them. "Help me eat these fries before I change my mind."

Lennox reached for the fries, not because she wanted them anymore, but because the action of reaching for a fry, placing it in her mouth, and slowly chewing gave her time to contemplate Nina's words. Was she surly? Yeah, probably a little anyway. She wasn't sure surly was something being in love was supposed to cure, but if it was, then she was content to remain surly and single for a very long time.

CHAPTER THREE

Monday morning, Wren parked her car in the courthouse garage and walked past the long line on the front steps of the courthouse to the security entrance around the side that led into the basement. The line there was a quarter the size of the one out front and the guards were less inclined to act like everyone was carrying a secret stash of weapons, probably because they knew most of the people in this line were courthouse personnel or defense attorneys showing up for hearings and the like. Whatever the reason, she was glad Ford had told her about the entrance because it shaved a good forty-five minutes off her morning trek to the office.

Once in the building, she took the escalator as far up as it would go and then located the stairwell to make the rest of her climb, remembering Ford's words about how the elevators, when they were working, were overcrowded Petri dishes to be avoided at all costs.

When she finally reached the ninth floor, she took a moment on the landing to try to catch her breath. With three trips to the gym a week, she wouldn't have described herself as out of shape, but she clearly needed to up her cardio game if she was going to continue to use the stairs in this building. Finally satisfied she would make the final few yards without losing consciousness, she started toward the door only to find it opening toward her. Three women walked into the stairwell, the redhead in front pulling up short with a gasp when she spotted Wren standing in front of her.

"Sorry," she said. "I didn't see you there."

Wren smiled. "No worries. I'm not sure there's much left of me after making the climb." She took a gamble and stuck out her hand. "Wren Bishop. I just started with the PD's office."

"Oh, you're the one," the woman said. "I'm Jill, and this is Susan and Donna. We work in the PD's office too."

Wren took note that Jill didn't volunteer last names or job titles or any sort of welcome. "That's why you all look familiar."

The three of them murmured something that could be interpreted as acknowledgement, but Wren read it as "We were having a nice conversation until we bumped into you. Now move along so we can continue." She got it. Offices, private sector and government, were all subject to the whim of personality, and newcomers didn't always fit nicely in the mix. "Well, I better get going. I've got an examining trial scheduled this morning."

Jill raised her eyebrows. "You know those are a waste of time, right?"

"Totally," the one Wren thought was Susan added. "Wait a week or so and you can look at the police report when the case hits grand jury."

Wren couldn't tell if they were making fun of her or offering concerned advice. Either way it was an opportunity to make conversation with peers—something she sorely missed since she'd left the law firm. "Maybe, but I figure if I go to the examining trial, I'll have a better opportunity to assess the officer as a witness." She grinned. "Maybe even score a few points on cross that we can use at trial."

Their expressions were identical—a mix of pity and the kind of curiosity commanded by the most freakish of beasts. Finally, Jill spoke, but her comments were directed to her pals, not Wren. "I'm thinking new girl here will change her mind the first day she shows up here and finds several dozen cases stacked on her desk. We'll see who has the luxury of requesting meaningless hearings then." Without catching her breath, she added, "Nice to meet you. See you around." She waved her hand, and Susan and Donna followed her down the stairs like they did this same routine every day of their lives.

They marched away and Wren barely resisted the urge to shout that she wasn't the one who'd requested the hearing, but she'd be damned if she didn't do a stellar job on it and every other mundane task she was handed. But she refrained, suspecting her words would be completely disregarded, especially if they knew she was only handling leftover cases.

She paused at the reception desk to ask if Ford was in, but Sally, the haggard receptionist, told her he was in a hearing. She pushed through the doors to the suite of offices and navigated her way through the maze of hallways to the tiny office assigned to her, checking the name plates on the doors along the way for the names of the women she'd encountered in the stairwell. Jill Bennet was the only one she saw, and her office was four down from her. She made a mental note to ask Ford about her since she seemed like the kind of person she should either get to know very well or avoid—maybe both.

The stack of files on her desk had grown over the weekend and she found a Post-it on top with a scrawled message. *Happy Monday! Here's a few more. Let me know if you have questions.—Ford*

Heavy workloads were the norm at the firm, but she'd had interns and secretaries to help with the administrative tasks. She had a feeling that Sally's main function was to transfer calls and hand out more work, not help with it. And that was fine. She'd known coming in things were going to be vastly different here and she was prepared to deal with the extra work in exchange for doing something more fulfilling than helping rich people get richer. She pulled out her phone to plug the new deadlines into her scheduling app, when a text popped up from one of her friends at Dunley Thornton, Emma Reed.

How's your quest to save the world going?

She smiled as she imagined Emma's half-teasing, half-earnest tone. *Getting there. Miss our lunches.*

Maybe you can sneak away on a slow day. Although I'm sure you've already made plenty of new friends.

Wren paused, her thumbs hovering over her phone. She didn't want to whine about the mean girl encounter in the stairwell. Not in a text anyway. She checked her calendar. Diane was out of town on a deposition for a few days. *Meet me after work at Sue's and I'll tell you all about it? Bring Katie.*

Katie's got plans with her maid of honor—something about wedding dresses and I've been told I can't go because it's bad luck. Sue's sounds great. Text me when you're ready to head that way.

Perfect.

The prospect of having a drink and debrief with a good friend at the end of the day made everything else seem doable. She logged in all the new files, set them aside, and focused on the one that was set for this morning, Jared Allen. He'd initially been charged with arson, but that was likely to be upgraded to murder because the investigators had found a dead body in the house, believed to be his wife. The DA's office would likely take their time deciding on the final charge since they had enough to hold him in jail simply based on the arrest for arson. She'd made notes based on the information on the file, but there wasn't a lot to go on since the contents consisted of a copy of the arrest warrant without the underlying affidavit detailing the facts in the police investigation that led the judge to issue the warrant in the first place. She'd attempted to see him at the jail on Friday, but his wing had been in lockdown because of a disciplinary issue. The visit might not have been fruitful anyway since her predecessor attempted to see him the week before and he'd refused the visit, stating he was hiring a lawyer and wouldn't need a public defender. Apparently, his situation had changed, and he was the PD's client now. Hopefully, she'd have a moment to talk to him before the examining trial started, but otherwise, she'd learn more about the state's case on the fly during the hearing which was exactly why her predecessor had requested the examining trial in the first place.

After a glance at her watch, she packed up the file and headed back downstairs to the magistrate's court on the sixth floor, relieved to be alone for the trip back down the stairwell. She used the few moments of solitude to gather her thoughts and review what Ford had told her about examining trials in general. The defendant wouldn't testify, so it was a perfect opportunity to gather information, risk free. The duty prosecutor would call the lead detective on the case to testify and ask them enough questions to establish probable cause—enough evidence to support that the law had been broken and chances were good the defendant had been doing the breaking.

There was a hearing in session when she arrived. She stood at the back of the room for a moment. Ford had told her Jared would've been brought over from the jail, but the only person she spotted dressed in prison garb was the woman whose case was currently being heard. She zeroed in on the bailiff and caught his eye. He waved her over to a desk situated near the currently empty jury box and in front of a door on the side of the room. "You're new," he whispered.

"That obvious?" She gave him what she hoped was a winning smile. "I'm Wren Bishop. Just started at the PD's office. I'm looking for Jared Allen. He's on the docket this morning."

He consulted the clipboard on his desk and then jerked his chin at the door behind the desk. "He's in the holdover. You want to see him now?"

"That would be great."

He opened the door and motioned for her to follow him. Inside the tiny room she spotted a counter and long plexiglass window with two cutouts. Another attorney was at one of the windows, engaged in fairly loud conversation with an inmate, and several other inmates, dressed in jailhouse orange, were milling around behind the glass. They all stopped and looked at her expectantly while the bailiff hollered for Jared to step up to the window closest to her. The bailiff nodded to her as he left the room, and the attorney standing a few feet away resumed his bellowing. There wasn't going to be any privacy here.

She smiled at Jared. "My name is Wren Bishop, and the court has assigned me to represent you."

"There was another lady."

She decided to take the statement as a question in an attempt to engage. "There was, but she no longer works for the public defender's office."

"And you do?"

"I do."

"You dress a lot nicer than the rest of them."

Wren looked down at her suit. It was a simple, classic black Armani she'd purchased on a trip to Paris last year and definitely one of her favorites. Probably a bit overkill for everyday at the office, but the sleek lines made her feel confident, and on this day in this place where not much was recognizable, she wanted all the support she could get. She shrugged. "I'm a clothes horse, what can I say?"

"My dad always said you can judge a person by the shoes they wear. Not that they have to be expensive, but they should be good quality and well kept." He pointed downward. "Those are both. Right?"

Wren was surprised at his focus on her clothes, but if the guy wanted to talk clothes and it got him to open up, she'd go with it. She leaned in close and whispered. "My mother always said that at least once in a woman's life, she should buy a pair of shoes that equaled her rent." She pointed at her Jimmy Choo's. "I followed her advice."

"You're a free world lawyer?"

She stared at him for a moment while she processed the unfamiliar term, but quickly figured out what he meant. "No, I'm not in private practice. I work for the PD's office. Are you planning to hire your own lawyer?"

"I was, but apparently everything I owned burned up in that fire and now that the police are pinning it on me, I can't even collect insurance. I'm stuck with whoever I get." He looked her up and down again. "I guess it could be worse."

It was vaguely unsettling to be appraised this way, but Wren got it. At her last firm, lawyers put on a show to woo new clients—fancy offices, lavish spreads, and other shows of wealth combined to showcase they were successful in all their endeavors and demonstrate that if a client chose to hire them, they could be successful too. And the matters there were mostly about contracts and money. Why should it be any different when a person's liberty was on the line?

"I'm sorry to hear that, but I'm here to help. Today's hearing is an examining trial. You won't have much to do but listen and I'll be doing the same. It's our chance to get a look at the police report and size up the lead investigator before the case goes to the grand jury. And it may give us information we can use to ask for a reduced bond." She pulled out a pad and a pen. "Were you employed at the time you were arrested?"

"Yep. I own a small landscape company. Just me and a few guys—they're all contract labor, but we've been working together for years."

She glanced at the file. "Your bond is currently set at a hundred thousand. If I could get that lowered, do you have anyone who would help with the funds? You'd need at least ten percent of whatever the final amount is as a fee if they can't post the full amount."

"Maybe my parents. We aren't really close, but if you make it so I can get my kids back from my in-laws when I get out, they might chip in."

She doubted that would be happening but pressed on. "Are they local? Could you stay with them if you are released? The judge will want to know you have a place to live and be assured you will show up for court appearances."

He hung his head. "I don't know. Maybe if you talk to them."

There was more to his reticence than mere embarrassment about being arrested, but she had limited time today and this fishbowl was not the place to have a deep conversation. She wrote a quick reminder to circle back to the topic later. "Give me their number and I'll give them a call."

She'd barely finished jotting down the number when the bailiff poked his head in the door. "I've got a line waiting out here. I need to put him back up."

"Okay, thanks," she called after his back as he exited, and she waited until the door shut, mentally reviewing everything else Ford had told her. "The hearing will be quick, but when it's over, I'll talk to your parents and get back in touch with you to discuss what happens next. Hang in there. And don't talk to anyone about your case. Not your cell mates, not the guards, not the police, not another attorney. Understood?"

He narrowed his eyes for a moment and then nodded. "Understood."

Twenty minutes later, Wren pushed back the stubborn lock of hair that kept falling into her face and studied her notes while she waited for her client's case to be called. While she'd been waiting, she'd watched two other examining trials before hers and it was becoming more apparent with every moment that things were a lot more casual than they were at the federal courthouse. Counsel stayed in their seats rather than stepping up to the podium to address the court and question witnesses, and proceedings were much quicker and to the point. The examining trial was kind of like a probable cause hearing in federal court where the United States Attorney would offer up evidence to demonstrate why the defendant had been arrested and the charges were valid. But unlike in federal court where usually several witnesses were called and the hearing was conducted formally, here an on-duty prosecutor called one law enforcement officer per case, asked a bare minimum of questions, handed the police report to the defense attorney who had about three minutes to scan it and give it back before they could ask as many questions as they could before the judge cut them off. In federal court, the judge would normally take the evidence presented under advisement before issuing an opinion about whether probable cause had been established, but based on what Wren had observed so far, such findings were pro forma here with the judge barely looking up before issuing his findings and every single ruling so far had been, "I find there is probable cause to bind the defendant over for trial." The only benefit to being here this morning was an opportunity to assess the cop on the stand and get a sneak peek at the police report which the DA's office wasn't required by law to turn over until the case was indicted by the grand jury.

"Is the officer here on your next case?" the judge asked the prosecutor.

Todd, the scruffy-looking ADA who looked like he still lived in his parents' basement, glanced up from his files. "Detective Braxton is here, yes." He glanced at his watch. "But I think Roy wanted to handle this one. Mind if we take a quick break so I can go check?"

The doors at the rear of the courtroom burst open. "I'm here. Sorry for being late, Judge."

The judge who'd shown absolutely no affect up to this point, broke into a grin. "Good to see you, Lennox. Aren't you supposed to be deep in the middle of punishment right about now?"

"Already done and the jury's out again. Figured I'd handle this one myself to pass the time."

Wren's head whipped between the two of them as she tried to process exactly what was happening. She'd last seen Lennox on Friday when she'd ducked into the back of the courtroom to watch part of the punishment phase of the Thomas trial. She'd been lucky to get a seat since it appeared the entire courthouse was interested in the outcome. She hadn't been able to stay long, but she'd witnessed enough to see that Lennox was as skilled at handling witnesses on the stand as she'd been at delivering a convincing closing argument. Not surprising. Lennox has good looks and earnest indignation that gave her extra credibility with a jury—another difference from federal court where judges determined the sentence, not a jury.

"You ready?" Lennox asked her.

Wren looked into Lennox's eyes and instantly spotted her overconfidence. She was riding high from trial adrenaline and had come to spend some of it on the new PD. Fine, there wasn't anything to win here except information. "Absolutely."

"Great. Judge, the state calls Detective Rick Braxton."

A tall, thin man entered the courtroom and sat on the witness stand, looking annoyed to be dragged away from real work to be forced to outline what any fool could discern from the police report. Lennox took him quickly through a list of questions about when and where the crime had occurred and the events leading up to the arrest.

"Tell us about this case. Were you the lead detective?"

"Yes. I received a call from a patrol unit about eight p.m. on the evening of March third. Emergency dispatch had been called by the fire department who had responded to a three-alarm fire in the Lochwood subdivision in East Dallas. I drove to the scene and met with the responding officers."

"Was the fire still going at that point?"

"Smoldering. The fire department was still at the scene as were two Dallas Police Department units."

"And why were the police called in the first place?"

"The fire unit found signs of an accelerant at the scene. They contacted the fire marshall and, as part of their standard operating procedures, they also contacted local law enforcement."

"Did you concur with their findings that the fire was the result of arson?"

"Yes."

"And you subsequently arrested the defendant. Is he in the courtroom right now?"

"Yes, he's wearing an orange jumpsuit and he's seated next to defense counsel."

"The arrest warrant is attached to this copy of the police report." Lennox stood and held it up. "Do you need to review this information before answering specific questions about the arrest?"

"I do not. I vividly remember the details."

Lennox set a copy of the police report on the edge of defense counsel's table and Wren pretended like she was only mildly interested in whatever evidence she was about to elicit with her own questions. Jared tugged on the sleeve of her jacket and she glanced over at him, mouthing the word "wait." She pulled a legal pad from her briefcase and wrote at the top in big letters, *Write down whatever you want to say*, and slid the pad and the pen toward him—a method she'd employed many times during civil trials. Then she turned her attention back to the front of the courtroom and waited for Lennox's next question.

"Was there anything else significant about your findings that day?"

"The fire department found a body in the house. It was later determined to be the wife of the defendant."

"Do you happen to know where the defendant was at the time the fire occurred?"

"He arrived at the scene while the fire department was still there, but according to neighbors, he'd been at the house about an hour before the fire started."

"What led you to focus your investigation on him?"

"A number of factors. There had been several domestic violence calls to the house over the course of the last year. Neighbors told us they often heard yelling and fighting going on at the property and threats of divorce. The couple was estranged and there were issues resolving custody over the children."

"What do you mean by that?"

"The defendant's wife had threatened to leave him on several occasions and take the children with her. At some point, she'd asked him to move out."

Wren heard her client scratching pen to paper, and she glanced over to see him writing *NOT TRUE* in all caps. She nodded and returned her attention back to the front of the courtroom.

"Where were the defendant's children on the day in question?"

"With the victim's sister. She told us her sister arranged to drop them off earlier that day, hours before the fire started. She believed her sister was going to meet with the defendant to discuss the status of their marriage."

"Were you able to confirm the type of accelerant that was used in the fire?"

"Yes. It was gasoline. The defendant purchased a gas can the week before, and video footage showed him at a nearby gas station a couple of hours before the fire."

"Was this one of the other factors that caused you to focus your investigation on him?"

"Yes, it was."

Wren took a moment to study the detective. He was calm and self-assured, his commanding, but easygoing tone indicated he was used to having juries believe his every word. She listened as Lennox ran him through a quick list of some of the other factors, like the fact Jared's wife might have been having an affair and made a few notes while her client bristled with anger beside her. When it was her turn to question him, she stood and asked for permission to approach the witness stand.

The judge shot a look at Lennox, like he was asking her permission, and the move riled Wren, but she stuffed it, figuring any show of defensiveness would cause the witness to clam up. When the judge finally nodded his permission, she casually strolled up to Detective Braxton.

"Thank you for all of this information. It is definitely illuminating." She pointed at the rolled-up police report in her hand. "I have to admit I was surprised by some of the things you didn't mention."

"Oh really. Like what?"

He didn't sound defensive, but she knew he was by the way he shifted in his chair. She changed her tact to keep him off guard. "Who else investigated this case with you?"

"The patrol officers. Their names are in the report."

"Any investigators from the fire department?"

"Yes. Also in the report."

"Thank you. Which one of you took the statement from Mr. Allen?"

"I think we all spoke with him."

"All of you? Well, that makes sense I suppose since it's pretty clear to me from this report that he was cooperative from the start."

"Not how I'd characterize it."

"Interesting. He arrived on the scene as the house was blazing. He called 911. I assume you've preserved the recording of that call?"

"I believe so."

"Have you listened to it?" She was out on a limb here since she hadn't listened to it either, but it was all she had right now and she was betting no matter what, Jared would sound distressed in the moment.

"I have. It was a quick call. He hung up after he reported the fire."

"He may have done so in order to try to help since he was on the scene, correct?"

"I don't know."

"True. You don't." She crossed her arms. "There may be other things you don't know. How about we run through them?" She didn't wait for his answer, but she could feel the judge growing impatient and she needed to move this along. "You don't know if the gas that was purchased was the same gas used as an accelerant?"

"No."

"In fact," she paused, wavering about whether to ask a critical question for which she didn't already know the answer. Ultimately, she decided it was worth the risk. "Does the video from the gas station show whether he was filling a gas can or his car?"

Detective Braxton shot a look at Lennox and Wren turned to look at her as well. Lennox kept her head down, faced toward her notes, giving him no cover. Finally, he cleared his throat and said, "The camera was on the opposite side of the car from where the defendant was operating the pump."

"Meaning you have no idea?"

"It's not clear whether he was filling the car or the tank. Or both," he added with a small smirk of triumph.

Fine, let him think he won that point. Wren pressed on. "And you don't know if Mr. Allen knew his wife was having an affair?"

"Not definitively, no."

"Do you even know if the rumored affair is true?"

"It's been confirmed, but we don't have to prove a motive."

"Is that a legal conclusion, Detective? Are you a lawyer? Or did Ms. Roy give you that little tidbit?"

His grin was cocky. "You want me to answer those in order?"

She shook her head. "How about you answer this? Do you have any eyewitness testimony to support your assertion that Mr. Allen started the fire or directed anyone to start the fire that killed his wife, the mother of his children?"

"Not yet, but I'm sure Ms. Roy will fill you in when we do."

Wren glanced over at the judge who was barely paying attention. She could object to the lack of a direct answer, argue her point some more, but winning this battle wasn't worth the energy. She had what she needed. The DA's office had nothing more than circumstantial evidence so far, and the lead detective on the case had as good as promised she'd be notified if anything else developed. "No further questions."

"Nothing more from the state," Lennox called out.

Suddenly, the judge perked up. "The court finds there is sufficient evidence to hold the defendant pending further proceedings in this matter." His words were monotone, and Wren doubted he varied from the script. Ever.

She turned to her client who was already standing on order of the bailiff. "I'll come see you in the holdover."

"I can keep him down here for a bit if you want to talk to him now," the bailiff said, "But he'll miss lunch. We'll get him a baloney sandwich."

Jared groaned and Wren sighed. She'd really wanted to get his version of the facts while it was fresh in his mind, but she supposed the holdover and a hangry client wasn't the best circumstance for gathering intel. "Okay, I'll come see you at the jail sometime this week. Remember what I said. Don't talk to anyone about anything having to do with this case. Understood?"

Jared nodded and shuffled away to his hot prison meal, and she stuffed her file in her briefcase and walked out of the courtroom to find Lennox waiting in the hall.

"You want to talk?" Lennox asked.

"Sure." Wren decided this was the perfect opportunity to ask for a bond reduction, especially considering it didn't appear the state had a rock-solid case. "Let's talk about an agreed motion to reduce the bond. My client owns a business and has children, and he can't take care of either while he's locked up. Both of those things demonstrate sufficient ties to the community, so he's not a flight risk. If he has a passport, he'll surrender it. How about it?"

"No way."

"Thanks for taking time to think it over."

Lennox cocked her head. "How about this instead? We can do a pre-indictment plea. Offer me something reasonable."

"You're kidding, right?" Wren stared at her for a moment, waiting for Lennox to burst out laughing, but she was totally serious. "What do you want him to plead to, because you don't have enough evidence to make anything stick at this point."

"There's evidence she didn't die from asphyxiation."

"What?"

"The fire may have been a cover-up. The ME found evidence of trauma."

Wren resisted the urge to dig through her briefcase for a look at the file, but she knew there was nothing about that in there. "Any reason you didn't bother mentioning that?"

Lennox shrugged. "The preliminary report from the ME just came in—we're still waiting on the official version. I knew I didn't need it to get the judge to hold him over, but I'm telling you now. As a show of good faith."

"Good faith?"

"Here's how I think it went down. Lisa Allen comes home from seeing her lover and your guy confronts her. He's taken the kids out of the house, so they aren't there to hear. She doesn't deny the affair and, in a fit of rage, he strikes out at her. Maybe he meant to kill her, maybe he meant to scare her, but she's not breathing, and he panics and sets the fire to cover it up."

Wren pointed back toward the courtroom. "A minute ago, you had this whole theory about how he's purchased gas before he got to the house so he could start a fire. Which is it?"

Lennox shrugged. "I have several theories. I can certainly sell it as premeditated murder, but if you'd like to agree it was a crime of passion and clear this case off my books, that's okay too. Look, I get you need to talk to him first. You have until next week. If it's a no, I'll present the case to the grand jury and ask them to return a murder charge."

Wren stood silently as Lennox turned and walked away. She didn't know how to react, but Lennox had definitely gotten the best of her in this round, and she vowed it wouldn't happen again.

CHAPTER FOUR

L ate Monday afternoon, Lennox looked up from the file on Jared Allen to see Johnny standing in her doorway.

"Jury's back," he said.

She took a deep breath. "Be right there."

Lennox walked to the rear doors of the courtroom and peeked in, noting it was packed. Shante Carter's family and activists from the LGBTQ community made up most of the crowd, but there were also plenty of courthouse personnel and press crowded into the space. She walked back into the workroom and lifted her suit jacket off of the chair. It didn't matter how long she'd been doing this. Every single jury verdict brought with it mixed feelings of dread and excitement. She took her time putting on the jacket and checked herself in the mirror before she strode into the courtroom, careful to keep her expression neutral. As she reached the front of the room, Shante's mother reached for her hand.

"What do you think is going to happen?" she asked.

She started to reply that if she knew that, she'd be out buying lottery tickets instead of trying cases, but this wasn't the time or place for levity no matter how much she could use a dose of relief right now. Murder cases, especially ones where the victim's family was in attendance for the duration of the trial, were the most wearing. Nothing she could do would ever bring the deceased back to life, and the deep loss to this family would never truly heal, especially considering the guilt they harbored since they'd been estranged from Shante in the months before her death. They hadn't even known she was living on the street until they'd been contacted by the lead detective on the case. The best she could do was bring a sense of closure, but every year on the anniversary of the victim's birth and death, the gaping hole would be visible once again. The best they could hope for was that on every one of those occasions, the defendant would be behind bars never to be free again.

She grasped Mrs. Carter's hand in both of hers and looked her directly in the eye. "I don't know, but I trust the jury to make the right decision. Stay strong. This will be over in a few minutes," she lied, knowing it would never be over for this family.

Lennox took her seat at counsel table next to Johnny and glanced over at Randall Thomas and Gloria. Gloria was standing near the rail, talking to Randall's family. Her expression was serious, but the rest of her body was relaxed—in a way Lennox recognized—like this was a casual proceeding. Like she was a spectator rather than someone with her client's freedom at stake. Of course, she would go home at the end of the day, no matter what happened. She saw her wave at someone in the back of the room and she followed her gaze to see the new PD, Wren Bishop, standing near the doors. Wren tentatively returned Gloria's wave and then looked in her direction in time to catch her staring. Were they friends?

"Any last-minute items before we bring in the jury?" Judge Larabee asked, shaking her attention from Wren.

Lennox turned her gaze back to the front of the courtroom and stood. "I know it's been a long day, but the family is here. If victim impact statements are appropriate," she paused, acknowledging the statements would only happen if there was a one-word verdict, "we'd like to offer victim impact statements before the end of the day."

"Agreed," Larabee said without even looking at defense counsel. She'd expected as much since he wasn't one to allow any time to be wasted in his courtroom. He'd been conducting other hearings the entire time the jury had been deliberating, and she was certain he'd like to move on when the new day started tomorrow.

"Before we bring in the jury, I want to caution everyone in here that there will be no outbursts when this verdict is read." Larabee raised his gavel and pointed it at the crowd. "So much as a peep and I will have you removed from the room." He paused and frowned at the crowd and then motioned to Sam, the bailiff, who disappeared into the door in the front of the courtroom and reappeared a moment later with the twelve-person jury in tow.

"All rise," Sam shouted as he led the jurors back into the box.

Lennox watched them carefully, knowing it was impossible to accurately read their minds from body language alone. Several didn't make eye contact with her, but not a one of them even glanced at the defense counsel's table. Years of experience taught her that could mean the defendant was going away for a long time or it could mean nothing. Gloria had hired a jury consultant at the beginning of the trial, and she wondered what the consultant would say now. Still, like every single other time she'd stood in a courtroom waiting for a jury verdict, she held her breath, prayed for the best, and focused all of her attention on the forty-year-old female engineer the jurors had selected to be their foreperson.

Judge Larabee instructed everyone to take their seats and faced the jury. "Have you reached a verdict?"

The foreperson rose and held out a piece of paper. "We have, Your Honor."

In slow motion, Sam strode over to her and took the outstretched form. He walked back to the bench and handed it to the judge who took the paper from him and studied it for a moment. Lennox didn't bother trying to read his expression. Larabee had years of practicing schooling his expression, and her guesses would be futile. Instead, she glanced back at the Carter family to find they were all staring directly at her. She nodded to them and turned back to the front of the room.

"And your verdict is unanimous?" Larabee asked the jury.

They all looked at each other for a moment and the foreperson rose again. "Yes. We all agree."

Before she sat back down again, she cast a quick and subtle glance at the defendant. The movement was so quick, Lennox wondered if anyone else had seen it, but she sure had and she sensed Gloria had as well. The next words out of Larabee's mouth confirmed her suspicion.

He instructed Thomas to rise. "The jury, having found the defendant guilty of the offense of murder, hereby sentences you to forty years in prison to be served at the Texas Department of Corrections."

"Motion to continue the defendant on bail pending appeal, Your Honor," Gloria said, almost as if it were rote.

Lennox started to speak, but Larabee beat her to it. "Motion denied. Following the victim impact statements, you shall immediately be taken into custody and held until you are transferred to an appropriate facility. Ms. Roy, are you ready to proceed?"

"Yes, Judge." She turned and placed her hand on the arm of Shante's mother whose eyes were full of tears. She walked her to the podium and stepped back to listen as Mrs. Carter read the statement the family had prepared. It was the one time in the case when the victims were able to address the defendant directly in a formal setting. Sometimes these sessions went off the rails with shouting and even attempted violence, but not today. Mrs. Carter read a succinct summary of the ways Randall Thomas's violence had changed their lives forever, robbing them of the chance to ever reconnect with Shante and show her she was loved. Sobs echoed in the courtroom when Lennox escorted Mrs. Carter back to her seat while Sam led Randall Thomas away for what should be the rest of his life.

After she said her good-byes to the Carter family, she walked to the back of the courtroom and spotted Wren, standing off to the side, saying good-bye to Gloria. The smile on Wren's face, the friendly way she shook Gloria's hand inflamed her, and she changed direction and walked toward her.

Wren turned as she approached. "Hi, Lennox. Congrats on the verdict. That guy was a menace and—"

"What's up with you and Gloria Leland. Are you friends?"

Wren's smile faded into confusion. "What?" She looked toward the doors of the courtroom where Gloria had just exited. "Oh, Gloria. She's a partner at Dunley Thornton. I don't know her well, but I did some research for her when I was a second-year associate. Apparently, she remembered me, and she called me over. She knows you trounced her, by the way."

"Of course I did. She was on the wrong side of this one." She shook her head. "She's always on the wrong side."

Wren laughed. "If only it were that easy."

Lennox was startled by her response. "What's that supposed to mean?"

"I mean justice doesn't always prevail and sometimes the good guys lose. Tell me you've never lost a case you're certain you should've won."

"That's not the point." Lennox was beginning to wish she hadn't opened this door. "Yes, sometimes the right side doesn't prevail, but that doesn't mean you shouldn't be on it."

"Let me guess, you're always on the right side of justice. True?"

Having the words repeated back to her and following their natural conclusion, Lennox felt a bit foolish, but not enough to back down. "I think the state of Texas would agree."

"That's a lot of pressure. Having the entire state's fate on your shoulders seems like a pretty big burden." Wren reached out and squeezed her shoulder. "But you seem like you can handle it."

Lennox looked at Wren's hand, a little appalled at the way Wren invaded her personal space, but oddly comforted by it. What she should do was shrug away the touch, but despite her resistance, she kind of liked the way it felt. Which wasn't how she was supposed to be feeling. No, she should be indignant. She should walk away. She should be celebrating the fact this horrible, triggering case was over but not with someone who worked hard to keep people from suffering the consequences of their behavior. She stepped to the side. "I have to go."

"Okay."

Did Wren look disappointed? Why did she even care?

"Yeah, okay. Bye." Lennox strode away from her quickly, wanting to redo the last few minutes so she didn't come off like the dorkiest person that had ever lived. She walked into the DA workroom and was greeted with applause. Johnny held up a shot-sized red solo cup.

"To the best trial lawyer I know."

She took the cup from him. "I'll drink despite the exaggeration. We did it together. And it didn't hurt that we were on the right side."

He grinned. "We're always on the right side, boss. Isn't that why we work here?"

She returned his grin but rolled his words over in her head. She'd echoed the exact same bold declaration a few minutes ago to Wren, but hearing someone else say it nudged her logical mind. True, most of the cases they wound up taking to trial were rock solid, but if she had to be completely honest, she had to admit a few duds came her way. The grand jury sometimes made wrong calls, based on a lack of experience and not always having access to both sides. Most of the time she managed to plead those problem cases out, but sometimes the defendant insisted on a trial and sometimes they won. What about the times they didn't, though?

She shook her head. She couldn't think about that. If she did, she'd make herself crazy. At the end of the day, if they didn't have a crowd of eyewitnesses and a smoking gun, no one ever knew who was really guilty. She did the best job she could with what she had and hoped for an outcome that made sense.

"Want to go to the Old Monk? It's a fundraiser, but I'm sure if you show up, it'll turn into a celebration."

Lennox considered the offer. She knew everyone expected her to feel like celebrating, but the case had been draining and all she wanted was a drink and a quiet night. "I'm going to pass. I'm whipped. You go and let everyone buy you drinks."

A few minutes later, she was in her Jeep and headed home. On the way, she considered her options, pretty sure there was nothing at her apartment to drink or eat since she'd barely spent any time there over the past week. She dialed Nina. "What are you doing right now?"

"Using this call as an excuse to duck out of this fundraiser."

"Meet me at Sue's."

"I wish."

"Isn't this one of those Dem group fundraisers? There's probably so many people there, they'll barely even notice you're gone."

"Way to boost my confidence."

"You know what I mean. Say you're not feeling good. Whatever. It's not like any of them are going to run into you at Sue's."

Nina breathed a heavy sigh. "Fine. I can be there in forty-five minutes. Grab a spot and I'll see you in a bit."

"Perfect." Lennox disconnected the call and stared at the road ahead. If she hurried, she could make it home to change before heading to the bar, but after several weeks of a harried trial schedule, she wasn't in the mood to rush around. She took the turn toward the bar and it was early enough that she found a parking spot near the door. She shrugged out of her suit jacket, tossed it in the back seat, and rolled up the cuffs of her sleeves. Still not bar attire, but better than lawyer drag.

The place was fairly empty which was to be expected on a Monday. She'd planned to head upstairs to the quiet bar so she and Nina could hear each other, but at least for now there wasn't any need, so instead she slid into one of the stools at the bar downstairs and waited for the bartender to finish ringing up a transaction for one of the few patrons already there.

She was reading news coverage of the trial on her phone when the baby butch bartender approached.

"What can I get you?"

Lennox set her phone down and surveyed the bottles on display. "Redbreast. Neat."

"You got it."

She watched as the soft butch spun the bottle and deftly poured a perfect two fingers into a short, thick glass which she placed on the bar in front of her. "That is why I could never be a bartender. I'd spend the whole night sweeping glass off the floor."

The bartender grinned. "You'd get the hang of it. What do you do?"

Lennox hesitated for a moment. She hated lying, but inevitably when she told people she worked for the DA's office, it opened the door to commentary about current events and complaints about all manner of things the community cared about. She wanted to sip her whiskey, meet up with Nina, and debrief about the case. She settled on a true, but incomplete answer. "I'm a lawyer."

Butch narrowed her eyes. "You look familiar. Where would I know you from?"

Lennox took a sip of whiskey and shook her head, figuring the question was more of a line than true curiosity. "No telling."

"Wait a minute." She pointed and then called out to another woman working at the other end of the bar. "Hey, Shelia, come here."

Lennox started to stand up to edge away when the woman named Shelia called out. "You're the one who sent that douche Randall Thomas to prison." And all eyes turned toward her.

She raised her hands. "Guilty as charged."

Shelia walked over and stuck out her hand. "Shelia Connor, nice to meet you."

Lennox returned the strong grip. "Lennox Roy."

"Shante was my favorite act next door back in the day," she said, referred to the Rose Room at S4, the largest bar on the block. "We were pretty torn up when we heard what happened to her." She turned to the baby butch. "Tear up her tab. Lennox doesn't pay for another drink in here. Ever."

Lennox felt the burn of a blush creep up her neck. "Thank you, but I can't accept."

"Of course you can," Shelia said, her voice bellowing throughout the bar. "I think we should even dedicate a portion of the bar to you. Any chance you could give us a play-by-play of the trial? I made it to some of the first day, but then had to work after that."

Damn. Coming here to avoid the courthouse crowd had apparently been a big mistake. She hadn't anticipated pop-up fame here. "Another time, maybe. I'm meeting someone." She glanced at her watch, wishing Nina would appear.

"Lennox Roy, I can't believe you started drinking without me."

Lennox recognized the voice coming from behind her, but it wasn't Nina's. She turned to see Wren Bishop standing directly behind her with a teasing expression on her face. "Uh…"

Wren smiled at Shelia. "She promised me we'd have the first toast together. Is the bar upstairs open? I need a little quiet time with this one."

Shelia shot them both a knowing look. "Of course. Head on up. I'll make sure you aren't disturbed."

Wren hooked her arm through Lennox's and led the way. "Thank you," she called to Shelia over her shoulder. Lennox went along with the ruse until they reached the top of the stairs.

"I'm not sure what we're doing here," she said, stepping away from Wren's grasp.

"You looked a little flummoxed back there."

"Flummoxed?"

"Yes, not your usual look." Wren leaned back as if to appraise her. "Not what I'd expect after your showing at the courthouse."

"I'm waiting on someone. I mean, for real. She'll be here any minute."

Wren smiled. "Don't worry. I won't interfere with your date. I just figured you could use a little rescuing and then maybe you might find it in your heart to be a little nicer to the new kid on the block. Maybe we can even have a civil conversation about a case or two."

"I can take care of myself." Lennox spotted a flicker of disappointment on Wren's face, and immediately regretted the harsh reply, but now that she'd committed to a course, she wasn't inclined to back off. "If you're looking for nice, maybe stick to your colleagues in the PD's office. You and me? We're adversaries."

"Wow. Okay. And here I was thinking we were both looking for the same thing."

"And what exactly is that?"

Wren stared at her for a long, uncomfortable moment before she answered. "Justice." She cocked her head. "Why? What did you think I was going to say?"

Lennox sensed she was being teased, but she wasn't entirely sure. God, she needed a manual when it came to dealing with this woman. Thankfully, Nina appeared at the bottom of the stairs. She waved in her direction and Nina waved back, a mischievous grin on her face. "I have to go."

Wren followed the direction of her gaze and nodded knowingly. Lennox knew what she was thinking but didn't bother to correct the misunderstanding if it would save her from having to deal with Wren any longer.

"Well, looks like you're in good hands. Have a nice evening. And congratulations again on the win."

Lennox watched her walk away, noting Nina grinning like a fool after they passed each other on the stairs. When Nina reached the top of the stairs, she grabbed her arm and pointed downward. "That's the new PD, right? She's family? Why are you letting her walk away? What did she say to you?"

Lennox shrugged out of her grasp and jerked her chin in Wren's direction. "Nothing and it looks like she doesn't need me to stop her from walking away." She stared for a moment as Wren hugged a woman who greeted her enthusiastically. They smiled and locked arms and headed to the bar. The other woman was tall and nice-looking. Like Wren, she wore a suit, but hers was sharply tailored and more classic than Wren's usual designer look. She shook her head. Since when had she become so obsessed with other women's clothing choices? She started to walk away, but curiosity drew her to give the striking duo a final look. Were they simply friends or were they lovers? More importantly, why did she care?

Finally, she tore her gaze back to Nina. "Buy me another drink before you shake me down for info." She pointed at the bar. "Seriously, I'll pay, but you'll have to get the drinks because apparently, everyone here wants to talk about the case."

Nina leaned over and kissed her on the cheek. "Face it, you're a local hero now. Get used to it." She headed to the bar and Lennox watched her go, stewing about the moniker and the encounter with Wren. When Nina returned with their drinks, they settled into a booth. Nina raised her glass. "Congratulations on the win."

"Thanks, but it wasn't enough," she said.

Nina's brow furrowed. "It was huge."

"I wanted life."

"But you asked for forty years."

"That's what Shante's family wanted. I told them I thought we should go for life, but they said she'd never been keen on the whole eye for an eye way of thinking. That she'd want Thomas punished, but with some chance at redemption."

"Maybe that was the more practical request. Juries sometimes have a hard time with the concept of 'life' in prison which can make it harder for them to pull the trigger when they feel like that's their only option. You gave them a concrete, solid punishment option. Besides, you and I both know that under either sentence, he'll be up for parole in about the same amount of time, and if he isn't paroled, he'll likely die in prison."

"I know, but part of me thinks I failed her. Her life is over. His should be too."

"You didn't. Her family is in a much better position to know how she would feel. Plus, a lot of prosecutors would have gone for the easy charge, not the hate crime. You fought big and won bigger." Nina raised her glass. "You deserve the accolades and you're the only one who is questioning your success."

Lennox clinked her glass with Nina's and they both drank. "Thanks for meeting me. I was too keyed up to go home, but I didn't want to be around the courthouse crowd."

"Happy to have a reason to escape another fundraising event. Though I guess you didn't escape the crowd entirely, did you?"

Lennox knew she was talking about Wren and Nina wasn't going to let the topic go. "I have to admit, I didn't expect to see her here. She strikes me as more of the uptown wine bar type than a drinks in the hood kind of girl."

"She is a bit fancy, but she wears it well. I bet she's still downstairs if you're interested."

"I'm not." Lennox rushed out the words before she could change her mind, but in the back of her mind she was mulling it over. To most people, Wren would be a total catch. She was hot and smart and passionate. But she didn't go for fancy types. Never had. And she knew from experience dating someone from across the aisle was fraught with peril. "She is pretty, but not my type at all."

"Have you even really talked to her?"

"She did the examining trial for that arson case—Jared Allen—this morning."

"Let me guess, even though you were in the middle of a trial, you went and did it yourself because you don't trust the duty prosecutor to handle it. Or was it that you wanted to get to know the cute new PD?"

"I always do all the hearings on big cases myself. I remember exactly how green I was when I was sitting in mag court doing dozens of examining trials a week. At some point, you don't even remember the defendants' names."

"How was she?"

"Who?"

Nina drew a circle in the air with her finger. "Focus, Roy. The PD."

"She had all the passionate idealism of a law school intern. Seriously, it's like she's fresh out of school."

"She's on loan from Dunley Thornton, right?"

"Yes, which makes it even worse. She left her cushy six-figure job to come slum at the courthouse for a few months. See, she's not my type at all."

"And your type always works out so well for you. Someday, you're going to get tired of one-night stands and get back in the dating game."

"It's much easier when there are no expectations. Plus, you know how it is." Nina constantly chided her about dating, but she was one to talk. As a judge, she had her own problems in that she spent most of her time at the courthouse, yet dating anyone there was a potential conflict.

"I do, but you haven't had a lot of success with your whole 'I will never get involved with anyone connected to the courthouse again' rule. It's where you spend all your time. How could you possibly expect to find anyone who understands you if they don't understand your work? Besides, if she's not going to be a permanent fixture, then dating her doesn't break your dumb rule."

Nina spoke the truth. Even when she had been looking for someone to date, she rarely found someone who meshed with her schedule, and on the rare occasions she had, no one seemed to understand that her job would always be first. They always said they did—at the beginning when things were all wine and roses, but after the first few dates were behind them, the gears shifted into commitmentville and inevitably they would get aggravated whenever work interrupted planned time together. And half the time, she couldn't talk about exactly what it was that was consuming all of her time and attention. She knew other prosecutors skirted the line on shop talk at home, but she didn't go there and her reticence to share had caused even more problems with potential girlfriends.

"If I say you're right, will you quit badgering me?"

"Maybe." Nina raised her drink. "If you'll bring a date to the banquet next month. And not just a date you met the day before, but someone with real girlfriend potential. Preferably someone with a cute sister."

"Aha, the true reason you're so interested in my dating life is finally revealed. You want me to find someone who will find someone for you."

"Hundred percent." She tilted her glass at Lennox.

"Challenge accepted," Lennox said, obliging her with a toast. "Now can we talk about something other than my nonexistent love life?"

They spent the rest of the evening rehashing the case and cases Nina had coming up and the election and everything else but Wren Bishop. The conversation was fun and engaging and took her mind off everything except the occasional wondering whether Wren was still downstairs and if the woman she was with was a friend or lover. Damn, she needed a life of her own.

CHAPTER FIVE

Wren rolled over in bed and slapped the alarm, but not before it woke Diane who rubbed her eyes with one hand and tugged on her arm with the other.

"Happy Friday," Diane purred. "I don't have to be at the Laramore depo until ten. Plenty of time for us to pick up where we left off last night."

Wren flashed back to the night before. They'd both worked late. In fact, she'd worked late every night for the past week, and the only fun thing she'd done was meeting Emma for drinks at Sue Ellen's on Monday night. When Diane called and suggested meeting at the Capital Grille for a late dinner and a nightcap, Wren had suggested take-out and her house instead, too tired for a fancy four course dinner and anxious to shed her suit and heels. She'd expected they would wind up in bed—lately, it was the only place where Diane didn't entirely annoy her, but Diane staying the night was a surprise since she usually bugged out after one round.

"I wish I could," Wren said, softening the blow with a light kiss on Diane's cheek, but I've got to get to the courthouse."

"They sure are running you ragged."

"It's fine." Wren didn't bother telling Diane she didn't have any court appearances scheduled today, but the grand jury was reporting out on the Allen case and she wanted to be there when the report was handed out. Diane would probably suggest she have a secretary retrieve the report or some other completely out of touch nonsense.

Okay, so that wasn't fair since up until a few weeks ago, she might have suggested the same thing. "I like it there."

Diane stroked her hand down her side, resting it in her lap. "Don't like it too much. We miss you at the office."

While she figured Diane was exaggerating, associates didn't have time to miss those who weren't there anymore, she pondered how much she missed working with a bunch of other attorneys who were at the same place in their career. Sure, there was plenty of competition, but overall, they were all respectful of one another.

When she walked into the PD's lounge an hour and a half later, everyone looked up at her, but when no one spoke to her, she contemplated the differences yet again. Tough crowd, but she wasn't one to be easily deterred. She raised her coffee cup in greeting. "Good morning," she called out to no one in particular.

Jill, the head mean girl, shook her head. "Our coffee not good enough for you?"

Wren looked at the cup in her hand. She'd taken advantage of running by her old office this morning to stop by her favorite coffee shop, the Pearl Cup. "Oh this? It's kind of amazing. They have this secret latte recipe. It's the owner's grandmother's recipe or something like that. A little sweet, but not too much. Definitely real vanilla, but I haven't been able to figure out the other ingredient. Maybe—"

Jill interrupted her by shaking a large coffee can in her direction. "We collect on the first and everyone chips in."

The non sequitur was disconcerting, but Wren got the gist. She could call Jill out for being rude or go with the flow. Only one response was going to get her anywhere with this crowd. She reached into her purse and pulled out her wallet. "Count me in. How much?"

She caught a couple of eye rolls from the others, but Jill was focused on the Louis Vuitton wallet in her hand. "What?"

"Is that real?"

The question was absurd, especially considering they weren't friends dishing about a purchase, and she could hear the disdain in Jill's voice. The wallet had been a birthday gift from her mother. To

Beth Bishop, it was a simple wallet, not an extravagant purchase, a trinket she probably picked up at Neiman's after lunch in the cafe with her friends. Not exactly Wren's style, but since it stayed stowed in her purse most of the time, she carried it out of sentimental value. She had two ways to play her reaction, be ashamed at the fancy or own it. She decided on the latter. "Yes." She shoved it toward Jill. "You can really tell the difference. Check it out."

To her surprise, Jill took the wallet and gave it a thorough inspection as if it were commonplace to thumb through the personal belongings of a person she barely knew. "I handled a few cases of counterfeits last year. This is definitely the real deal. How much did it set you back?"

It was the kind of question you asked a close friend, not someone who was practically a stranger and certainly not someone you'd expressed disdain for since the moment you met. Wren had reached her nice girl limit for the morning and her tone was clipped when she responded, grabbing the wallet back. "It was a gift."

"Right."

Desperate to find an excuse to ditch this conversation, Wren started to glance at her watch, but reconsidered when she anticipated the reaction she'd get if Jill caught a glimpse of her Rolex. "I should go. I'm meeting with Ford in a few minutes."

No one bothered responding, but Wren was convinced she heard whispered mentions of her name as she left the room. Whatever.

Ford's door was open as usual, but Wren knocked anyway. He looked up and smiled, beckoning her in. "Have a seat."

She kept her hand on the door, hesitating. She wanted to close the door and ask him for frank advice about how to get the rest of the PDs to accept her or at least stop acting like she was the enemy, but while Ford might be her mentor, he was also her boss and ratting out the others' bad behavior was likely to make things worse. Resigned to deal with the situation on her own, she took a seat in front of his desk.

"Isn't the grand jury supposed to report out on the Jared Allen's case today?" he asked.

"Yes. Any wager on his chances?"

"The package you submitted was good, but don't get your hopes up. The case has gotten a lot of publicity and none of it good for him. It's bound to influence the jurors."

He was right, of course. Grand jurors served a longer term than trial court jurors, returning day after day to hear bits of evidence about various cases and make decisions about whether to indict. While they were cautioned not to read about the cases they heard in the news or discuss them with friends and family, the warnings didn't have the same effect as they did on jurors who were immersed in the details of a single, all-consuming case that took place over the course of a week or two. "I'm trying to remain positive, no matter what. He was pretty clear he wasn't interested in a plea. If it's a true bill, he's going to want to go to trial soon."

"They all say that," Ford said. "It's because they think if they can get to trial, everyone will see the truth, and they'll get out sooner. If he were out on bond, he'd be singing a different tune. The longer he's in jail, the more he's going to start thinking about ways to get out."

"I hear you, but unless the state has more evidence, I'm not sure giving them extra time to build their case is to our advantage. You know Lennox Roy better than I do. Would she be holding evidence back or would she use it all at grand jury?"

"Lennox is one of the best. Her only fault is that she defers to law enforcement too often. If the police bring her a case, she trusts they did their due diligence. Most of the time, she's able to recover from any stumbles they made, but occasionally, her reliance on their work has tripped her up."

"Fair enough. If the case gets true billed, can we get an investigator?"

"Yes, but we only have two investigators assigned to the entire department, and you have to share them with the rest of the PDs. Speaking of which, how are things going with the rest of the crowd up here?"

Here it was. Her opportunity to ask him for advice about how to get the rest of the group to like her, but no matter how many times she rolled the question around in her head, her complaint sounded petulant and immature. No, she'd work out her issues with the other PDs on her own. Somehow. "Everything's fine," she lied. "Everyone seems really busy. I can see why you needed to add staff."

He nodded. "Damn right about that. If it weren't for these lawyer-on-loan programs, I don't know how we'd make it. DAs have no trouble funding more lawyers, but boosting the budget of criminal defense lawyers has never been politically expedient."

"We need better messaging."

"Look at you with the 'we need better messaging.' A few more months here and I'll lure you into a permanent position."

They both laughed, but Wren wondered if he meant it. She'd never considered leaving Dunley Thornton permanently and she doubted the PD's office could afford to pay her a fraction of what she made there. Plus, it wasn't like she was making any friends here. Despite the ostensibly cutthroat environment among the associates at the firm, she'd enjoyed having a peer group. Here she was a level below a junior attorney because everyone assumed she didn't know jack about criminal law and they knew she wouldn't be sticking around long enough for them to bother building rapport with her. Well, she couldn't do anything about the second part, but she could show them she knew her stuff. "If the case gets true billed, let me handle negotiations and trial prep for you."

"This case may not get resolved before your time here is up."

"I know, but there will be a lot of heavy lifting in the meantime. It's not like you have time to handle it. I'm not here looking for a vacation. I've been racking up hours for fat cats looking to save a buck here and there. Let me put my incredible work ethic to good use."

"Fine. The case is yours to prep. If, by some miracle, it gets no-billed, I'll find you another one."

"Excellent. You won't be sorry."

He grinned. "No, but you might be."

They spent the next twenty minutes going over the other cases Wren had been assigned. When they were done, she ditched her files in her office and headed up to the eleventh-floor grand jury desk. There was no one at the counter and no one in the back was dumb enough to make eye contact with her. Wren waited patiently for a few minutes and then she started to pace. Her wait time would probably pass faster if she were at her desk working, but now that she'd committed full-on to the case, she wanted to know where things stood as soon as possible. On her seventh pass by the desk, she nearly ran into Lennox Roy.

"You're going to wear out the carpet if you keep this up."

Lennox's arms were crossed, and she wore her usual stern expression, but Wren caught a glimpse of amusement in her eyes. "Girl's got to exercise."

"You probably had a fancy gym back at Dunley Thornton."

Wren cocked her head. She certainly hadn't mentioned her other employer to Lennox. They hadn't spoken at all since the night she'd run into her at Sue's a few weeks ago. She'd seen Lennox in the halls of the courthouse, and she'd dropped a grand jury packet for the Thomas case off at her office, but there'd been no real interaction. Which meant Lennox had asked around about her. "You know a lot about my last firm?"

"I thought it was your current firm. Aren't you just here on loan?"

Tone. There was definite tone in Lennox's voice, and Wren was tired of facing opposition from all directions, so she didn't bother to hide her aggravation when she responded. "I'm here to do a job, just like you, but you seem to be more interested in my pedigree than this case."

"Oh, I'm plenty interested in this case. I'm a little worried that attorneys from your firm don't know how to do what's right for their client."

Wren chewed over the words until it struck her what Lennox was talking about. "You think because I worked at the same firm as Gloria Leland that I'm like her? Dozens of attorneys work there. Do you honestly think we're all alike?"

"You sure seemed friendly with her after sentencing."

"She's a partner at the firm. She asked me a question and I responded politely. It's how people get along in the real world, which is apparently very different from how things function here where everyone is in a clique and if you didn't rise up through the ranks, you should slink away and eat your lunch by yourself." Whoa, she hadn't meant to get that personal and she could tell by Lennox's shocked face, she'd stepped over a line. "Sorry, that was uncalled for. I guess I'm used to a more congenial workplace. It's been an adjustment."

"It's okay."

Surprisingly, Lennox's voice was laced with genuine sympathy, and Wren felt the need to continue to explain. "I had this vision of everyone working together toward a common purpose. I mean, I'm used to fighting with opposing counsel over money, but when people's liberty is at stake, I figured we'd all have the same goal."

"A little naive, don't you think?"

Lennox's tone was surprisingly gentle and she wasn't wrong, but Wren was sticking to her guns. "I prefer to think of it as being human. The world could use a whole lot more of that, don't you think?" Before Lennox could answer, the grand jury secretary appeared with a stack of papers.

"Y'all waiting for the true bill report?" she said, peeling two of the papers off the top and handing one to her and one to Lennox. "Here you go."

Wren skimmed the report. Allen's case was the third one listed. First degree felony murder. Well, shit.

"Looks like we'll see each other in court again," Lennox said.

"Maybe. It's Ford's case. He'll be sitting first chair no matter what."

"Oh, I'm sure we'll work something out long before trial. Your guy doesn't want to face a jury with these facts."

Damn her and her infuriating smugness. Wren forced a smile. "We'll see." She turned to walk away, but only made it a few steps before Lennox called out to her.

"It's the suit."

Wren looked over her shoulder. "What?"

"It's the suit." Lennox gestured at her clothing. "The one you're wearing and the ones you've worn every other day you've been here. They're obviously tailored to fit you, you have dozens of them, and they look like you paid more for them than most of the other PDs make in a week. Or a month."

"You're saying if I dress down, I'll have more friends?"

Lennox shrugged. "Maybe." She pointed at the paper in her hand. "Come see me if you change your mind about the plea offer. I'll leave it open for the rest of the week." She strode away.

Wren watched her go, knowing she should be thinking about the plea offer, but all she could think about was the fact Lennox Roy, heartthrob of the courthouse, noticed what she wore every day, and the revelation was both startling and titillating.

Lennox sat at her desk and watched Detective Braxton skim the police report. When he finally looked up at her, she said, "You ready to talk about how a green public defender took you to school during that examining trial?"

He bristled in his seat. "She was shooting blanks. Didn't land any good shots."

"Not true. Little bits of doubt start to add up. Have you checked the gas station to make sure there are no other camera angles that might have caught Allen filling up a gas can?"

"We're still going through footage, but I don't think so."

"How about pulling the receipts of everyone who was there at the same time and talking to them?" She asked.

"And if none of them remember seeing anything? You're going to have to turn all of those interview notes over to his lawyer and she'll say that proves he wasn't doing anything wrong. Besides, you already have your indictment. Why are you so worried about making it stick?"

"You know better than that." She stared him down for a moment. "I could get an indictment on your five-year-old son, but the making it stick part comes now. If we wind up going to trial, I want a tight case and that means shoring up all these pesky little details well in advance." She thumbed through the file to the section containing interviews with the family. "What's the situation with the boyfriend? Have you interviewed him again?"

"We've talked to him twice. He has a solid alibi for the time of the fire and three hours beforehand. Vic's parents really like the guy—he's the son they never had—so he's still hanging around. They say he's a source of comfort and helps the sister with the kids since they don't have a father figure anymore."

"That's laying it on a bit thick. Their dad's in jail, not Mars." She didn't relish the part of her work that involved breaking up families, even when she knew kids might be better off raised by strangers than cold-blooded killers. The problem was it wasn't usually such a stark contrast. If Jared Allen's actions had been a crime of passion, that didn't necessarily mean he was a bad person, but she'd expend little energy on that line of thought because it wasn't her job. That was something for Wren to worry about, work to combat, and judging by what she'd seen at the examining trial, she'd be a worthy foe.

An hour later, after an extensive grilling, Detective Braxton left her office with a list of assignments. Lennox leaned back in her chair and shut her eyes, swearing she would only take a five-minute nap before plunging back into the police report on her desk.

"Caught you."

Her eyes flew open, and she focused on the grinning face of Reggie Knoll, Judge Larabee's court coordinator. "Hey, Reggie. Can't a girl catch a tiny bit of sleep around here?"

"Maybe if you didn't work around the clock, you could sleep in your own bed. Or someone else's…"

Reggie's comment hung in the air like a tree branch about to put a hole through the roof. Lennox was used to the flirting. They'd gone out a few times when she was assigned to another court. It had been fun, but she'd quickly grown tired of everyone at the courthouse knowing her business and had broken things off with the standard "let's just be friends" line. Reggie had pushed the boundaries since, but only in a way that could be plausibly denied as harmless flirting and Lennox hadn't called her on it because it was too awkward, further reinforcing her ultimate decision that dating people from work was a bad idea. "Does Larabee need me?"

"No, but Judge Mackey next door does. He needs someone to take a plea. It's Roger's case, but his wife went into labor and he had to take off. Roger told Mackey you could handle it. All the paperwork's done."

"Can't one of the mag court prosecutors do it?" she asked, referring to the assistant DAs who handled pleas by the dozens before a magistrate judge when everything was agreed upon in advance and no discretion was needed.

Reggie shrugged. "He wants you. What can I say?"

"Fine. I'll be right there." Lennox stood and put on her suit jacket. It wasn't that she minded filling in for Roger, but she hated handling the end of a case she hadn't worked all the way through. She checked her phone and found Roger had sent her a text with lots of thank yous and the pertinent case info. Better. Much better.

She walked next door and entered the courtroom from the door by the jury box. The defendant was easily recognizable since he was dressed in an orange jumpsuit and slides with white socks, but the woman seated next to him was a surprise. "Parker, good to see you."

Parker grinned. "If I'd known Roger was sending in the big guns, we wouldn't have pushed so hard for this deal."

Lennox rolled her eyes. "He told me to go easy on you." She hadn't seen Parker since the fundraiser at Sammy's. "You all set?"

They went through the motions of the plea and Judge Mackey rubber-stamped the agreement. As Parker was packing up her stuff, she said, "You're coming over Saturday, right?"

"Wouldn't miss it. Can I bring anything?"

"No food—we have that covered, plus Nina promised to make her famous margaritas and we'll have beer and sodas and stuff like that. You're welcome to bring a date though."

"I think I'll stick to some microbrews."

"What?" Parker feigned surprise. "The great Lennox Roy can't get a date for a simple afternoon picnic?"

"Shut up. The great Lennox Roy hasn't had time to date lately." She looked around to make sure no one was listening in. "Besides, where am I supposed to meet anyone?"

Parker waved her arm. "Word is you have no problem making good use of the resources at your disposal."

"My reputation is greatly exaggerated. I've gone out with maybe three people who work here and none of it amounted to anything. Unfortunately, a couple of them like to talk, which makes me seem like more of a Casanova than real life. Not interested in dipping back into the pool."

"You might try venturing out into the world at large. You never know where you're going to find 'the one.' I met Morgan in the alley behind Sue's after she accidentally locked herself out of the building."

"How have I never heard this story?"

Parker shrugged. "Everyone assumes we met while I was in law school. We save the alley story for good friends." She grabbed her bag and started to the door. "See you Saturday. By the way, it won't just be courthouse people. Expand your horizons. It'll be good for you."

"I'll try to make it," Lennox said, not fully committed, but definitely considering the idea. If nothing else, she could use a small break from work. Hanging out poolside with a beer and a burger sounded like the perfect way to decompress. Adding a date to the mix would only complicate things, and she needed a day without complications.

CHAPTER SIX

Wren leaned back in the recliner in her living room and read the report from the arson investigator for the third time, but she still didn't have a handle on his findings. She was used to reading technical gibberish from a number of product liability and medical malpractice cases she'd worked on at the law firm, but this was a combination of scientific jargon and law enforcement terminology, and she needed a dictionary to translate. Bottom-line, the state's expert appeared, on paper anyway, to be convinced the fire was arson, and with the evidence of Jared's estrangement from his wife and the insurance money he stood to collect upon her death, there was plenty of circumstantial evidence to point to his guilt.

She felt hands on her shoulders, massaging gently.

"I rolled over in bed and you were gone."

Wren cringed slightly at the tinge of annoyance in Diane's voice, but she kept her tone light. "You were sleeping so soundly, I didn't want to bother you." She pointed at the file in her lap. "Figured I'd try to get a little work done before the cookout."

Diane's smile faded. "Every time you say the word 'cookout' I envision sitting on the ground, picking flies out of our food, while screaming children run around us."

Wren laughed. "I'm pretty sure it's not that kind of event. It's more the gather in someone's backyard and ooh and ahh over their new landscaping while eating good food and drinking beer."

Diane wrinkled her nose. "Beer, huh?"

"Or whatever. I'm sure we can bring something you would like better." Wren paused, knowing this was the part where Diane expected her to give her an out. Say something like, "Hey, I know you'd rather not go, so let's stay in and have brunch and go back to bed for the rest of the day."

But she wanted to go. After finding no friends at the PD's office, she was eager to attend an event where she could meet other people who frequented the courthouse but didn't necessarily make it their entire life. Besides, Ford had invited them, and she'd promised she'd be there. "I'm looking forward to it," she said emphatically.

"Fine. I'm sure I can endure anything for an hour or two."

"You don't have to go." The words tumbled out before she could stop them, but Wren decided it was for the best. She didn't know if they'd have a good time or not, but she was going for sure, and she didn't need to be saddled with Diane who she knew would spend the entire time there pestering her about how soon they could leave.

Diane's eyes sparkled and her relief was palpable. "Are you sure you don't mind if I bag on you?"

"Not at all," Wren replied, surprised at the strong sense of relief that swept over her. "I'll call you tomorrow."

Diane's lips formed a small pout at the obvious dismissal, but Wren had no interest in placating her. She really did want to get some work done before the party, and right now reading mind-numbing arson reports was infinitely more appealing than returning to bed for a few hours with a woman who couldn't be bothered to be by her side for a simple backyard picnic. She filed away the feelings to be examined later and returned to her reading while Diane gathered her things.

"If you're feeling lonely tonight, give me a call. I'll probably grab dinner out, but you know where to find me later."

Wren resisted the urge to tell her she wasn't interested in being her booty call any longer, deciding not to expend the energy. Besides, she wasn't interested in starting a fight when she was determined to have a fun day. Instead, she returned Diane's wave and said she'd talk to her later.

An hour later, she shoved the reports in her bag, and took a long, hot shower and contemplated what she should wear. Ford had invited her to this shindig at Morgan Bradley and Parker Casey's house, and assured her it was casual. Part of the reason she wanted to go was to get to know Morgan better, especially since Ford held her in really high esteem. He'd taught with Morgan at Richards University before Wren had attended, and he and Morgan had become good friends, even trying a few high-profile murder cases together. When he'd asked her to the cookout, he'd folded the invitation into a mention of how it would be good for her to meet some other criminal defense attorneys outside of the courthouse environment, and she wondered if he'd gotten wind of exactly how much the other PDs didn't like her. Or maybe they'd all be at the party but would be nicer because they weren't on the job. Whatever the case, she'd been craving social interaction since her break from the firm, and a backyard barbecue sounded like exactly what she needed.

After she toweled off from the shower, she settled on a blue and white floral maxi dress and a pair of flat sandals. Satisfied she looked casual, but still nice, she reached for her go-to crossbody Prada, another gift from her mother, but the interaction with Jill over her Louis Vuitton wallet replayed in her mind and instead she selected a slim leather wallet and shoved it along with her lip balm in her pocket. No one was going to accuse her of being a fashion diva, even if it was a little bit true. She grabbed a few bottles of her favorite Zin Rose and headed for the car.

Morgan and Parker lived across the expressway in east Dallas, but it was an easy drive and she rode with the top down. Dallas was one of the worst places to have a convertible. It was really only the right weather to have the top down a couple of months a year—the rest of the time it was either raining or sweltering hot, but on days like today when the sun was shining and there was a light breeze in the spring air, it was perfection.

She turned on their street and immediately spotted the house, partly because of the long line of cars parked out front. She circled the block twice, unsure if her car would fit into one of the few tiny spaces left on the street. She'd slowed to a crawl, about to start her third time around, when she spotted Lennox Roy walking toward her, and she was riveted by the sight of the uptight prosecutor dressed in shorts and a T-shirt. Damn, she had long legs. Tanned, toned, gorgeous legs. Dangerously sexy. She tore her gaze away and resumed her slow crawl down the block.

"Hey," Lennox yelled. "Wait up."

Damn. Had Lennox caught her staring? Too late to avoid her now. She stopped the car and braced for their encounter.

Lennox jogged toward the car and leaned against the passenger door. "Are you stalking me?"

"Are you in the habit of chasing moving cars?"

Lennox laughed, the sound a distinct contrast to her usual brisk tone. "In my defense, you were kind of stopped when I first saw you." She pointed to the street in front of them. "Do you live here?"

"What?" Wren cursed her frazzled brain and the sexy legs that had shorted her circuits. "No, I'm headed to a party." She stared at Lennox for a moment as realization dawned. "You too?"

Lennox grinned. "Backyard barbecue. Beer and games. You're at the right place."

"Kind of. I've circled the block twice and can't find a parking place. That's what I get for being fashionably late, I guess."

Before she could process what was happening, Lennox opened the door and settled into the passenger seat. "I'll be your copilot." She pointed ahead. "Try up here. Toward the end of the street."

Who was this woman in the seat next to her? Certainly not the surly attorney who'd treated her like she didn't know jack about criminal law. Rather than dwell on the inexplicable juxtaposition of stiff-suited courthouse Lennox and this beachy version, she decided to go with it. She pressed her foot to the accelerator. "Okay, work your parking magic."

They were almost to the end of the block when Lennox reached for her arm and pointed across the street. "I think you can fit in there if you turn around and come at it from the other side."

The words blurred a bit as Wren was fully focused on the feel of Lennox's hand on her arm. As if she sensed it, Lennox pulled her hand back and Wren instantly missed the touch. Weird. But nice. Really nice.

"You got it?" Lennox asked.

So many possible answers, but all Wren could manage was a nod. She turned the car at the end of the street and headed back in the direction they'd come from. She pulled alongside the SUV parked on her left and stopped. "This is the part where I confess I failed parallel parking three times before I got my driver's license. I'm still suffering from the trauma."

"You want me to try it?"

She kind of did, but she didn't want to hand over the keys and admit there was anything Lennox could do that she couldn't. "No, I got this. Just promise me you won't laugh at my fifty-point turn."

Thankfully, she was able to make the maneuver into the tight space fairly easily and with a sigh of relief cut the engine after aligning fairly close to the curb.

"See," Lennox said, slapping the dashboard. "That wasn't so bad, right?"

"Now that it's over, sure."

"Consider it practice for when you can't find a valet. Although I'm sure those are rare."

"Excuse me?"

"You strike me as the valet type."

It was true, she did have a valet at her condo building, but that was more about managing the parking lot than because she was too lazy to park her own car. "I park my car every day at the courthouse."

"Hard to believe. There's not a scratch on it, and if you parked it there, you'd have plenty of dings."

"Maybe I'm careful about where I park."

"Maybe."

They sat in silence for a moment. "I guess we should go in," Wren said, feeling a little funny about entering a party full of people she didn't know. Would Lennox ditch her now or would she stay by her side?

"Sure." Lennox pointed at a bag on the floor containing the wine bottles. "Does this come inside?"

"Yes." Wren noticed Lennox's skepticism. "What's wrong?"

"Nothing." She reached down and pulled out one of the bottles and examined the label. "This looks fancy. Maybe you'd like to save it for a backyard French cuisine dinner instead?"

Wren caught the teasing tone, and relaxed. "Look, I'm the new kid looking to make a good impression." She paused, considering whether to share more. This was her first time having a conversation with a courthouse colleague about something other than work. Maybe she and Lennox could actually be friends. She decided to test the waters. "Look, I tried dressing more casually at work, but the other PDs still treat me like I'm a pariah. Ford invited me here today, but I don't know these people, so I grabbed a few of my favorite bottles to buy some good will."

"Relax. You'll like Parker and Morgan. They're good people. And they wouldn't care if you showed up empty-handed." Lennox stuck her hand in her pocket and pulled out a piece of royal blue ribbon. "Here, use this." She tied it around one of the bottles and thrust it toward her. "Look, it's a hostess gift. Leave the others here. It's cool enough for them to keep in the car."

"Do you always carry ribbon in your pocket or is it only a weekend thing?"

A hint of a blush pinked Lennox's cheeks and the effect was adorable. "Uh, I was wrapping a present earlier and I didn't have a place to toss the extra."

Wren resisted making a crack about how Lennox was so law-and-order she couldn't bear to litter, and instead said, "I'm impressed." She tucked the bottle under her arm, reflecting on this softer side of Lennox—the one who wrapped presents and helped women park their cars. "Thank you."

"You're welcome."

Wren followed Lennox up the sidewalk to the house and waited while Lennox knocked on the door.

"They won't hear you. I'm sure they're out back. Go on in."

She turned toward the voice to find two blondes holding hands with a young girl who stood between them. Lennox clapped the shorter haired one on the shoulder. "I guess they let anyone into this party."

"Right back at you." The woman jerked her chin at Wren. "Who's your friend, Roy?"

"This is Wren Bishop."

"Nice to meet you." She stuck out her hand. "I'm Skye Keaton, and this is my wife, Aimee Howard, and our daughter, Olivia."

"Nice to meet you."

"Good to know you. I mean, any date of Lennox has questionable taste, but we'll give you the benefit of the doubt."

"Oh, we're not here together," Wren blurted out. "We just showed up at the same time," She checked Lennox's face for confirmation, surprised to see she looked deflated. What was up with that?

"My bad. I thought I saw you drive up together."

Lennox shook her head, and her friendly demeanor disappeared. "She's right. We're totally separate." She held open the door and they all walked into the house. She took off before Wren had a chance to say anything else, but Aimee and Skye hung back and began a spirited interrogation.

"How do you know Parker and Morgan?" Aimee asked.

Wren immediately felt awkward. "I don't, actually. Ford Rupley invited me as his faux plus one."

"Ah, you're the new PD."

Wren cocked her head at the ah-ha tone in Aimee's voice, but didn't react. "Indeed, I am. How about you two? Are you attorneys?"

"Hell no," Skye said, quickly casting a look at Olivia who rolled her eyes. "I'm a private investigator and Aimee is a Realtor."

"Careful," Aimee said. "Next she's going to ask you if you already have a house here in Dallas. Assuming you moved from somewhere else."

Wren filed away the fact Skye was a private investigator—to be examined later. "I'm originally from Houston, but I've lived here for a while." She hesitated before mentioning her former job but decided these two seemed like regular folks. "I used to work at a firm downtown in Thanksgiving Tower, I live near there."

"Dunley Thornton?" Aimee asked. "They're top tier. They've handled my parents' business for years."

A bell went off in Wren's head. "Are your parents the Howards of Howard Enterprises?"

"That's them."

"They're the biggest real estate developers in the city. Probably in all of North Texas." She looked to the side to see Lennox, who had disappeared in the crowd.

"Also true. Did you work with them?"

Wren forced her attention back to this nice couple "I met your dad once when we were working on some litigation for them. Savvy businessman."

"That he is. I, however, have never been too interested in the family business, so my empire consists of a little boutique agency in Highland Park."

Skye rolled her eyes and put an arm around Aimee. "Little, my ass."

Aimee laughed. "It's all relative, right? My family thinks my decision to work outside the family business is lame, but it's the best thing I ever did. I'm kind of a go my own way girl."

With that response, Wren decided she instantly liked Aimee. Very much. "I can totally relate."

"Let me guess, you come from a family of lawyers."

"Not even." She hesitated a moment before dropping the family name, ultimately deciding if anyone would be unfazed it was Aimee Howard. "My parents own Bishop Development."

"Ah, so you're like my Houston twin." Aimee turned to Skye. "Her parents are to southern Texas what mine are to the north." She linked arms with Wren and grinned. "We're going to get along famously."

Wren had no choice but to follow Aimee and Skye into the thick of the party. Next up? Pretending like she wasn't secretly trying to spot Lennox the entire way.

❖

Lennox walked into the kitchen at the exact moment Nina emerged through the narrow entry with a tray of margaritas. They'd been on the rocks, but now they were all over her.

"Dammitt, Lennox," Nina said. "That was my best batch."

Lennox pulled the end of her shirt up and twisted it in her hands while watching Nina's creation dribble from the cloth. "Some sympathy here, please? I'm the one who's going to smell like a margarita machine all day."

"Oh, please. I bet you're dying to show off how great you look in your swimsuit. I made sure Morgan invited a few single women for that very reason. But before you dazzle them with your six-pack, help me clean up this mess."

Lennox joined her on the floor, picking up the glassware and mopping up the tequila that hadn't managed to make it onto her shirt. "Why must you continually try to hook me up?"

"I'm living vicariously. I have too much going on to get involved with anyone until this campaign is over, but I always have time to help a friend out."

"Did it ever occur to you that I won't be around as much if you marry me off?" Lennox frowned. "That's it, right? You're trying to get rid of me?"

Nina laughed. "Who said anything about marriage? Besides, if you ditch our friendship because you meet a woman you like, then it wasn't much of a friendship to begin with." She stood and extended her hand. "Come on, help me make another batch of drinks."

Lennox clasped Nina's hand and pulled them both upright. She did have a six-pack, the product of much time spent working out, but she wasn't in the habit of showing it off and definitely not here where so many people she knew from the courthouse were in attendance. But it was a swim party, and she was doused in tequila, so she decided to go with it. She pulled her T-shirt over her head, rolled it into a ball, and tucked it under her arm at the exact moment Wren Bishop barreled into the kitchen.

"Hi," she said in a perfectly normal voice that quickly fizzled into rambling. "Uh, Aimee asked me to get some, um…juice. Right. She said you might have juice. For Olivia? Juice?"

Lennox wondered if Wren realized she'd said the word juice three times in the span of as many seconds, but then she realized Wren's eyes were trained on her abdomen and her own self-consciousness took over. She folded her arms across her chest. "I'm sure we can rustle up some juice. Right, Nina?" She turned to face her friend who was grinning like an idiot. She glared hard. "Juice? Suitable for children. Do you know if Morgan and Parker have any juice?" There, she was now tied with Wren in the juice ramblings.

"Juice?" Nina wrinkled her brow. "Parker said there's drinks for the kids in the garage fridge. Lennox, you know where the garage is, right? Can you show Wren?"

"Yeah, okay." Lennox shot Nina a withering glare before turning back to Wren. "Come on, I'll show you the way." She led Wren to the garage, acutely conscious her almost entirely bare back was on full display, but what was she supposed to do, walk backwards?

"This is a nice house," Wren said.

Thankful for an innocuous subject, Lennox jumped right in. "It is, isn't it? They've done a lot of work on it over the years, but still managed to keep the integrity of the original architecture, but with a cohesive design." A few beats passed and when Wren didn't respond, she stopped and turned around to find Wren staring at her like she'd grown a second head. "What?"

"Add architectural commentary to her list of talents."

Lennox narrowed her eyes. "Why do I think you're making fun of me?"

Wren shrugged. "I don't know, but I assure you, I'm not. Can't a girl be impressed when another girl talks all smart and passionate like?"

Lennox tried, but couldn't suppress a grin. What was it about Wren that kept her from being serious? She didn't know, but she made a decision to lean in. For today, anyway. "Yes, a girl can do those things and God forbid anyone try to stop her." She grabbed the knob for the door to the garage and pushed it open. "After you."

Wren sighed. "I knew the view had to end sometime soon."

"You're kind of impossible."

"You're kind of half-naked." Wren fanned her face. "It's a little distracting."

Lennox knew she should point to the fridge and walk away, but the allure of Wren's flirting was too strong. She stepped closer, putting herself entirely in Wren's space. "Is this better?"

Wren's breath hitched. "Depends on what you mean by better."

Lennox stared directly into Wren's eyes, searching for some sign this wasn't going to end poorly, but all she saw reflected back at her was bare desire, and it felt good. It shouldn't, but it did. She pushed away her doubt and her dumb rules, and surrendered to the moment. "I mean this," she whispered as she leaned closer until her lips were millimeters from Wren's.

Wren's lips parted and a slight moan escaped. "I—"

A loud voice boomed into the garage. "Lennox, are you in here?"

Damn. Lennox stared at Wren's waiting lips and forced herself to pull away. "Over here," she called out. She cast one last look into Wren's eyes before turning to face whoever was looking for her. It was Skye.

Skye pointed to Ford who was standing beside her. "He's been looking everywhere for Wren. Nina said she thought you two were in here." She grinned. "Something about juice boxes which I'm pretty sure was code for something."

Wren appeared at her side with several juice boxes in her hand. "No code," she said. "The boxes are real." She shoved one toward Skye. "I think one of these is for Olivia."

Skye glanced between them, her brow scrunched like she was trying to make out if they were making fun of her or not. "Okay." She took the juice box. "Better deliver this. See you at the pool." She turned and walked out of the room, leaving Ford standing in the doorway looking puzzled.

"I showed up to introduce you around, but it appears you're already making friends," he said, with a pointed look at Lennox. "You're being nice to my new hire, aren't you?"

"Who me?" Lennox raised her hands in the air, anything to distract from the almost kiss between her and Wren. "I'm always nice. Outside of the courtroom. Otherwise, all bets are off."

"Uh-huh." Ford motioned to Wren. "There are a few people I'd like you to meet. Come on and I'll get you fixed up with one of Nina's margaritas."

Lennox started to make some smart remark about her chest and margaritas, but doing so would be a signal she was trying to keep Wren at her side, which was right in line with the fact she'd almost kissed her a moment ago. But that was a moment ago, and in the span of time between the almost kiss and the almost being discovered, she'd recovered her senses enough to realize the near miss had been a mistake. Or had it?

CHAPTER SEVEN

Wren slapped at her phone, but in her sleepy haze, she kept missing the button to turn off the alarm, which only served to increase her agitation. Perfect start for a Monday morning.

"I brought you coffee, but it's probably cold now."

She opened her eyes to see Diane standing at the end of the bed, dressed in a sharp red suit. She looked annoyed. "What's wrong?"

"Nothing at all," Diane said, her tone and frown signaling the opposite was true. "I have to go."

Wren rubbed her eyes. Something was wrong, but she couldn't figure out what without either more sleep or coffee, cold or not. She fluffed her pillow, sat up in bed, and reached for the mug on the nightstand. The coffee was definitely cold, but she drank it anyway, needing the fuel. "See you later?"

"Probably not. I have a long day ahead and I'm meeting the investors for the new downtown development for dinner. I'll probably stay at my place tonight. Maybe you can find some of your new friends to play with. Have a great day."

She turned on her heel and strode off, leaving Wren to chew on the fact she'd tossed out that last statement like it was a piece of trash. "Have a great day," Wren said and then mumbled under her breath, "whatever." Diane was annoyed with her, and she didn't really care why which should tell her everything she needed to know about the future of their relationship.

It had been a week since the party at Parker and Morgan's and the atmosphere between her and Diane had definitely chilled. She hadn't bothered calling Diane last Saturday when she'd gotten home from the party, partly because she'd gotten home later than expected, but mostly because she hadn't wanted to cap off a great day with listening to Diane whine about how hard she worked and what stress she was under. Every single one of the people at the party was under way more stress than a fancy corporate lawyer—they all managed cases that involved actual life and death and liberty. Yet, they still managed to be nice and kind and have fun, which was a striking difference from the competitive environment of the firm. Even adversaries in the courtroom had put aside advocacy to come together, break bread, and share stories of victory and defeat. The only hint of competition was the fierce water volleyball game, and she'd paid way less attention to the score than Lennox's ripped body as she led her team to victory.

Wren let her eyes flutter shut as she remembered their near kiss. The tension in the air had been incredibly thick and intense, and she could not believe she'd been about to take Lennox's lips between her own. Who knows what would've happened next if Ford hadn't appeared, ready to drag her off to meet everyone else at the party. She liked to think she wouldn't have succumbed, but she couldn't be sure, which meant two things: she needed to decide if she was going to continue to date Diane, and if she wasn't, what was she going to do about the stirring feelings she was having for Lennox?

The rest of that afternoon had been a blur that consisted of beer, food, and sneaking glances around the yard, ever conscious of where Lennox was standing, who she was talking to, whether she'd put her shirt back on. Spoiler alert: she hadn't. When Wren got home that night, she climbed into bed and spent way more time thinking about the woman she'd left at the party than the woman who'd shared her bed off and on for the last few months, which was a problem for more reasons than she'd had time to sort out in the week since. To her relief, she hadn't run into Lennox, at least not in close proximity, since the party, but the memory of their almost kiss and the prospect of turning a corner at the courthouse and bumping into Lennox had disrupted her ability to focus on her work.

She downed the rest of the cold coffee, swung out of bed, and padded to her dining room table where she'd left her laptop set up from the night before. The best way to diffuse a situation was to learn everything about it that she could. She stretched her arms over her head, then brought them back down to the keyboard and typed Lennox Roy into the search bar. Within seconds a cascade of entries filled her screen: press releases, conference bios, and headline news. She scanned the first page and clicked on a particularly eye-catching headline: *Prosecutor keeps vow.*

Lennox Roy rarely comments about the cases she tries, but she did have this to offer following the trial of Edward Vincent, notorious rapist who terrorized the Richards University campus over the course of the fall semester. "He will never walk the streets of Dallas or anywhere else again. The defense spent days during sentencing trotting out expert after expert to try to mitigate his crimes and engender sympathy from the jury, but the truth prevailed. Nothing, and I mean nothing that ever happened to this man can remotely compare to the horror he inflicted on the dozens of women he raped. Their lives will never be normal again, but they will have some relief knowing this devil will spend his life behind bars."

Okay, so she was a passionate advocate for victims. Plus-one in the good human category. Wren clicked on a few more articles that bolstered her initial impression, but she did notice a pattern of black and white, good versus evil in all the accounts of Lennox's trials, and the revelation gave her pause. She'd worked both sides of dozens of civil litigation cases in her career and rarely were the issues so clear-cut. Usually both parties were right about some things and wrong about others, and the key to working out a case was finding the middle ground. She could almost hear Lennox in her head right now, saying criminal cases were different and there was no middle ground when it came to retribution and punishment, but she doubted that was the case every single time. Besides, what kind of ego did it take to assume that because you'd charged someone with a crime, they were definitely guilty no matter what a jury ultimately decided?

Deciding she wasn't going to solve that mystery today, she moved on to checking for info on Lennox's personal life, telling herself she was doing so now in order to know her enemy, not stalking the woman with the kissable lips. Details were scarce.

Lennox didn't appear to own a house, she wasn't on social media, and none of the news articles about her cases contained personal info. Wren scrolled through several pages of Google and stopped on an article about a Daniel Roy who'd been sentenced to twenty years in prison. The same surname was likely a coincidence, but she clicked on the link anyway, curiously drawn to find out more.

The mugshot that appeared on her screen was a stunning likeness of Lennox, and Wren was riveted to the screen. Daniel Roy was currently in his fourth year in prison, housed at the Allred unit of the Texas Department of Corrections near Wichita Falls. Wren kept clicking and learned that Daniel had been charged with murder in neighboring Tarrant County, and had pled guilty. Could this inmate really be a relative of Lennox, or was it only a coincidence that they looked so much alike?

What Wren wanted to do was go down the rabbit hole of the internet and find the answer, but she was already risking being late for court as it was. She reluctantly closed her browser and headed for the shower. As the hot water cascaded over her body, her mind kept wandering back to Lennox with her shirt off at the party. Her well defined abs and kissable lips were very much a hot topic, but if Daniel Roy was related to her, Wren was even more curious about what else Lennox had to reveal.

Lennox glanced around the courtroom, but there was no sign of Wren and she could feel Judge Larabee's agitation from across the room.

"When's the last time you spoke with defense counsel?" Larabee asked, fixing her with a stern scowl.

Lennox swallowed hard as her mind flooded with the memory of Wren standing in front of her in Parker and Morgan's garage, lips parted, ready and willing to be kissed.

"Have you talked to her this morning?"

Lennox exhaled and shook her head. "It's been at least a week, Judge, but I've had no indication she wouldn't be in court today."

Larabee's forehead bulged. "She's new, isn't she? Not big on making good first impressions, I see." He turned to his bailiff. "Set your watch for five minutes. If she's not here by then, arrest her when she walks in the door."

Lennox shot a look at the back door, half hoping Wren would burst through the door and save them all a full display of Larabee's wrath. As the old-fashioned clock on the wall kept ticking with no sign of Wren, the silence in the courtroom became almost unbearable. At the four minute and thirty second mark, she stood, no longer able to stand the suspense. "Judge, I'd like to propose—"

The double doors flew open, and Wren strode into the room like absolutely nothing was wrong. "Good morning, Judge Larabee, Ms. Roy. I'm sorry I'm late, but—"

Larabee smacked his gavel on the bench. "Sam, take her into custody."

Lennox half stood to protest, but Sam, the bailiff, beat her to it.

"All due respect, Judge, she had ten more seconds on the clock," he said, his usual drawl laced with a hint of pleading.

Larabee's face reddened. "You sure about that, Sam?"

Sam nodded slowly. "Yes, sir." He held up his wrist. "Fiftieth anniversary present and the wife sprang for the good stuff."

Leave it to Sam to be the only person left who kept time on a wristwatch. "If it matters, Your Honor, I was watching the time too and I agree with Sam."

"Fine," Larabee said, his tone making it clear it wasn't actually. He pointed the gavel at Wren. "Counselor, present your motion."

Lennox expected Wren to be flustered, out of sorts, first from showing up late and then from having the judge discuss her fate as if she wasn't even in the room, but she appeared to be unflappable.

"Thank you, Judge." Wren pulled a legal pad covered with scribbles out of her bag, which she set in the seat behind the defendant. "We'd like to begin by renewing our motion for reasonable bail. Mr. Allen has identified several items he can put up as collateral, and he has identified a suitable place to live pending trial."

"You have anything to say?" Larabee glared at Lennox.

"The State of Texas opposes any reduction to the current bail amount and asserts that no amount of bond could secure the defendant's presence at trial."

"Well, that's ridiculous," Wren said. "I'd like to hear specific evidence that supports that assertion."

Lennox didn't bother responding, figuring the judge would shut her down. Larabee wasn't big on doing any favors for defense counsel, especially not public defenders, though he'd never come right out and said it. She was pretty sure his theory was that if a person couldn't afford to pay for a lawyer, they shouldn't have gotten into trouble in the first place. Troublesome perspective for sure, but what kind of advocate would she be if she didn't take advantage of every opportunity in her favor?

A moment of silence passed, and Lennox stared at the judge, wondering what was up. He was staring down the edge of his nose at Wren, but instead of looking angry, he looked curious.

"Ms. Bishop, do I know you?"

Wren stood to address him, a totally unnecessary move, but Lennox figured she was being extra deferential to make up for being late. "I'm not sure we've met, Your Honor."

He scratched his chin and stared at the ceiling. "Wait, I know where I know you from. Don't your parents live in Houston?"

"Yes, Judge, they do. Do you know them?"

"Hell yes, I do. I'm pretty sure everyone in the southern half of the state does as well."

This conversation wasn't going the way Lennox hoped it would, but it would make her seem like a jerk to object to what some would characterize as harmless conversation. She, on the other hand, knew exactly what was happening.

"Didn't you use to work with them?" Larabee asked.

Wren shook her head. "No, sir. Well, unless you count summers spent babysitting my younger brother. Mom and Dad were always very generous, but when it comes to career, they believe their children should carve out their own path."

Lennox didn't think Wren, who sported designer suits and accessories, knew the first thing about making her own way in the world. Not really, but again, speaking up now would make her sound like a jerk.

"That's a nice philosophy. And you decided to make your own way at the public defender's office?"

Wren cleared her throat and looked down. "I wish I could say I was that socially conscious. Actually, I'm in my fourth year with Dunley Thornton, but I'm on loan to the PD's office for now."

Larabee's ears perked up at the mention of Dunley Thornton. Lennox could almost see the dollar signs floating above his head. Like Nina, Larabee was up for reelection this year, and he could use a cash infusion from a big law firm. Let the sucking up begin.

"What a huge sacrifice. Good for you." Larabee pointed at Jared Allen. "You're very lucky, you know. Not everyone gets a top-quality defense lawyer for free." He consulted the file in front of him and steepled his fingers. "I've given this some thought and I think it would be best for your defense if you were allowed a more reasonable bond." He smacked the gavel, purely for effect, and pronounced, "Bond is reduced to fifty thousand, cash or surety. Defendant is required to wear an electronic monitoring device while on bond and must report in weekly to the court probation officer."

He rattled off a few other conditions while Lennox stared at him, unable to believe he'd gone from don't I know your parents to a ridiculously low bond. Allen would only have to put up five thousand to get a bondsman to grant surety. When Larabee finished, the bailiff came to gather him to head back to the jail for a hot second until he could source the funds. Lennox tried to catch Wren's eye, but she followed her client into the holdover without a backward glance. She wondered how long it would take Wren to give her client the real picture—that the judge may have lowered his bond, but even if he could now make bail, the conditions were so restrictive, he'd likely wind up back in jail within a week or two. Guys like him thought they were above the rules, but she'd gladly show him differently.

She spent another few minutes slowly gathering her things. She told herself it was procrastination regarding the stack of files in her office she needed to review, but she knew the delay was more about hoping Wren would emerge from the holdover and they could talk. She'd been wanting to talk since their near kiss. She'd been cocky and careless, and she'd almost crossed a line. Thank God Ford and Skye had shown up when they did, or she might have made a huge mistake. She closed her eyes and relived the moment. An image of Wren's full lips filled the screen of her thoughts. She hadn't had a chance against that kind of temptation, and she thought the only solution was to steer clear of Wren anywhere outside of the courthouse, that doing so would help her avoid the risk of giving in to her feelings, but now that they were in the same room, she knew her urge was deeper than she'd thought.

"Sleeping in the courtroom, huh? So, do you win your cases by osmosis? Now I know your secret."

Lennox opened her eyes to see the woman she'd been daydreaming about standing right in front of her, and while she had been hoping to see her again, she didn't like being caught off guard. "Not sleeping. Nope. But I was thinking about this case. Care to grab a cup of coffee and talk about it with me?"

"Sure."

"Great, I just need to check in with my number two. Meet you downstairs?"

"In the cafeteria?" Wren frowned. "Oh no. That's not going to work at all."

"What's the problem?"

"Well, you asked me to join you for coffee, but all they have downstairs is colored water devoid of any flavor beyond burnt rubber. Check in and then head up to my office." She started toward the door. "See you in a bit."

Lennox watched her go, curious about what Wren had in mind. She wasn't wrong about the quality of the coffee in the cafeteria—it resembled late afternoon diner coffee that had spent too much time on the burner—but she wasn't big on leaving the courthouse in the middle of the day just to go in search of decent coffee, especially since there weren't a lot of good coffee shops in the warehouse district near the courthouse.

But meeting with Wren wasn't about coffee, it was about the case and she'd do well to remember that. She checked in with Johnny and took the stairs to the ninth floor. The PD's secretary, Sally, was on the phone when she approached the desk, but she waved her on back where Lennox wandered the halls until she found Wren's cramped office. Wren was on the phone but waved her into the room. She settled into the chair across from her desk and tried not to eavesdrop on her conversation.

"I'd love to see you…Saturday night is perfect…No, I'll make the reservations. I'm not that busy. Okay, love you too."

Lennox shifted in her chair as she analyzed Wren's tone. Was that a romantic "love you" or a friendly one? Was she talking to the woman she'd seen her with at Sue Ellen's or was this someone else?

"Sorry about that," Wren said as she hung up the phone. "My parents are going to be in town this weekend and I haven't seen them in a while. Apparently, they have big news. Don't you hate when people tell you they have something big to tell you, but refuse to give any hints so you're left wondering if they're going to drop a bomb or simply buy you a private island? Anticipatory dread is how I'll be spending the next few days."

Lennox reflected on pretty much every time her parents called her. She was certain the accompanying sense of dread she felt when she spotted their number on an incoming call could top anything Wren's parents had to offer, but she'd never confided that fact to anyone other than Nina and she wasn't about to start now. Instead, she murmured a simple, "The worst."

"Are you close to your parents?"

The question caught her off guard. It wasn't like she hadn't been asked before. It was the kind of topic that people usually assumed didn't carry a lot of baggage, but when it did, it was usually explosive. She'd become good at leaving the pin in the grenade and she wasn't about to release it now. "Not really, but it's a mutually acceptable arrangement." Sensing from Wren's expression she was about to ask a follow-up question, she quickly changed the subject. "Didn't you promise me coffee?"

Wren's smile was contagious. "I did." She turned around and pulled a French press and two mugs from behind her filing cabinet. "This is a nice Sumatra. Even but intense, with a nice finish." She pointed to a mini-fridge next to her desk. "I have cream if you want, but I suggest you try it first because it's delicious on its own."

Lennox stared at the top of Wren's desk, now transformed into a hipster coffee shop. What was happening right now?

Wren filled a mug and handed it to her. "What's the matter?"

Lennox paused for a moment before accepting the mug from Wren. "How long have you been handcrafting coffee drinks here in your office?"

"Pretty much since my second day. Don't get me wrong, I still contribute to the whatever is the cheapest at the warehouse super saver whatever to fit in, but there's no rule that says I have to drink the stuff just because I helped pay for it."

Lennox laughed.

"What?" Wren asked, like she really didn't have a clue why what she'd said was so humorous, a naivete Lennox would normally find annoying in most people, but on Wren it was adorable.

Lennox pointed to the French press. "You're a junior barista who has set up shop in her office. You really think none of the other PDs have noticed your home brew is different from whatever they're all drinking. This along with the designer suits and you drive a car that cost more than a few of them combined make in a year."

Wren sipped her coffee and stared at her, but she didn't say a word.

"You don't have anything to say?"

"I'm mulling it over." Wren took another sip and then abruptly set down her mug. "All done mulling. Who cares how I get my coffee fix and what kind of suits I wear? And what I drive is no reflection on my ability to practice law. Well, maybe that's not right. I was hugely successful at my last job which is why I'm able to afford a nice car and have nice things. Why is that something I should be ashamed of? Tell me?"

Lennox threw up her hands. "Hey, drive, drink, and carry whatever you want. I don't care. I was simply offering some insight into your coworkers. They aren't big on anyone who doesn't do their kind of work, or if they did, doesn't express enough chest beating to show off their sacrifice."

"I see. I haven't earned the right to be self-righteous and mean."

"They're a tight-knit group."

"That's one way of putting it. How about prosecutors? Are they a tight-knit group too?"

Lennox paused for a moment to consider the question. She was close with her colleagues, but she couldn't deny there was a bit of competition within the ranks. Who got the most guilty verdicts, who would get promoted from a misdemeanor to a felony court? Those kinds of questions lurked below the surface during the happy hours and the backyard barbecues. The PD's office, on the other hand, didn't have the same hierarchal structure, and they seemed to celebrate all victories and mourn all losses together as if they were banded together against the man. "Unlike you, we all represent the same client."

"That's not an answer."

Lennox sighed, knowing Wren wasn't going to let this go. "We're a tight-knit group for the most part, but there is an element of competition. That said, I don't recall any real mean girl crap." Her memory nudged and she held up a hand. "Okay, I've seen it once, but that was back when I was in misdemeanor court." She frowned. "It was about a lawyer on loan—like you, although I've never seen the DA take in one for a felony court like the program you're in. But we get scads of lawyers vying for real world experience, and the big firms send their castoffs down here all the time. They get to write it off as pro bono and we get a warm body to fill a seat in the DA's office."

Wren frowned. "You think I'm a castoff?"

"To be perfectly frank, I don't know anything about your legal skills, but even if you've handled a few white-collar cases for big shot clients, you haven't been in the trenches doing criminal defense work and you've never been a prosecutor." She paused, realizing she'd just revealed she'd done a little digging into Wren's past. "This is a different world from what you're used to, and the fact that this is only temporary for you makes you less likely to fit in. That's a fact." She waited a beat, but Wren didn't say anything. "So, that's it? You don't have anything to say in response?"

Wren took a sip of her coffee and then set down her mug. "I'm mulling."

"You do a lot of mulling."

"It's a skill. You should try it."

Wren's tone was even, but Lennox knew her words were a bit of a dig. "Maybe, but I tend to trust my instincts."

"And what do your instincts tell you about me?"

"That you're a good person and you want to do good, but for all your well-meaning intentions, you don't have a clue how the system really works, and you'll be out of here before you will ever be able to figure it out." She hunched a shoulder. "The rest of us will still be here, doing the work." She stood. "Tell Ford, when he's ready to have a serious talk about a plea deal for Jared Allen, he knows where to find me." She set her mug on Wren's desk. "Thanks for the brew. It was a nice change, but I don't want to get used to it."

She left without looking back, but she could feel the burn of Wren's intense gaze on her back. The truth was she enjoyed the coffee and the company more than she liked to admit. It was time to stop this silly flirtation before it started to distract her from her work. Besides, it wasn't like it was going to go anywhere since Wren would be leaving in a few months.

Then you could date her, and you wouldn't be breaking your no dating at the office rule.

Lennox pushed the voice away. Not constructive. Not helpful at all.

CHAPTER EIGHT

Wren huddled against Ford in the tiny space in the visiting area of the north tower of the main Dallas County jail, because she had no choice if she was going to hear anything they discussed with Jared. The window with one handset was designed to be a perfect fit for one visitor, and there were no other choices. Even with the truncated space, it was still nicer than some of the other jails she'd visited during her brief tenure at the PD's office. So far she'd been to three different jails, all in Dallas County. One was a small group of cells located on the tenth floor of the civil courthouse downtown—a fact she'd never known even though she'd been in that building on many occasions in the past. Another was a converted hotel off I-35, whose claim to fame was that Doris Day had stayed there back in the day. She doubted most of the young inmates at the hotel even knew who Doris Day was, and she only knew because her grandmother used to sing "Que Sera, Sera" to her when she was little.

"Do you want to take the lead?" Ford asked. "He seems to trust you."

Wren appreciated the vote of confidence, but Lennox's speech about how she was only here on a temporary basis was still ringing in her ears. "I think you should. What if he decides not to take a plea, and I'm gone by the time this case goes to trial? He should make a decision with the one who's in it for the long haul. Besides, I'm not entirely sure I know what he should do."

Ford smiled. "No one does. He's the only one who can really know if he's guilty and whether he wants to gamble on a jury. Our job is simply to give him all the information and expertise we can and let him make the decision."

"And if he asks outright what he should do?"

"What does your gut say?"

Wren wanted to say the only thing her gut did when she thought about the range of punishment on this case was churn, but that was a cop-out. She didn't have to give his question any real thought. "He should go to trial. The evidence appears damning, but scratch the surface and there's nothing there. Anyone could've started that fire. If he did it, he sure went about it stupidly, which I get doesn't preclude his guilt, but it takes away the argument that he had a lot to gain. People who have a lot to gain generally go to greater lengths to protect their prize. Even if he gets found not guilty by a jury, the life insurance company will probably tie the benefit up in court for the rest of his life." She took a breath, about to launch into the rest of her logic, but Ford was grinning at her. "What?"

"And this is why you should talk to him. Let him think about it for a moment before you plunge in with the epic underdog anthem. Okay?"

She gave an exaggerated sigh. "I'll do my best."

"You should reconsider going back."

"Context, please?"

He waggled a finger between her and their surroundings. "You're good at this."

She wanted to accept the compliment at face value, but she could tell doing so would lead this conversation down a path she wasn't interested in exploring. "I'm happy to have this opportunity, but I've worked really hard to be on a partner track, and all I'm doing is applying all the fun litigation skills I've learned along the way."

"I hear you, but it's more than that." He held his hands up in surrender. "I'm not going to push it. When you're ready, there'll be a place for you."

She pushed the proposition to the back of her mind, knowing it wouldn't stay there, but determined not to let it derail her plans. She'd spent years building a place for herself at Dunley Thornton, and if she made partner, then she'd have some sway to be able to help others in ways she could only dream of as a first-year public defender. And making it at Dunley was an achievement she'd accomplished all on her own, without the help of her parents—mostly. She couldn't deny the family name opened doors, but she'd put in the labor to prove she was worthy in her own right. Tossing it all away now would defeat all her hard work.

The creak of the door in front of them saved her from having to respond. Jared shuffled toward them and slunk into the lone chair. He wasn't looking good. He was pale and his clothes and hair were disheveled.

"Everything okay in there?" she asked.

"What do you think?" he growled.

She stared in shock, taking a moment to reconcile this guy with the mild-mannered man she'd met in the holdover at the courthouse.

"Sorry," he said, hanging his head. "Being in here…it's getting to me. Any word on lowering the bail? Were you able to get in touch with my cousin about posting the surety?"

"Wren got the bond lowered to fifty thousand, but we haven't been able to reach your parents or your cousin," Ford said. "You only need to come up with five thousand and someone who'll sign for you. Is there anyone else we can call?"

Jared shook his head. "You say *only* like it's nothing. I don't even have enough money on my books to buy some decent food in here. Believe me, if I had a way out I'd take it."

"We'll keep trying."

"I can't take much more of this. I haven't seen my kids since the day I was arrested. Who's taking care of them? It's my in-laws, isn't it?"

He directed his question to Wren, and she grimaced and nodded to acknowledge the gravity of the situation. "I know it has to be incredibly hard to be in here, feeling powerless, but your kids are with your sister-in-law. I'm assured they are being well cared for."

"And indoctrinated. I mean, I know she loves them, but Denise has never been a big fan of mine." He sighed. "If I could just get out of here, explain to them that I didn't do anything to hurt their mother."

His intense dejection signaled it was time for her to lay out his options. "About that. I've met with the ADA assigned to your case and she's made a plea offer."

"She wants me to plead guilty?" He shook his head vigorously. "Not going to happen."

"I hear you. You've been clear since the beginning that you are not interested in a plea, but I—we—have an obligation to tell you everything about your case, and that includes letting you know when there's an offer on the table for you to consider. You can take two minutes to consider it, or you can reject it outright, but we have to tell you about it. Understood?"

"I'm thinking it's not that great or you would've led with it."

Jared's smile was tortured, and Wren realized she kind of liked this guy. He was a mess for sure, but he was smart and cared about his kids, and it was time to put him out of his misery. "No, it's not great. She's offered twenty years. It's way less than a life sentence, but way more than walking free after a not guilty verdict."

"Shit. Twenty years. What does that actually mean in terms of how much time I'd have to do?"

It was the first time he'd even entertained talking about the details of a plea, and she had to think his mixed reaction was motivated by spending time inside, stewing about what was to come and talking to other inmates, many of whom probably had more experience than he did with the criminal justice system. But when it came to experience, she knew the details about the specifics would be better coming from Ford. She nudged his leg with hers, and he instantly got the clue.

"You'd do at least half of that time because it's an aggravated offense, so you'd be up for parole in ten years. Whether or not you'd get it, is a wild guess."

"Even ten years is a long time."

"Yes, yes it is," Wren said.

"And it could be more."

"Yes."

He stood and paced the small enclosure, the snap of his sports sandals against his heels growing louder with each pass. "You should sit down," Ford said.

"Why?" Jared asked. "Because if I don't, they're going to burst in here and end this visit? This cordial little meeting to tell me my life is basically over?" He threw up his hands. "Look at me. I'm wearing a canvas jumpsuit and shoes other people wear to the beach. I don't get to choose when or where or what I eat. I live in a space not much bigger than this room with a stranger in the bed two feet away. And here you both are and all you have to offer is a chance that I'll be doing this only another decade. There's not a lot more that can be done here to strip me of who I am."

Wren pressed her palm up to the glass. "Jared, come over here and listen to me."

He dipped his head and shook it slowly. "Please don't tell me any more bad news."

The pain in his voice stung, but it spurred her mission. "I won't. Please sit down."

He shuffled back into his seat, but the hopeful light was gone from his eyes.

"Look at me," Wren said, waiting to continue until he lifted his chin and looked up. "You don't want to take the plea, right?"

Silence stretched between them and she watched his face contort through a range of emotions.

"Not twenty."

His voice cracked on the words, and she could tell he was torn between the desire for a sure thing and the gamble of going all the way. "Is there any amount of time you would do to put this behind you?" She hated asking the question, but she sensed he'd been hoping for something more palatable that would allow him to move on with his life.

He shifted in his chair. "I don't know. Five maybe. Word is that would put me up for parole in less than two. Ben and Angela would still be young."

It was the first time he'd referenced his kids without insisting he was innocent. Wren shot Ford a look and he nodded for her to respond. "That's unlikely. They'd have to reduce the charge."

"But you'll ask, right?"

Ford should be the one answering this question since he'd be stuck with whatever mess she left behind. She could hear Lennox laughing now at the lowball offer. Not surprising since she'd told Ford twenty years was a gift. "Yes, we'll ask. And if they don't accept?"

"Then get me the quickest trial date you can."

They spent the balance of the hour discussing questions he had about his family and business. When she and Ford walked out of the jail and through the breezeway to the courthouse, he offered to convey Jared's counteroffer to Lennox. "It would be good experience for you, but if you're seeing her…you know, outside the courthouse…"

She'd never seen him at the loss for words, and she'd laugh if she weren't concerned about clearing up the misconception. Of course, he thought something was going on after he'd walked in on them almost kissing. Key word: almost. "We're not. And thanks for offering, but I've been talking to her most of the time so far. Let me see it through. I promise I won't get her so riled she doesn't even consider it."

"Oh, I doubt she'll consider it for very long," Ford said. "But if you can get her to think about it at all, that might stall things a bit. I know he wants to go to trial soon, but there's still a lot of bad publicity out there, poisoning potential jurors' heads. Plus, we're going to need our own expert at trial, and we'll need time to get him prepped."

Wren silently counted how many times Ford said "we." Under the same circumstances, every single partner at Dunley Thornton would be saying "I did this," "I thought of that," with little to no consideration for the fact the associates were the ones who did all the real work, leaving the partner free to show up and act like they'd saved the day. Ford's approach made her feel like her work was valuable, that it was more than a bunch of busy work designed to keep her occupied while the grownups did the real work. For her first couple of years at the firm, she'd worked only one piece of a case with no insights about how what she was doing fit in with the rest of the team, and it had been aggravating. The balance of autonomy and teamwork Ford had given her in the short period of time they'd been working together was refreshing—she actually felt like she was his colleague instead of a puppy nipping at his heels, begging for scraps along with the rest of the litter. If this was what feeling like a big dog was like, she could get on board. Now, she just had to convince Lennox to take her seriously. And that might be the biggest challenge yet.

Lennox stood at the back of the courtroom and watched Johnny argue pretrial motions in a burglary case to Nina who was sitting in for Judge Larabee who was out the rest of the week having a minor medical procedure done. Nina was roughing Johnny up a little, likely as a favor to her so she could see how he handled the pressure, but she hoped it wouldn't have the opposite effect. Johnny was a solid prosecutor, but he tended to take the safe route when it came to whether or not to take a case to trial, and she was ready for him to step up and start taking more risks. Nina raking him over the coals might not be the way to accomplish that goal, and she made a slicing motion across her throat, hoping her pal would get the hint.

"Ms. Roy, do you have anything you wish to add?" Nina called out from the bench.

So much for sneaking in to watch the proceedings. Cursing her best friend under her breath, Lennox merely waved. "No, Judge. Just passing through. This is Mr. Rigley's case." She ducked out of the room and headed back to her office, running smack into Wren Bishop as she burst through the double doors.

"Oh my gosh," Wren said as she backed up. "I appear destined to crash into your path at every turn."

"Not the worst thing that could happen." Lennox immediately regretted the words when she spotted Wren's pink cheeks. "I mean, there are a lot of defense attorneys who I'd like to run into less." She placed her hand on her forehead. "Never mind." She pointed back toward the courtroom. "If you're looking for the judge, she's in the middle of a hearing, but it should be over soon."

"Actually, I was looking for you."

Her head told her Wren seeking her out was for purely professional reasons, but her body experienced a surge of excitement at the proclamation. "Is that so?"

"We met with Mr. Allen, and I'd like to talk to you about your offer."

The excitement faded as fast as it had come. Silly really, since purely professional was exactly what she wanted, but she didn't have time to examine her conflicted emotions with Wren standing right in front of her waiting to talk about a case. She reached for the door to the DA workroom. "Great. Let's talk."

She led the way into her cramped office and offered Wren a seat.

Wren looked around before sitting down.

"What's wrong?" Lennox asked.

"Your office is so clean and organized. Admittedly, I haven't been working here long, but almost every prosecutor whose office I've been in has files stacked everywhere."

Lennox pointed to two large, space-hogging, file cabinets. "All my files, carefully ordered by date of disposition and then alphabetically. I can't function in chaos."

"I don't know about that. A lot of what happens here is pretty chaotic and you seem to handle yourself well."

"Thanks for the compliment, but it's never chaos to me. I'm probably the most prepared attorney you will ever meet." She held Wren's gaze, wondering how the conversation had gone from discussing a plea offer to how she handled her caseload. "You wanted to talk about Jared Allen's case?"

"Right." Wren took a big breath. "We have a counteroffer."

"Twenty is as low as I'm willing to go. I'm already starting to regret coming in that low."

"Then you better brace yourself." Wren took a breath and then rushed her words. "He'll do five, but it will have to be some other offense, non-aggravated."

"Five? Years?" Lennox held back a laugh. It wasn't funny, but it was bizarre. "That's ridiculous."

"Is it? Your detective and the fire inspector built their case backwards, based solely on supposed motive. But just because you think you have a juicy motive, doesn't mean the facts add up."

Lennox tried not to be distracted by the display of fiery passion that lit up Wren's eyes. "The facts add up just fine as far as I'm concerned."

"We'll have our own experts if we go to trial."

Lennox held back a smirk. The PD's office was nowhere near as well funded as the DA. "I'm sure you will."

"And arguments to combat your supposed motive."

"That's how this works."

"If you're so certain you have this locked up, why are you offering a plea at all?"

"My goal is to keep the family from having to testify in any capacity. Your client, if he cares about his family at all, should want the same thing."

"Which is why I'm here with a counteroffer."

"Five years is not a counteroffer, it's an insult."

"When's the last time you did five years in a state penitentiary?"

Bam. Wren's words barreled into Lennox's brain and shut everything down. She could almost hear the eerily similar last words her brother had shouted at her echoed in the refrain. She clenched the edge of her desk and focused on staying in the moment as the room started to swim in front of her.

"Are you okay?"

Lennox felt something warm and looked down to see Wren's hand on hers and then she looked back up into Wren's gentle, caring gaze. She jerked her hand away. "I'm fine."

Wren's hand remained on the desk for a moment before she eased it back into her lap. "Something just happened."

"No."

"Okay."

Wren drew out the word and looked at her expectantly, but she merely stared back unable to focus.

"So you won't take the offer to the family?" Wren asked.

Lennox forced herself to breathe. To remember what they'd been talking about. *Offer. Plea. Five years.* "I shouldn't."

"But you will because if your goal is to make this easy for them, you have to consider it."

"No. They may want to consider it, but whatever they decide is not binding on me, and just so we're clear, I'm not on board. At all. Speaking to them is a matter of respect, not persuasion." Lennox paused and noticed she was still gripping the desk. She eased her hold and shook out her stiff, aching fingers. "Don't expect me to encourage them to take the easy way out."

"Fair enough," Wren said, like it made her no never mind either way. She stood. "Any idea when you will be talking to them?"

Lennox almost asked who before she remembered what they were talking about again. "I've got a meeting scheduled with them tomorrow. I'll call you after, but I can assure you it won't make a difference."

Wren smiled. Not a cocky smile or a smirk, but a genuine happy, picking daisies in the park with birds flying around her head kind of smile. "I'll look forward to hearing from you then."

Lennox wanted to yell, "Didn't you hear me? I said it's not going to make a difference," but she didn't want to be the person who caused that smile to disappear, because as much as she didn't believe anyone could be that happy, seeing Wren smile like that kind of made her want to have faith such happiness could exist. So, instead she opted for a mumbled, "Okay, then."

Wren walked to the door and opened it and even took a step across the threshold before Lennox started to breathe again, confident she could focus much better with Wren out of her space.

"Hey."

She looked up to see Wren in the doorway, facing her. "I thought you left."

"I did, but I didn't make it far."

Lennox waited, but when Wren didn't speak, she did. "Did you forget something?"

Wren bit her bottom lip. "What are you doing tonight?"

"Tonight? Me?"

Wren made a show of looking around. "Is there someone else here? Yes, you. I want to buy you dinner."

Warning bells clanged and Lennox was quick to respond. "Oh no. I'm sorry if I gave you the impression—"

"That you're a person who likes to eat? Goes to restaurants? Socializes with other people?" Wren rolled her eyes. "No secret expectations on my part. It's a simple invitation, and no, it's not a date. Simply two professional people getting to know each other over a meal. It's done all the time by all kinds of people and rarely does anyone die from the encounter, although I did see this *20/20* episode where—"

Lennox couldn't handle waiting anymore to announce her decision. "Yes, dinner. I'll meet you wherever, just leave me in peace so I can get some work done."

"Great. I'll make a reservation and text you the details. What's your phone number?"

Lennox rattled off the number and ended with a sigh. Fine. She'd do this—whatever it was, but she wasn't entirely sure it wouldn't kill her.

CHAPTER NINE

Wren clicked the reserve table now button on her phone and cut and pasted the restaurant info into a text to Lennox. *See you at seven thirty*, she typed. She stared at the screen for a moment, but when no quick reply materialized, she decided to stow her phone in her bag to keep from checking it compulsively. No sooner had it left her hand than it started buzzing repeatedly. She grabbed it and swiped it open.

Sounds good. See you there.

Wren smiled, relieved Lennox wasn't the kind of person who felt the need to abbreviate her texts, but kind of wishing she'd added some emojis to indicate she wasn't being dragged to this dinner against her will. Not that Lennox seemed like the kind of person who did anything against her will. Of course, she didn't really know anything about her, but hopefully after tonight that would change. She was determined to pry as much information as she could out of Lennox on her mission to find a way to burrow beneath that hard exterior and get her to come around to her way of thinking about Jared Allen's case.

You know that's not the only reason you asked her to dinner.

Her inner voice wasn't wrong. She was attracted to Lennox— who wouldn't be? But in a curious about the enigmatic, successful, good-looking woman kind of way. She hadn't been lying when she told Lennox this wasn't a date. Lennox wasn't her usual type at all. She was way too buttoned up and inflexible about her beliefs.

Wren could never imagine them having a productive conversation because Lennox was too convinced her way was the right way. That might work in a professional setting, but on a date, it was a death knell. Which begged the question of why she'd asked Lennox on a date-like outing to discuss business. She didn't have the answer, but she did know she was looking forward to it. But there would be no kissing.

Damn, why had that thought and the accompanying flashback to the almost kissing popped into her head just now? Dumb question since she knew the truth—it had been lying there, below the surface for days.

Her phone buzzed again, and she glanced at the screen.

Dinner tonight?

Diane. She set the phone down while she considered her options. They hadn't seen each other in days, and Wren was a little disturbed to realize she hadn't missed Diane at all. That and the fact she was thinking about kissing other women—make that one woman in particular—signaled it was time to officially break things off. They hadn't been together all that long, and they'd never even pretended to be exclusive, but she knew in her heart, that as tempting as it was to thumb out a Dear Jane text, she had to talk to Diane in person. But not right now. She picked up her phone and typed a quick response. *Can't tonight, but we should meet soon and talk.*

The response was swift and confusing. *You changed your mind already?* Wren stared hard at the screen, mortified to realize she'd sent the reply to Lennox instead of Diane. She scrambled to remedy her mistake. *Sorry. That wasn't meant for you. We're still on. See you there.*

To avoid making the same mistake again, she picked up the phone and called Diane.

"Hey, I was expecting a text."

Wren bit back a retort to the passive-aggressive way of telling her not to call in response to a text. "I've had to do a lot of texting today and my thumbs are tired. I've got a work dinner thing tonight."

"Okay. How about you come over later? I'm sorry I've been so busy lately. It's been a week and I've missed you."

The smooth, sultry voice usually roped her right in, but this time she recognized it for the click bait it was. Diane didn't miss her. She missed the concept of "them"—two successful women who could make a formidable couple if they joined forces. She faked a yawn. "I better not. I've got an early morning and I'm tired. I'll probably crash as soon as I get home."

"Well, if you change your mind, let me know." Diane purred the words. "I'm always up for a surprise visit."

When had Diane's over-the-top flirting started to get on her nerves? She wasn't sure, but she did know that there was no way she was going to stop by Diane's place for a late-night booty call tonight. Or ever again. "I'll give you a call when things settle down."

"Sure, sure. Call me when you can."

Wren heard the annoyance, but she couldn't summon up enough feeling to commit to anything other than a 'talk to you soon'. After they hung up, Wren wondered what Lennox would think of Diane. She wasn't sure why that question popped into her head, but now that it had, she couldn't stop comparing qualities. They both worked hard and were good at their jobs. They both had incredible sex appeal, but it came across in completely different ways. Diane's was all out there like a diamond tiara, but Lennox's was like granite, hard and strong and full of surprises the closer you looked. Both were impactful, but Lennox's subtlety captured her imagination and left her wanting more.

She shook her head in frustration. She needed to stop thinking about Lennox as anything other than an adversary or she was going to be in trouble.

An hour later she was home, standing in her closet, trying to decide what to wear. Del Frisco's Grille was laid-back, but it was also kind of hip and trendy, and except for the random tourist who might wander in, it was likely to be full of fashion-forward thirty-somethings. Not that she didn't fit that description, but she'd chosen it for the food and location. Trying to picture Lennox enjoying the vibe made her head hurt a little. What had she been thinking? She should've picked a quieter place, one that was more diner and less date night. She checked the time. If she changed the reservation now, she'd come off looking flaky and she didn't want to look flaky. She wanted to look put together and confident and not the least bit like she was overthinking this evening. Which she totally was.

Fine. Without thinking, she yanked her favorite jeans, a white scoop neck tee, and her new favorite clothing item—a crop trench linen jacket—from the closet and quickly changed. She completed the look with a pair of sandy beige, buttery soft gladiator sandals, and stood back to examine her reflection in the full-length mirror in her bedroom. Casual chic and not a designer label in sight. None visible, anyway.

She'd left the car with the valet, but she called downstairs to tell them she changed her mind and wouldn't need it. She shoved a lipstick in her jacket pocket along with her phone and ditched her designer purse on the table just inside her front door. It was a nice night and walking to the restaurant seemed like a good way to burn off her anxious energy.

McKinney Avenue was packed—not unusual for a Thursday night—and everyone appeared to be pre-celebrating the weekend by raising a glass during happy hour. She loved the vibrant feel of the neighborhood. The mix of old and new architecture, trendy new eateries mixed with venerable mainstays. And she loved being able to step outside of her building and be right in the thick of the action or, when she was ready to commune with nature, walk the Katy Trail, mere yards from her door. She wondered where Lennox lived. Was she an apartment or house kind of person?

The better question was why she cared. She could pretend her curiosity was directed at sussing out more about Lennox as a prosecutor, but she wasn't having similar questions about every other prosecutor she'd dealt with at the courthouse. She might be a little obsessed with this one, and that could be a problem.

She chewed on that thought on the final steps to the restaurant and came to the conclusion her attraction to Lennox was only a problem if she let it interfere with work, and she resolved that wasn't going to happen. First off, she was only at the PD's office until the end of August. Second, she wasn't a teenager with a crush. She could manage a physical attraction by staying on top of her emotions. Likely, part of her attraction to Lennox was the fact the woman she'd been dating was missing the mark for her on so many levels. On paper, Diane was the perfect girlfriend. Beautiful, accomplished, and successful. In real life though, her good looks and accomplishments didn't outweigh her complete self-centered focus, which led her to think she was, in turn, nothing more than a good on paper girlfriend to Diane and one who'd lost favor since she'd started working at what Diane viewed as a less-than job at the PD's office. In comparison, Lennox might not be able to see her side of things, but at least she understood her work at the PD's office was meaningful, representing real people in the midst of tragedy, rather than big corporations fighting over their piece of the financial pie.

When she reached the door of the restaurant, she paused before entering and took a deep breath. This dinner was purely business. She would talk to Lennox about the case and enjoy some good food and that was it.

Two steps in and her resolve dissolved on the floor in a puddle of lust.

Lennox was dressed in jeans and a black leather jacket and, hard to believe, she looked even more delicious than she had with her shirt off at Morgan and Parker's party. Wren took advantage of the fact Lennox hadn't noticed her yet to stare, unable to pull her eyes away. She looked badass—the complete opposite of the buttoned-up, law-and-order prosecutor she'd sparred with earlier in the day. This Lennox was as powerful and confident as the other version, but she was edgy too, riding the boundaries of other people's expectations and blasting them all to hell.

Lennox smiled and strode toward her, and Wren knew she should stop staring, but she was riveted.

"Hey," Lennox said, her voice low and husky. "You're right on time."

"And you're early." The simple observation was all Wren could manage.

"Habit."

They stood and stared at each other for a few minutes. Wren knew she should say something, do something—anything to break whatever this spell was that had rendered her unable to think and speak, but she was paralyzed. Finally, Lennox pointed toward the hostess stand. "You said you had a reservation?"

Right. They were here to eat dinner. Talk. Work stuff. Wren let out a breath. She could do this. Yep. "Yes. Come on."

Cindy, the hostess, greeted her enthusiastically. "Hi, Ms. Bishop. I figured you were out of town since I hadn't seen you in the last week." She very pointedly gave Lennox a scan. "Just the two of you?"

Wren tried not to grimace at the public announcement of her dining out habits, thankful that at least Cindy hadn't asked about Diane. She'd shared this favorite spot with Diane a few times, but Diane favored restaurants with white tablecloths and fancy waiters who hovered and had never warmed to the casual vibe. "Yes, two for dinner, please."

Cindy shot her a knowing smile and led them to a secluded table in the far corner, still in the thick of things, but not in the midst of all the noise. She pointed out a few specials on the menu, and left, but not before shooting Wren a knowing wink.

"I should've picked a quieter place," Wren said, praying Lennox hadn't picked up on Cindy's "have a great date" signals.

Lennox looked around, her expression neutral. "It's not that loud. You come here a lot, I take it."

"I live down the block. It's easy and they do great takeout." Wren leaned her arms on the table. "It's kind of nice being a regular. I don't have to explain any special orders and they're always offering me new stuff they're trying out in the kitchen."

"I guess that makes you a VIP then." Lennox set her menu down. "I have to confess, I'm not much of a food person." She patted her stomach. "I mean, I eat, of course, but mostly for fuel not for flavor. My go-to at night is usually a turkey sandwich and, if I'm feeling wild, I might add in some chips, but only if I'm going to get a run in the next morning."

Wren gasped. "Oh no. We live in a city full of some of the best restaurants in the country. So much good food worth working out for."

"I'm aware." Lennox's cheeks reddened. "I mean I know good food when I eat it—take Sammy's barbecue for example, but it's not like I seek it out."

"Well, now I feel like us meeting is fate." Wren leaned forward and stared into Lennox's eyes, hoping she wasn't freaking her out, but unable to resist the urge to plunge forward. "Do you trust me?"

Lennox tilted her head slightly, like she was considering the question, and after a long pause, she responded. "Oddly enough, in this very moment, I kind of do."

"Excellent." Wren reached over and grabbed Lennox's menu and set it next to hers at the edge of the table. "At the end of this meal, if you are not completely satisfied, I will owe you."

"You'll owe me? That's a pretty open-ended statement."

"Deliberately so." Wren held Lennox's gaze for a long moment. She was openly flirting now, and she didn't give a thought to the consequences. It was possible this dinner was a big mistake, but right now, in this moment, it felt like this was exactly where she should be, and she decided to embrace the moment, the feeling, and the way the light played on Lennox's hair.

Yeah. She was in trouble.

CHAPTER TEN

L ennox couldn't tell if the waitress was flirting with Wren or merely being super attentive, but for the second time tonight one of the employees greeted Wren by name and chatted with her like she was a long-lost friend. She wondered what it was like to live in a high-rise and stroll to fancy restaurants every night. Not that this was ostensibly a fancy restaurant. No, it was one of those trendy places that put off a casual vibe while it siphoned off the equivalent of a car payment for dinner and drinks.

"Shall we split a bottle of wine with dinner?" Wren asked, almost as if she'd read Lennox's thoughts.

She'd only had a glance at the wine list when the hostess had set it down, but it was long enough to know that everything on it was way beyond the range of both her knowledge and budget. Besides, if this really was a business dinner, she should stay sober. She motioned to her water. "I'm good with this."

A flash of disappointment appeared and just as quickly disappeared in Wren's eyes before she turned her attention back to the waitress. She handed her the list. "No wine tonight, but I would like a martini. For dinner, let's have my usual times two. Thank you."

The waitress nodded and whisked away. "You could've ordered the wine for yourself," Lennox said, feeling a bit like she'd ruined Wren's experience and unsure why she cared.

Wren waved a hand. "I don't need it. Besides, a martini seems much more business dinner, am I right?"

Business dinner. Lennox was surprised at the twinge of disappointment the two words carried even though she'd characterized it the same way in her head a moment ago. She filed the emotion away to be examined later. "I suppose you're right, but does it count if you're the only one with the martini?"

"Can I talk you into one?"

"I'm more of a beer person."

"They've got some great microbrews on tap."

Lennox wavered for a moment. If this was really business, she would never have a drink, but they were past that now and a beer might take the edge off. But a martini would put her on equal footing with Wren and she needed that right now. "I think I'll keep it business and join you with a martini."

"Vodka or gin?"

"Hey, I thought you were doing the ordering."

Wren grinned. "Look who's letting me be in charge for the very first time since we've met."

"*Letting you.* See how that works?"

"Duly noted." Wren called out to the waitress as she walked by and added another martini to the order. "Now that we have the housekeeping out of the way, let's talk. Did you grow up in Dallas?"

Lennox picked up the cocktail napkin the waitress had left on the table and started twisting it into a knot. "I thought we were here to talk about the case."

"Oh, we'll get to that. I ordered a four-course meal. I thought we'd start with some appetizer-like information to break the ice. So…did you?"

Why was the simple question so hard to answer? Because that's how it always started. People make a few innocent queries, and next thing you know they wanted to burrow deeper and deeper into who you are. But everything about Wren's engaging smile, her carefree tone, appeared innocently curious, and it really was a pretty innocuous question. Surely, she could handle sharing a tiny bit of information. "Yes, but not this part of town. I grew up in Oak Cliff."

"I love that area. My favorite thing to do on Sundays is have lunch in the Bishop Arts District and then walk around and visit all the shops, ending the day with coffee and wine at Wild Detectives. It's my favorite bookstore. Have you been there? Do you love it?"

Lennox wanted to reel back the last two minutes, listen to her instincts, and refuse to answer the original question, but it was too late now. "Not that part of Oak Cliff." She injected her words with a somber tone and punctuated them with a stare. "Our apartment was on the other side of the highway, Kiest Park area. More gunfire and drug deals than brunches and art galleries." She examined Wren's face for any signs of pity or disgust, but detected only genuine interest, like she was waiting for her to say more. Fat chance. She'd already said more than she'd meant to.

A man walked over carrying two martini glasses. He set them both on the table and greeted Wren enthusiastically. Wren introduced him as simply Bruce, the manager of the restaurant, and then answered his question about how she was doing. Lennox expected to feel relief at the interruption, but instead she was agitated. Wren obviously knew everyone in this place, which was great for her, but the familiarity put her on edge. She was a regular at the sandwich shop around the corner from the house she rented in old East Dallas, but other than that, she tended to walk through the outside world anonymously. She didn't have any social media accounts, she didn't discuss her personal life with anyone other than Nina, and her only other friends were people she'd worked with for years at the courthouse. Yet here she was in a bustling restaurant with a practical stranger, sharing details about her upbringing that only Nina knew.

While Wren chatted with Bruce about some new restaurant going in around the corner, Lennox became consumed with the desire to get the hell out. She started formulating excuses for why she had to leave and had almost settled on one when she heard Wren say, "It was great to see you." She motioned for him to lean closer. "Lennox and I need to discuss a sensitive work matter. Do you think you can get them to deliver the apps and then hold off coming by for a bit? We're not in any hurry. Right, Lennox?"

She nodded her reply, an automatic response, and watched Bruce assure her he would take care of it personally. Seconds later, he was gone, and Wren was back to looking at her with that intense gaze that made her feel like she was the only person in the room. Not agreeing with her felt rude and unnatural. "Right."

"You were telling me about the neighborhood where you grew up," Wren prompted her.

"I was done."

Wren studied her for a moment, like she was trying to decide whether to push the point. "Do you like living in Dallas?"

Relieved that Wren had switched topics, Lennox was quick to answer. "Love is a strong word. I like it okay. Working for the county here gives me a much broader scope of experience than I'd get in any of the surrounding counties." Wren chuckled. "What?"

"Everything circles back to work for you."

"It's my life." The words spilled out before she could stop them, but she wasn't sure she'd change her response, given the opportunity. It was honest. Work *was* her life. She was certain it had saved her from a rocky fate, and she was determined this anchor would be the one thing she would never lose. "I don't do much else."

"I gathered that. Which is probably why you're so good at it."

"Flattery is not going to win me over."

"Another reason you're good at what you do." Wren raised her glass. "A toast to the restorative benefits of work."

Lennox raised her glass and clinked it against Wren's. The icy vodka mixed with the olive brine led a smooth path down her throat, and she warmed to the heat. Be careful, her brain said. You could learn to like this. "You seem like the kind of person who thinks restorative properties come from something other than work."

"I'm not sure, but I think I've just been insulted."

"No, just an observation."

Wren raised her eyebrows. "Based on?"

Lennox gestured around the restaurant. "All of this. Nice restaurants, expensive clothes, and high-end cars. Work seems like a means to an end, not the other way around."

"Believe it or not, I've worked hard my whole life. It may not be the kind of work you value, but that doesn't mean it doesn't have meaning or require lots of skill and effort. I know I'm privileged. Why else do you think…"

Lennox cocked her head, waiting for Wren to finish, but instead she raised her martini glass and finished her drink. "You were saying…"

Wren cleared her throat. "I was going to say that it's possible to spend too much time on any one side of things. Lack of perspective can cloud a person's ability to empathize, to see other viewpoints."

It was Lennox's turn to feel indignant. "And you think I lack perspective?"

"Maybe. Think about it. Cases come to you, supposedly vetted by law enforcement. You can't help but take it for granted the defendants are guilty of something even if it's not the crime they were charged with. You see a lot of really bad stuff. Autopsy reports, gruesome crime scene photos, victims whose lives have been wrecked and shattered. Of course you're jaded. How could you not be? But your position comes with a responsibility to step outside of preconceived notions and try to find the truth."

"Wow." Lennox stared across the table, fighting her gut reaction to get up and leave. "You're pretty preachy for someone who deigns to work among the downtrodden, knowing it's not a permanent fate."

"Preachy? I didn't mean to sound patronizing, but I can see where what I said came across that way, and for that I'm sorry. But I stand by my intent. I don't see why it's a bad idea to look at the world through a variety of lenses."

"I'll tell you why." Lennox noticed she was shredding the napkin again and tossed the pieces onto the table. "Because if people don't have principles, they will lose their way. And the only way to set them straight is with real life consequences." She looked up as the waitress reappeared with a platter in her hand.

"You're going to love these," the waitress said in a smooth, silky voice. She picked up the shreds of napkin as if it was perfectly normal to find them on the tabletop. "Would either of you like another drink?"

"Yes," Wren said. "We both would." Her expression dared Lennox to defy her.

"Sure. Okay." Lennox waited until the waitress left the table before launching back into the conversation. "I kind of thought you might want to cut dinner short."

"Why would you think that?" Wren asked. She narrowed her eyes. "You mean because we're having a spirited debate?" She shook her head. "You should see my family around a dinner table. This is nothing."

Lennox saw a memory of her own family around a dinner table. Her parents fighting. Her brother too strung out to care. The entire evening ending in sobs of apology for behavior that would never change. "Not everyone has the privilege of a spirited exchange without consequences on the back end."

Wren leaned forward and captured her with an intense gaze. "I know. It's a fact I don't take for granted. I promise you." She started to pick up her drink but paused. "Oh, and people can like to shop and have nice things but still have principles. I promise."

Lennox nodded. She still didn't think Wren had a basis for her arguments, but she couldn't argue that she was professional about it. Too bad she wasn't sticking around at the PD's office—she'd be a worthy adversary. "I spoke to Lisa Allen's sister this afternoon. To give her a heads up that I'd have a few additional things to discuss at my meeting with her and the rest of the family tomorrow."

"Let me guess. She wanted Jared to spend the rest of his life in jail."

"On a good day. Most of the time, the family wants to stake him to a post and light him on fire."

"Do you think you can talk them down?"

Lennox tensed, worried she was about to bring this somewhat pleasant evening to an end. "I'm sure I could if I was inclined to."

Wren slowly nodded. "But you're not."

"Correct."

"Care to tell me why?"

"You don't want to hear it."

"Humor me."

"This isn't like the cases back at your firm where one side trims some items off their damages and the other one pays a little more to make it all go away. This family lost a daughter, a sister, the mother of their grandchildren. Those children will grow up without a mother and it will affect every aspect of their lives for as long as they live. There is no way to make it better."

"Except revenge."

"It's called justice."

"Even if he didn't kill her."

"Then he has the right to go to trial. If he didn't do it, he has no business taking a plea of any kind, even one that's a slap on the wrist."

"It's a sure thing versus a gamble. It's practical."

"Would you stand up in open court and say you did something you didn't do because it was practical?" Lennox watched Wren's face contort through a variety of expressions until she finally shook her head no. "I didn't think so."

"The truth is I don't know what I would do in that situation, but this isn't about me. Will you at least present them with the option? If they decline, let it be their choice."

She didn't want to, but she would. Only because she didn't want the fallout if the family later found out he'd been willing to take a plea and were mad at her for not letting them know. But she wasn't going to sell it to them because a pretty woman asked her to. Wren might have principles, but she had a reputation to uphold, and throwing cases wasn't part of it. She'd treat this case like any other. Just the facts, and no amount of cajoling from Wren was going to change her approach. "I'll tell them what you've offered. That's it." She braced for Wren's demeanor to change, and it did, but not in the way she expected.

"Fine. Now, can we truly enjoy these cheesesteak egg rolls because I've been craving them all day." Wren picked up an egg roll and waved it like it was a magic wand, and Lennox couldn't help but smile. She liked Wren—there wasn't any sense denying it, and the way her body reacted when Wren walked in the room confirmed there was definitely an attraction. But no amount of like or lust would get in the way of doing her job. Sweet smiles and cheesesteak egg rolls notwithstanding.

CHAPTER ELEVEN

"Good evening, Harry," Wren said to the doorman who leapt to attention as she approached her building.

"Good evening, Ms. Bishop. Did you have a nice dinner?"

It shouldn't be a complicated question, but Wren paused before answering as she took a moment to replay the entire evening. The food was delicious as usual, and once she and Lennox had put aside discussion of Jared's case, they'd discussed a myriad of other topics, like movies and books and the city—none of which were overly antagonizing. Lennox had laughed and smiled more than Wren had ever thought possible, but the entire evening she'd had the distinct impression Lennox was keeping herself in check, restrained, like there was an undercurrent of steel and that if she scratched the surface, they would clash and then this friendly Lennox would disappear. But for the first time since she'd met her, she considered Lennox's reserve wasn't a distasteful reaction to her, but merely the way she moved through the world all of the time, that it was intrinsic. Like she really was made of steel with only a veneer of regular human vulnerability. She'd heard the undercurrent of pain in Lennox's voice at the brief mention of her childhood, and Wren wondered what had happened to cause her to become so tough, so resistant to connection?

She was still thinking about it when her head had hit the pillow, but her phone rang interrupting her thoughts. She wanted to ignore it, but late-night calls usually signaled some kind of foreboding, so she reached for the phone and jabbed at the answer button. "Hello?"

"Were you sleeping?"

"Hi, Dad. Not yet, but close." She sat up in bed, suddenly alert, and checked the clock. It was almost one a.m. "Is something wrong? Are you and Mom okay?"

A second voice came through the line, and her mother said, "We're fine, but we weren't thinking about the time difference. We're in Scotland for the week, and up early for a golf game at one of the resorts we've been thinking of purchasing. We changed our flights and now we're connecting through Dallas tomorrow night instead of Saturday and we were hoping we could change our plans. I know it's Friday night and you probably already have plans, but our flight gets in in time for us to make an early dinner which should still give you plenty of time to do something else. You know, if you have a date or something."

Wren sighed with relief and ignored her mother's thinly veiled attempt to fish around for details about her personal life. "I don't have plans and I'd love to see you." She wanted to ask if the trip was for business or pleasure, but she wanted sleep more. They could talk tomorrow. "I'm not sure we can get into the restaurant I'd been planning to take you to, but I can get a different reservation."

"You still have a membership at the Tower Club, right? Let's go there. Your dad's been waxing nostalgic about their tortilla soup."

"Lots of James Beard finalists serving up great food all over this city and you two want to go to a private club instead." She playacted a heavy sigh. "Fine. It'll be nice to see you."

"Okay, sport," her dad said. "Now, go back to sleep. We'll text you when we land, but don't worry about meeting us at the airport. We'll take a car to the club and meet you there."

After Wren hung up the phone, it occurred to her that her parents forgot she wasn't working at the firm downtown, but across the tracks at the criminal courthouse. Oh well, they'd have a lot to talk about at dinner. When she'd first told them about her plan to enlist in the lawyer-on-loan program at her firm, they'd been all in favor of her giving back to the community, but now that she was immersed in it and enjoying the work, would they feel the same way?

The next morning, her alarm seemed to go off way too early, but she sprang out of bed and plunged right into her day. Coffee and a bagel to start, a brisk hot shower, and her favorite suit. It was Friday and it was sunny out and it was going to be a good day. Lennox would talk to the family, they would see the wisdom in the deal, and Lennox would come find her at the courthouse to tell her the news. Of all of the things that she envisioned happening on this day, seeing Lennox again had her the most excited, and right here, in the privacy of her home, she didn't mind admitting she had a little bit of a crush going.

An hour later, her excitement dimmed when she walked through the door of the PD's lounge to add her contribution to the monthly coffee buy and the cluster of other PDs gathered there abruptly stopped their conversation. She tried to shrug it off, but the shunning was starting to get to her. She put her hands on her hips and faced off. "You don't have to stop talking simply because I walk into the room. If you have something to say about me, I'd rather you say it to my face."

Jill cast a nervous glance at the rest of the group, clearly caught off guard by the confrontation. Good. It was time these people realized she wasn't a pushover. Wren kept up her stare, not willing to let them off the hook too easily. "I'm waiting."

"You may be Ford's pet project," Jill said. "But that doesn't mean we're going to stand for you waltzing in here and acting like you own the place."

Wren was startled by the vitriol. "What are you talking about?"

"We only have two investigators assigned to our entire office and they're both completely overworked, but we manage to function with the few resources we have, making sure we all get what we need, but Ford pulled one of them from half of his pending cases to help you out with your precious arson case. What do you have on him, anyway?"

Wren didn't immediately respond, taking time to process the anger behind the accusation. Jared Allen was technically Ford's case, not hers, and if he wanted to assign an investigator to it, he was within his authority, especially since he was head of the department.

But Jill's anger was deeper than that. Obviously, they all thought she was teacher's pet and getting special treatment because of it. It was time to address the root cause of this conflict, head-on.

"Ford was one of my law school instructors, and he's been a mentor to me for years. True, I didn't choose a career in criminal defense, but Ford taught me the importance of making sure everyone has solid representation without regard to their financial resources. I've been blessed with financial security and, over the years, I've contributed to causes like the Southern Poverty Law Center and the ACLU and Lambda Legal, but it never felt like enough. When the opportunity came up to participate in this program, to spend a few months doing hands-on work with your office, I jumped at it." She paused. "But I never thought the people who did this really important work would be so territorial, so resentful of anyone offering to help. I didn't expect to make any best friends when I walked through the door on my first day, but I'd hoped for a short while I could be part of a team that was doing big, important work, and that together we could do more than we could apart. Hell, I've seen better teamwork in the cutthroat world of big law than I have here."

She strode over to the coffee can and shoved a twenty inside. "Keep your investigators. I'm resourceful and I'll find another way to make sure Jared Allen and any other case I work on gets the very best representation." With that declaration, she turned her back to them and strode out of the room.

When she made it to her desk, she found a stack of new files and a Post-it from Ford. *I need you to cover these examining trials this morning. Thanks! Ford.*

Lovely. She'd be stuck in mag court for the next few hours, unable to figure out a plan to go with her grandiose declaration she didn't need an investigator for Jared's case. Now that she was out of the heat of the moment, she realized she'd completely overstepped her authority and when Ford found out, he was going to be pissed.

What if there was another solution? Jared couldn't hire an investigator because a) he couldn't afford one, and b) if he could, the judge would question why he needed a public defender. But there was no rule saying she couldn't hire a private investigator. Not one she was aware of anyway, and if it didn't cost the taxpayers of Dallas County any money, the judge and Ford shouldn't care. Right?

She opened her computer and typed a few quick searches until she found the number she was looking for. One phone call later and she had a meeting set up for the next day. If she got good news from Lennox today about the plea, she could easily cancel and, if not, she could hit the ground running on Jared's defense. Satisfied she'd managed to clear one worry off her desk, she focused on the stack of files Ford had left. It was a lot, but focusing on them would keep her from thinking too much about whether Lennox would get the family to agree to the plea. And about how Lennox had looked in that black leather jacket.

She was in the middle of a hot little daydream about Lennox and the jacket—and Lennox out of the jacket—when she heard a knock and looked up to see Ford standing in the doorway.

"Sorry for the file dump, but I figured these examining trials are good experience."

"No worries." She hesitated for a moment as she considered whether she should confess she'd cut loose the investigator on the case, but then she'd have to get into the why of it all, and she didn't want to rat out the other PDs for treating her like the outsider she was or confess she'd overstepped her authority. Instead, she fanned the files out on her desk. "Lots of variety here."

"For sure. Don't worry about trying to win any of the examining trials. There all in mag court six, Judge Bell's court, and she'd die before she'd question a single move the cops make. Just use the opportunity to get whatever info you can about the cases and make a lot of notes. Any word from Lennox?"

The question brought back a flash of her daydream and she could feel the burn of a blush inch up her neck. "She's meeting with the family this afternoon. She's not interested in the deal, but if they are, it's possible she could be persuaded."

He crossed his fingers. "Don't get your hopes up. If she's hell-bent on sending Jared to prison for a big stretch, she's likely to convince the family that a trial is the best way for them to get the justice they believe they deserve."

"You're probably right, but I think we have a lot to work with. The police didn't even bother to look at Lisa's new boyfriend before they arrested Jared. We should take a close look into him and everyone else in Lisa's orbit to see who else might've had a motive to set the fire."

"You're right. I reassigned one of the investigators, Lance Ryker, to help out with this case, but it may be a bit before he can get to you. We only have the two, and they're swamped with cases way older than this one. If you don't work out the plea and Jared wants a speedy trial, I've already told Lance to clear the rest of his schedule." He checked his watch. "I've got a motion hearing in Judge Aguilar's court. Yell if you need me."

She called out "will do" to his retreating form, but he was already gone. She felt a smidge of guilt about not telling him her solution to the lack of investigator resources, but no sense causing a stir until it was a done deal. Satisfied she had a plan, she shoved all of the files into her bag and headed downstairs. She was going to resist the urge to go by Lennox's court, but if she happened to run into her, it would be a total bonus.

Lennox walked into the lobby of the eleventh floor and greeted Lisa Allen's family. She'd spoken with them several times by phone and read all of the police interviews, but this was the first in-person meeting and she'd been dreading it all day. No matter what the outcome, there was no winning this case. Lisa had died a brutal death, and these people, her loved ones, would never be able to remember her without the accompanying horror of the details of her demise. She had only one thing to offer them—justice.

Which brought her back to what she was going to do about Wren's plea offer. Sure, a plea would allow them to have some semblance of closure, but how was she supposed to sell that when she knew their pain would linger way after Jared Allen went to prison, no matter what the length of his sentence?

The right thing to do would be not to sell it at all. She'd tell the family matter-of-factly what Wren had offered and, if asked, she'd offer her honest opinion. That was the best she could offer, and way more than she was obligated to do, but if for some reason they decided to accept, she wasn't confident she could get her boss to sign off on it because she wasn't going to go on record approving such a lenient sentence, no matter how charmed she was by Wren Bishop.

And she was charmed. Who wouldn't be? Between her pedigree and her winning smile, Wren was probably used to getting her way more often than not, and that spelled danger. Both professionally and personally. Lennox had had more than enough encounters with slick defense attorneys who appeared charming at first but turned out to be all flash and no substance, and she wasn't about to repeat any of her past mistakes.

She took a deep breath and faced Lisa's parents, Mr. and Mrs. Sloan; her younger sister, Denise; and Lisa's boyfriend, Chet Evans. Not a large group, but enough to make the possibility of a lack of consensus real. She was a little surprised the family had included Chet in this meeting considering Jared and Lisa hadn't been officially divorced at the time of her death, but asking him to step out would make her seem like a jerk. Her job was to tell them where things stood and corral them into a consensus as to how to proceed, and if having the victim's boyfriend in the room helped that along, she wasn't going to question it.

"I appreciate you all coming in today," she said. "We've reached a critical point in the case, and I need to make some decisions about where we go from here and I'd appreciate your input."

Mr. and Mrs. Sloan looked at each other for a moment, but surprisingly, it was Chet who spoke first. "Isn't it a little soon? He wasn't indicted all that long ago, right? I've been doing some research, and it appears most serious cases linger on the docket for the better part of a year before they get resolved."

Lennox spotted Denise shaking her head at the remark, probably wondering what her sister had seen in the guy. She took a moment to study him. He was a salesman, and he looked the part—flashy suit, expensive looking watch and rings. While Jared Allen had a wind-blown, loner biker look about him, this guy dressed to impress and acted like he was used to bending people to his will. Lisa had clearly gone for the complete opposite of her husband when she was seeking out a new love interest. The relationship smacked of rebound, where the interim lover was the antithesis of everything you'd left behind.

"When cases linger, it's usually the defense dragging their feet," Lennox said, plunging ahead. "The defendant might be out on bond and knows the facts are stacked against him, which only fuels the desire for delay. But Jared's in jail and he can't make bond. It's my understanding, he plans to invoke his right to a speedy trial, meaning the only delay from here on out will be due to the court's docket, and you should know that Judge Larabee has a reputation for keeping a rocket docket. While the jury in one trial is in the jury room deliberating, he'll go ahead and use the courtroom to start picking a jury for the next one. He's not going to allow either side to delay the proceedings."

"Okay, so what are we looking at in terms of resolving this?" Denise asked.

"It depends," Lennox said. "The defense has passed along a message that Jared would be willing to accept a plea."

Denise sucked in a breath and her father put his hand on her shoulder. "Tell us," Mr. Sloan said.

"Five years. It's the minimum for a murder case." Lennox took a breath. Easier to simply spit it out than let the dread linger. "As it stands now, he's charged with a capital felony, murder committed during the course of committing arson. If we agree to this plea, we'd have to let him plead to the lesser included charge of murder."

Mrs. Sloan tore the tissue in her hand in half. "Five years?" Her voice cracked with pain. "Are you serious? He took her life. He left her children motherless."

She shuddered at the last words, and her obvious pain stirred memories, but Lennox forced herself not to look away. "He did. That's what he's charged with, but the jury will have an opportunity to consider the lesser included charge as well, and the punishment range for that is five to ninety-nine years. If we go to trial, I intend to seek a conviction for the capital murder charge and mandatory life sentence."

"Then why are you coming to us with this, this ridiculous plea offer?" Denise asked.

They were stressed and with stress came anger. Lennox was all too familiar with the stages of grief as they worked their way into the resolution of a case, and she summoned her inner reserve of patience to keep from snapping back her answers. "It's part of my job to give you all the information as we move forward. We are preparing to go to trial. Nothing has changed in that respect, but just like the defense attorney has a duty to convey any offers we make to the defendant, we have a duty to discuss with you, as the family of the victim in this case, possible alternative resolutions. As you know, early on, I offered twenty years to resolve the case, but they rejected that offer, and this is their counter. It's a lowball offer and it doesn't reflect the severity of the case. It will save you the suffering of sitting through a trial where you will have to relive the consequences of this crime all over again, but only you can determine if that is a fair price to pay for what I consider a complete subversion of justice."

"So you're telling us not to take the offer?" Mr. Sloan asked.

Lennox cast about for a nice way to let them know it wasn't their offer to take. "Ultimately, my boss, the DA, is the one who would have to sign off on a plea with these terms, but I know she will welcome your input. If it's what you really want—to put this case behind you right now—then I will tell her where you stand." She paused, wavering about whether to offer her own opinion before blurting out. "But if you're asking me what I would do, the answer is I would reject this offer. Anything less than forty years, is a travesty." *Sorry, Wren, but I have to be honest.*

The room was silent for a few moments, weighted with the grief of loss and portent of the decision they needed to make. Lennox resisted the urge to say anything else, reluctant to try to sway them in one direction or the other. Finally, Denise spoke.

"No deal. The bastard goes to trial. Let the world see what he did." She looked at Chet and her parents who all nodded back at her. "He'll stay in jail until his trial, right?"

"Unless he makes bail. He's not a flight risk and he's entitled to a fair bail, but so far it appears he isn't able to raise the funds, which is probably why he's trying to get a minimum sentence."

"That can't happen."

Lennox merely nodded, but she noted the urgency and passion in Denise's voice, and the way Chet put his arms around the huddled family, like he was the big man, taking care of them all. Denise would make a good witness during sentencing, but something about Chet's actions bothered her. He was a little too cozy with this family to be a guy who hadn't been dating Lisa Allen all that long, and his presence gave off a bit of an ick factor.

An hour later, she was in her boss, Mia Rivera's, office. She reeled off the details of the meeting with the family and waited for Mia's reaction which was exactly what she expected it to be.

"Yeah, that offer is junk," Mia said. "Who's the PD handling it?"

"The offer came from Wren Bishop," Lennox said.

"Is she any good?"

Talk about a loaded question. "She seems to be, but I think Ford will wind up trying it. Wren's on loan from Dunley Thornton, and chances are good she'll be back there by the time this case goes to trial."

"Interesting. I know Ford likes to let his lawyers find their own way, but he can't think we'd go for this." She glanced over the reports from the police and the arson investigator. "Am I missing something?"

Lennox shrugged. "I've gone over the case with the investigating officers several times." She ticked the facts off on her fingers. "Defendant is a jealous, soon to be ex-husband. There's some history of domestic calls, but no evidence of physical violence—mostly loud yelling. The ME's report says Lisa suffered a trauma before she died, but we don't have a weapon and it may have burned at the scene. Jared is the named beneficiary on her life insurance policy."

"Who collects if he doesn't?"

"The kids. Two, sweet motherless kids." Lennox pulled up a picture on her phone of Lisa Allen with her two young children. "The jury is going to hate him."

"Okay, so this lowball offer is the result of an inexperienced public defender and nothing more."

"Yes." Lennox hated saying it. Wren wasn't a bad lawyer but she didn't get how the system worked here at the criminal courthouse where you can't toss a little something something at a problem and make it go away. "It appears so."

Mia made a note on the file and handed it back to Lennox. "Set it for trial. Are you going to have Johnny try it with you?"

"Yes. He could use the experience, and the arson facts are fairly straightforward. Accelerant, timing, etc."

"Sounds good." Mia looked back down at the pile of work on her desk and Lennox paused, unsure if this was a good time to bring up something else she'd been considering.

"Anything else on your mind?" Mia asked.

"Have you made any decisions about the promotion to super chief?" She hated to have to ask, but it wasn't often she got an audience alone with the big boss. Her first assistant aka gatekeeper rarely let her past.

Mia smiled. "Ian warned me you might ask. All I can tell you is we're close to a decision and you're definitely in contention." She picked up the handset on her desk. "I have a conference call with the commissioners, but thanks for checking in."

Lennox took the hint, stood, and started toward the door. She was a few steps away when Mia called out, "Put this guy away for the rest of his life or get him to plead to thirty years. Either result will make a very convincing case for a promotion."

She nodded in response, hiding her surprise at the twist. Great, her promotion and her feelings for Wren rested on how this particular case was resolved. Determined to face it head-on, she stopped by the PD's office, but Wren wasn't in and neither was Ford. Fine. She'd call one of them later. And she knew exactly which one it would be.

Chapter Twelve

Wren strode out of the elevator and toward the host stand at the Tower Club. She hadn't used her membership once since she'd been working at the PD's office, but the head waiter, Henry, greeted her as if she came in every day.

"Ms. Bishop, we've missed you. Your parents are already seated. Shall I have Thomas bring a bottle of your usual to the table or would you prefer something different tonight?"

Wren laughed. "I'm surprised I still have a usual considering how few times I've been here this year. But I'm also grateful you remember, so yes, please have him bring the wine. Thanks." She waved good-bye at him and walked to the table with the very best view of the Dallas skyline at night. And more importantly, her parents.

Her mom and dad stood as she walked toward them, and there were hugs all around before she joined them at the table. "It's great to see you," she said. "And you don't look jet-lagged at all. How do you do that?"

Her mother laughed. "I'd like to say I'm impervious to travel exhaustion by now, but really I just slept like a baby on the plane, and I didn't eat a bite." She pointed at the menu in front of Wren. "And now I'm famished. Please tell me you're ready to order."

Wren pushed the menu to the side. "I've been thinking about the lobster bisque all day. Thomas will be here in a minute with some wine, and we can order right away." She turned to her father. "Dad, are you starving too?"

He grinned. "Always, but not because I didn't eat on the plane." He held up his hands. "I confess, I ate your mother's meal and mine, but I'm still starving."

Wren returned his grin. Her parents had a private jet, ready at a moment's notice to whisk them to wherever they wanted to go and all the money they could ever want, but they were both very down-to-earth and still took a personal interest in all of their business enterprises.

"We'll be going back to Scotland next month to check out the renovations on the new property," her mom said. "You should come with us. We'll add on a few day trips to local distilleries to make it fun. We met a few of the owners while we were there, and they'd be happy to set up a personal tasting for us."

"As tempting as private Scotch tastings might be, I'm a little busy right now. Ford has me working a pretty big case with him, and I'd like to spend as much time on it as I can before I have to get back to the firm." She spied her mom exchange a questioning look with her father. "What's up?"

Her mom shook her head and then buried it in her menu. "Let's eat and then we can talk. Is the halibut still good here?"

Wren raised her eyebrows at her father, but he merely hunched his shoulders. Thomas appeared at that moment with the wine, derailing her plans to interrogate them, but she resolved to find out what was up as soon as they ordered.

Thomas opened the bottle of Cristom Pino Noir and poured them each a glass with a flair many of the younger waitstaff didn't have the patience to perform. He'd been with the club through its many iterations, and she had fond memories of him sneaking her and her brother special snacks whenever they would visit Dallas with their parents. "Mr. and Mrs. Bishop, it's a delight to see you. Are you in town for a special occasion?"

Her parents exchanged looks again. "It's always a special occasion when we get to have dinner with our daughter," her mother said. She sipped her wine. "This is delicious."

"Thank Wren," Thomas said. "She insisted we start carrying it last year."

"True story," Wren said. "I represented the winery, and the winemaker sent me a case to thank me for a good result. I'm truly addicted."

"As are many of our guests," Thomas said. "If you ever think about leaving your law practice, I'm sure there's a place for you as a restauranteur."

"You're sweet, but I think I'll stick with the law, thanks."

After they placed their orders, Wren steered the conversation to the reason for her parents' visit. "If you think I'm waiting until after dinner to find out what the two of you are up to, you are wrong. Spill."

Her mother shifted in her seat and her dad cleared his throat. "It's funny Thomas should bring up changing occupations," her father said. "That's kind of what we wanted to talk to you about."

Wren sighed. "What? Are you worried, I'm going to leave the firm and start working for the public defender's office?" She immediately wondered why she'd seized on that and was a little surprised to find she didn't find the idea completely ludicrous.

"What?" Her dad scrunched his brow as if puzzled, and then shook his head. "Oh, no. That's not it."

"Then what is it?"

"We'd like you to keep doing what you've been doing at Dunley Thornton—providing great representation for your clients—but we'd like you to do it for us. Exclusively. And by us, I mean Bishop Development."

Wren paused, mid-sip, and set her glass on the table. "You're going to need to repeat that."

Her mom play-punched her dad. "Austin, I told you not to spring it on her like that. Wren, your dad and I want to travel more. For pleasure, not business. Your brother has stepped up and we're planning to promote him to COO. When we do, we'd like to restructure all of the C-suite office positions, and we'd like you to come on board as our new corporate counsel."

Wren stared at them both, flummoxed. Of all the things they could've possibly wanted to talk about tonight, she'd never imagined this would be one of them. Serving as the top attorney for a huge corporation was a big get, even if she only scored the position by virtue of being the daughter of the owners.

"And it's not because you're family," her father said, reading her mind. "Not entirely anyway. Don't get me wrong, we'd much rather have someone we know and trust in the position, but we wouldn't be offering it to you if we weren't convinced you'd be a great fit for the job."

"She knows that, Austin."

"Of course, she does, but it doesn't hurt to hear it, right, Wren?"

She wasn't sure how to answer. Her parents had always made it clear she and her brother were welcome to work for the company, but they'd have to work their way up like any other employee. Her brother, Wyatt, had taken them up on the offer, starting in the mail room and he'd moved up the ranks while he obtained his degree from Rice to be close to the action. He'd continued to work for the business while he took classes, and once he had his MBA, he became a manager while she enrolled in law school in Dallas, after deciding the only way, she could prove her own worth was to go a completely different route. Her parents had never pressed her to come work for them and she'd never brought it up, but hearing their offer now, she realized she'd always wondered why they didn't push her to stick around before. "Actually, I do think I'd be a great fit, but I never realized you thought so too."

"Of course we do," her dad said, reaching across the table to squeeze her hand. "You're a brilliant lawyer."

"Well, you say that now, but I've been away for years and you've never even hinted at me coming back to work for you."

They exchanged looks again, but she couldn't tell what they were trying to say to each other. All she knew was someday she wanted to meet someone she could communicate with with only a glance. It occurred to her there might be a particular reason they were making this request. "Wait a minute. Is something wrong? Is one of you sick? Is that why you're retiring early?"

"Who said anything about retirement?" her mother asked. "We're simply stepping back a bit. What's the point of all this success if we work too hard to enjoy it?"

"What about the foundation?"

"We'll still be involved, but not in the day-to-day. Don't worry, we don't have any plans to shut it down, but we have considered transferring it to another established nonprofit that's doing similar work. Between it and company business, there's no time for anything extra. If you were to come on board in management with your brother, we would feel more secure about taking a step back."

A cacophony of thoughts assailed her, and she wasn't sure where to begin sorting them out. The only thing she knew for sure was that she shouldn't make this big of a decision on the fly. "This is big news, and I appreciate everything you've said, but I'm going to need some time to process this before I can give you an answer. Plus, I'm still committed for a few months to the PD's office."

"That won't be a problem," her dad said. "We think the work you're doing there is great. If you want to stay on longer and come work for us at the end of the year, that works too."

She nodded, slowly chewing over her options. She had given some thought to asking the firm for an extension on her time on loan to see Jared's case through to the end, but she'd hesitated because of how a longer absence might affect her partnership prospects. She'd never even considered vaulting from the PD's office into a position as head legal counsel for Bishop Enterprises.

She met her parents' expectant gazes with a smile to cover her hesitation. "I'm honored to be asked. Really, I am. I guess I'm just surprised. You've always said you thought it was great that I went my own way after college. I guess I assumed you didn't want both Wyatt and me steeped in the family business."

"That's my fault," her mother said. "I figured that it would be better for you to find your way in the world before coming back to the business. The appearance of nepotism is bad enough with your brother, but because you're a woman, there will always be people who assume you needed the benefit of family to come out on top. But you've become quite accomplished, and any corporation would be lucky to have you on board. And to be fair, you've never really expressed an interest in anything other than the foundation work. When it came to the development side, you kind of zoned out whenever we talked about it."

Her mom was right. She had tuned out all the dinner table discussion about the business, mostly because it dominated everything about their lives. Vacations, dinners, attendance at school events—all were at the whim of whatever was going on with Bishop Enterprises, and she'd lost a large chunk of childhood to the business. To have it offered up to her today, should be the perfect revenge. Then why did she feel so conflicted?

The rest of the dinner, the three of them avoided the subject, and when they parted for the evening, she promised them she'd give the offer serious thought. She doubted she'd think of anything else for a while, but when she pulled out her phone to find a text from Lennox, her attention was instantly diverted.

Ready to talk about the case?

She stared at the text for a minute. She wasn't really interested in talking about Jared Allen's case right now, but she also wasn't interested in passing up the opportunity to talk to Lennox. She started typing a response to say she could talk now if Lennox wanted to call, but back-spaced the words before she finished the message. After staring at the screen for a moment, she thumbed out a new message.

Sure. Come over if you're not busy. Down the street from Del's.

She added her address and hit send before she could change her mind. It was a bold choice, but she had no regrets, telling herself a discussion about plea deals should be had face-to-face, but knowing her motivation for wanting to see Lennox in person ran deeper.

The response was almost immediate. *See you in ten minutes.*

Damn, she hadn't expected Lennox to accept her invitation, let alone so quickly. She jumped in her car, and maneuvered through downtown traffic, but her journey was thwarted by a construction crew setting up for the weekend. When she finally pulled up to her building, Lennox was standing outside engaged in a lively conversation with the doorman. Whatever they were discussing involved exaggerated expressions and the waving of arms.

Wren left her keys with the valet and hurried to the door. "What's going on?"

Lennox turned toward her, and her expression quickly went from stressed to relieved. "Thank goodness you're here. Can you tell this guy that I know you?"

"It's okay, Harry. She's here to see me, and although she looks a little rough around the edges, she's a pretty famous prosecutor at the DA's office." She motioned toward the door and started walking toward it but stopped when she realized Lennox wasn't following. She reached out her hand. "Are you coming?"

Lennox stared at her outstretched hand for a moment before grasping it in hers. Wren marched them to the elevator, glad to find a car waiting because Lennox looked like she was about to bolt at any moment. Despite the long ride to the top floor, neither one of them spoke. When the doors opened, Wren grabbed Lennox's hand again, and led her to the door to her apartment, letting go only because she had to fish her keys out of her purse and unlock the door. She pushed open the door and glanced over her shoulder. "You're coming in, right?"

Lennox nodded and followed her in.

"Have a seat," Wren said. "I'll be right back." She didn't wait for a response and strode quickly to the bedroom. Once behind her bedroom door, she caught her breath. What in the world had she been thinking, inviting Lennox Roy to her apartment?

Get it together.

She took off her heels, tossed them in the closet, and then paused for a moment before taking them back out and putting them back on. She wanted to change, but the longer she left Lennox in her living room to fend for herself, the weirder this situation would become. Besides, Lennox was dressed like she'd come from the courthouse, in one of her trademark dark suits that fit her like a glove. Keeping her own suit on was a way to maintain the illusion of a power balance.

Who was she kidding? She was so off kilter right now, in this moment, Lennox Roy had all the power. She squared her shoulders and put her shoes back on. Time to go find out how she planned to use it.

❖

Lennox didn't know what she'd been thinking by accepting Wren's invitation, and it was rapidly becoming clear she hadn't thought it through. She certainly hadn't imagined lounging on the couch in expensive digs. As if the uniformed doorman wasn't enough, from what she could tell, she could fit her entire house in here. Times two.

She stared in the direction Wren had disappeared. Was that the master bedroom down that hall? Was Wren changing clothes right now? Was she the kind of person who hung everything up on a hanger or was she a toss everything into a pile in the corner kind of person?

She shouldn't care about any of these things. But she did. Since they'd met, she'd been intrigued by every aspect of Wren, from wondering why she'd volunteered for the lawyer-on-loan program to being fascinated by the coffee bar she was running in her office.

She paced the room, too agitated to sit. She'd made several passes when the door down the hall burst open, interrupting her thoughts, and Wren strode back into the room, dressed as she'd been when she'd left. "Sorry about that. I had to…send a text." She winced as if she realized how weak the explanation sounded.

"No worries." Lennox shoved her hands in her pockets. "I had just left the courthouse and was only a few minutes away when I got your text. It didn't occur to me you weren't already home."

Wren pointed at the couch. "Do you mind if we sit down? My feet are killing me."

Lennox shot a glance at the sexy heels. "Why don't you take off your shoes? It's your house, after all."

Wren frowned for a sec, and then she reached down and pulled off her shoes, tossing them to the side. "You're right. Speaking of being more comfortable, can I get you anything?"

Why did the simple question seem so suggestive? *Because you're like a teenager when you're around her—all hormones and no filter.* "No, I'm good. Thanks."

"Okay then. I guess you want to get right to it."

"What?"

"The reason you stopped by?"

Pull it together. "I met with Lisa Allen's family this afternoon. It looks like we're going to trial." Wren nodded slowly but didn't say anything. "Did you hear me?"

"I did."

"And?" Lennox wondered why she was so agitated while Wren, whose offer had just been rejected, seemed so calm.

"And I'm sure they felt justified in rejecting the offer," Wren said with a sympathetic tone. "Did they at least consider the possibility of a plea?"

"Not this one, but remember I offered twenty years preindictment."

"You know what I mean. Did they consider the five years?"

"I do, but I'm trying to illustrate the point that we already made a reasonable offer, early in the case, but that one's off the table. The new offer is still reasonable, but I doubt you'll think so."

"Try me."

"Thirty years. It's better than life with no possibility of parole."

"It's forever if you're not guilty," Wren said.

"You act like you know what that feels like."

"You act like its nothing."

Lennox wanted to say there was a reason for that. That she couldn't afford to worry about the cost defendants had to pay because she was too busy worrying about their victims, but the truth was she did have an idea of what it was like to be on the other side. "You don't know me well enough to make that assessment."

"You're right. I only know your reputation."

"And that is?"

"You're kind of a hard-ass. You are more deferential to law enforcement than most, and you have a tendency to believe that every defendant deserves whatever they have coming."

Lennox knew her reputation. Hell, she'd cultivated it, but hearing it summarized by Wren in such a matter-of-fact tone was like a punch to the gut. Did Wren really think she was completely unfeeling when it came to seeing both sides? Suddenly, she was desperate to dispel the impression.

"My brother's in prison. Serving a twenty-year sentence."

There it was. She blurted out the words before she could consider the consequences. It wasn't like people didn't know. The case had been at another courthouse in another county, but the rumor mill wasn't confined by geography. Besides, Gloria liked to brag about what she considered victories, but Lennox didn't consider convincing her druggie brother to plead to twenty years for a crime he had no recollection of committing a victory. She could imagine Wren drawing a comparison between that and her trying to get the supposedly innocent Jared Allen to sign up for a long stint in the pen, and she got the irony.

"When was he sentenced?"

Wren's question struck her as odd. Most people asked what he'd done wrong, but Wren seemed more concerned about how long he had left to do, like the other details were extraneous, which at this point she supposed they were. "Four years ago."

"Aggravated?"

"Yes."

"So at least six more to go."

Lennox nodded. This conversation was so clinical she half expected the next question to be where her brother was serving his time.

"What's his name?"

"Daniel." She choked out the word. No one ever asked his name as if it wasn't a factor in the equation of his life. It was so much easier to discuss his fate if they didn't have anything to call him. "He's thirty-two. Two years older than me." Why had she added that fact? Why were they having this conversation at all? "I know what it's like to be the family of the guy on the other side of the equation. Probably better than you do."

Wren reached for her hand, a gesture that was becoming all too familiar. "You're right. I'm sorry for acting like an ass."

"You didn't know."

"I was being a holier than thou, privileged jerk." Wren squeezed her hand. "If you want to talk about it, I'm a pretty good listener."

"I don't talk about it." *At least I didn't until today.*

"Ever?"

It was a valid question, but it gave Lennox pause as she tried to remember the last time she'd discussed Daniel with anyone. "No one else really knows about it. Except Nina. Judge Aguilar," she added.

"You two are close."

"We both started at the DA's office together. There's not a better bonding experience than being tortured by experienced defense attorneys over misdemeanor cases."

"I bet."

Lennox drifted off into her head as she remembered another bonding experience with one of those experienced defense attorneys. When she'd first met Gloria Leland, she'd loomed larger than life with her movie star good looks and arresting confidence, and she'd allowed herself to buy into the facade. Too bad she hadn't figured out the truth before imploring Gloria to represent Daniel.

"Where did you go just then?"

Wren's voice sounded slurry, like she was standing by the side of the pool while Lennox was underwater. Thinking about Gloria always made her feel like she was drowning. She shook her head to clear away the thoughts. "I made a mistake with my brother's case. I hired someone I knew…someone I was involved with…to handle it and…Well, you know how it turned out." She looked up to meet Wren's eyes, dreading sympathy, but finding only intense interest that spurred her to add, "Needless to say, we're not dating anymore."

There she went again with the overshare. She set her drink down on the table and stood. "I should go."

"Please don't." Wren's smile was gentle. "You're upset. You shouldn't drive when you're upset."

Was she? Agitated was more like it. She was agitated a lot lately—a throwback to the day Daniel was sentenced. Or maybe she'd never stopped being agitated and something else had changed. It didn't take a brain surgeon to figure out what the something, make that someone, was. Wren made her feel things. It was like she'd reached in and opened all the portals to her feelings and they were coursing through her, overriding all her tendency toward self-preservation, and she was hurtling toward Wren without regard to where she might land and how hard.

"I'm not upset," she said. Wren answered by drawing her eyebrows in, in the most adorable way. "I promise. It's been a long time and I've figured out how never to be in that position again."

"That's good. What was your solution?"

"I don't get involved with anyone who works on the other side."

"Defense attorneys?"

"Exactly."

"So, about fifty percent of the attorneys at the courthouse are off limits?"

"I guess that's right." Something about the way Wren said the words made her rule feel silly and arbitrary, but if it made her feel better to have a boundary erected, who was Wren or anyone else to judge?

Wren didn't say anything for a moment, but the silence that hung in the air between them was more comforting than uncomfortable. After a few moments, she stood and walked toward Lennox until they were standing only a few inches apart, and Lennox's breath stalled as she wondered if they could be closer still. When Wren finally spoke, she surprised Lennox once again. "I'm sorry that woman, whoever she is, hurt you. That's a deep wound, understandably."

"I'm fine."

Wren reached up and ran a hand along the collar of her shirt, letting her fingers trail along her neck, leaving a slow burn in their wake. "You are fine." She breathed deep. "So very fine. But you have every right to be upset about what happened."

Lennox didn't want to think about her own mistakes, or Gloria, or anything to do with Daniel. Every one of those things were in the past. They'd been dragging her down for years, but right here in front of her was a woman who made her feel things she absolutely never felt before. Who was affirming her feelings and comforting and arousing her all at the same time. All she wanted to do was give in to her desire, dangerous as it was, and Wren's parted lips were the perfect invitation to feel again.

The second their lips touched, she knew she was in trouble. Soft, silky, hot, and hard. By turns, Wren's touch soothed and enflamed her. She heard the echo of a groan and vaguely recognized it as her own voice, expressing pleasure she hadn't thought possible again. She pulled back for a second to get air, but within seconds, Wren's tongue traced her lips and when she pressed her way in, a cascade of feelings washed over her. Lust, satisfaction, followed by fear and the sense of danger lurking nearby. She pushed the fear away, but it roared back full force, refusing to be deterred. Unable to stay in the moment, she pushed back from Wren, immediately missing her touch.

She saw her own pain reflected in Wren's eyes, but she didn't have room for other people's feelings. Hell, she couldn't even manage her own. She had no business being here, at Wren's apartment, on a Friday night ostensibly to talk business, which anyone with half a brain would know was only an excuse. Apparently, she'd learned nothing when it came to boundaries. But that stopped right now. She backed up, feeling the doorknob against her back and anchoring herself in the physicality of it. Turn the knob. Open the door. Walk away. Three steps to safety.

She took them and the last thing she remembered was Wren's face, her expression full of sympathy, calmly watching her go.

Chapter Thirteen

Wren walked through the front door of the Capital Grille at the Crescent, about ten minutes early for her reservation. After checking in with the hostess, she took a seat in the lobby and used the few moments of quiet time to relax. Since Lennox had left her apartment Friday night, she'd barely been able to concentrate on her work while simultaneously burying herself in it to keep from thinking about what the kiss and Lennox's subsequent mad dash to the door had meant. Five days later and she was no closer to an answer.

The kiss had been mind-blowing, and she knew Lennox had felt it too, but obviously they had very different ways of reacting to searing passion. Lennox, after fleeing her apartment like she was running from a fire, had ghosted her, while she'd been consumed with replaying every moment they'd spent together, trying to figure out exactly when things had shifted from adversary to…She wasn't sure what, but she was certain she wanted more of whatever it was.

She was deep into a mental replay of Lennox's well-toned abs at Parker and Morgan's party when she felt a tap on her shoulder. She turned and came face to face with Skye Keaton, and she scrambled to her feet hoping she hadn't been breathing as hard in real life as she had been in her daydream. "Thanks for meeting me," she said while catching the hostess's eye to let her know she was ready to be seated.

"Your message said it was a matter of life and death." Skye cocked her head. "I'm thinking now that maybe you were exaggerating, but I didn't want to be responsible for the demise of civilization if you weren't."

Wren ducked her head. "Sorry for sounding so worked up. I tend to get a tad excited when I'm trying to solve a problem."

The hostess appeared before they could continue their conversation and, at Wren's request, led them to a booth tucked away in a corner. "This is perfect," Wren said. "Can we get some water and a few minutes alone?"

"Absolutely." The hostess set down the menus and scurried off.

Skye slid into the booth and stared across the table with an odd look on her face. Wren didn't know her well enough to know if she was mad or annoyed or something else. "What is it?"

"Well, let's see. You call me to say it's imperative that we meet. You invite me to an expensive restaurant, have us seated in a cozy spot, and tell the staff we want to be left alone. You know I'm married, right? Happily?"

"What?" Wren mentally replayed the sequence of events. When what Skye was implying finally struck her, she rested her face in her palms. When she looked up, Skye was grinning at her. "I'm so sorry. My goal was to meet far enough from the courthouse that we wouldn't run into anyone we knew, and…" She shook her head. "I keep digging a deeper hole, right?"

"Kinda."

Time to get to the point. "I want to hire you to do some work. Are you available to take on a new case?"

Skye studied her for a moment. "Are you leaving the PD's office?"

"No. I mean, at some point yes. My loan is up at the end of the summer."

"Doesn't the PD's office have its own investigators?"

"Not really. We have two for the entire department and they're both swamped. And all of the other PDs hate me so no one is about to time-share their detectives with the new girl."

"You have a lot going on."

"You're not wrong. But now back to you. Are you available?"

"Tell me about the case."

"You probably heard about it in the news. Jared Allen, estranged husband of Lisa Allen. Lisa died in a fire at their house, and the cops, fire department, and Lennox Roy believe Jared hit her over the head, set the fire, and left her to die."

Skye nodded. "I do remember that case. Husband had just taken out a life insurance policy."

"Whatever." Wren was tired of the sound bites all designed to "prove" Jared was guilty when not a single one related to actual evidence. "There's the story in the media and then there's Jared's story."

"And something in between is likely where the truth lies."

"How poetic."

"I'm no poet." Skye stared at her for a moment. "But I do know a thing or two about rooting out the truth. It is what it is and if you don't want real answers, you shouldn't go looking."

"You're saying you won't pull back if you find something incriminating."

"Something like that. I mean if you're paying, you get to decide when to pull the plug, but I'm letting you know up front, facts are facts. I don't slant my investigation in a particular direction based on who's hired me." She shrugged. "I learned that lesson the hard way when I used to be a cop—a long, long time ago."

Wren found Skye's honesty refreshing. "Assuming I hired you, when could you start?"

"You caught me at a good time. Parker and Morgan just wrapped up a big case earlier than expected. I've got some time now. Do you have all the discovery? When's the trial set?"

"I have most of the discovery. The ME seems to be dragging his heels with portions of his report, but I have the bulk of it. We're due in court Friday to set a trial date."

"Is Mr. Allen out on bond?"

Wren appreciated Skye referring to him as Mr. rather than "Allen" or "the defendant." "No, we got the bond reduced as low as it's going to get, but he's having trouble finding someone who'll pay the five-thousand-dollar surety and sign for him."

"That doesn't bode well for finding witnesses who are going to say he's a stand-up guy."

"I know." She'd considered that fact but decided that just because someone didn't have a lot of friends, didn't make them a killer. "But I'm counting on you to find people who can testify on his behalf."

"I'll find what I find. Is this a good time to talk about my fee? If you get the judge to sign an order, he'll probably authorize payment. I take a few cases a year at court appointed rates."

She had considered the fee and done some discreet asking around. For a court appointed attorney authorized by the court, the judge would often authorize a small amount for an investigator, usually a few hundred dollars, a pittance when it came to standard PI fees. Plus, she'd have to file a motion to get those funds which meant she'd need to ask Ford about it and he'd wonder why she wasn't using one of the PD investigators and then she'd need to explain about how the other PDs were all over her about the prospect of her stealing their resources. She'd made an executive decision to pay the cost herself and worry about the details–asking forgiveness rather than permission. "I'll cover your usual fee." She pulled out her wallet. "How much do you need up front?"

Skye stared at her wallet, the Louis V, for a second. "I'll bill you. You look like you might be able to afford it. I assume you'd prefer to keep this between us?"

"I'm sure it's going to get out eventually, but I'd rather you not announce it until I have a chance to clue Ford in. Maybe you could start by going to see Jared."

"I can go first thing in the morning if you'll let him know I'm coming. I'll need a letter of representation from you to get into the jail. Can you get that to me today?"

"Absolutely." Wren picked up her phone, instinctively ready to send the letter writing assignment to her secretary before she remembered she didn't have one. So far, she'd been able to do all of her work at the PD's office digitally, but it looked like she was going to have to figure out where the printer was or run by her apartment and take care of it, which might actually be easier than interrupting Sally on one of her long personal calls. Satisfied she had a plan in place, she pointed at the menus. "Now that we have all that out of the way, tell me you're hungry, because I'm starving."

Skye smiled. "I'm always hungry."

After they placed their orders, she said, "So, I guess you know everyone at the courthouse really well if you were a cop for years."

"Do you want to know why I'm no longer a cop?"

"Nope."

"Let me guess, you already checked me out."

"I did. You made a mistake, but that was years ago, and you've been commended since."

"True. Back to your question, I do know most everyone at the courthouse. And I guess you're asking that question because there's someone in particular you would like to know about."

"See, I knew you were a great investigator." She cast about for a way to bring up Lennox, but Skye beat her to it.

"Lennox Roy is a top-notch prosecutor, but she has a couple of blind spots."

She wanted to know what those were. Had to know if she was going to do her job, but discussing Lennox with anyone she barely knew felt like a form of betrayal. "I can tell she's a great adversary for the state."

"That's a nice way of saying she is myopic, but yes, she is."

"What's the other blind spot?"

Skye fixed her with a hard stare. "Are you hiring me because you think Lennox and I are friends and that will give you an inside track?"

Skye's intuition was going to make her a perfect investigator for this case. "Not exactly. I mean, I don't know any other criminal investigators and you come highly recommended. I guess it doesn't hurt that you know Lennox, right?"

"Well, that leads me to the other blind spot, and it may cause you to change your mind about having me work on this case. Lennox doesn't believe in redemption. She's a hard-ass that way. She thinks defendants deserve to rot in hell and second chances are a waste of time. She and I have known each other a while and there's mutual respect between us, but she'll still attack my credibility on the stand without a second thought because she believes in her heart of hearts that one thing I did in the past defines me. I'm telling you this because if I wind up testifying at trial, she'll try to bring it up."

Wren mentally reviewed what she'd read online. Skye and Parker had been partners on the Dallas Police force, and one night while investigating a case, Skye and two other officers assigned to the case had planted a gun at a crime scene. Parker had turned them in and eventually left the force to go to law school. Skye had resigned from the force. She wasn't sure about all the in-between, but Skye and Parker were friends and Skye had established a reputation as a highly sought-after PI which told her the story was more complicated than any of the media sources implied. "That was years ago, and you paid the price."

"True. Most judges rule it inadmissible since it happened so long ago, but you asked me about Lennox, and I figured that's the kind of thing you'd want to know." She narrowed her eyes. "Unless you were asking for something more personal."

She was. She desperately wanted to know everything about Lennox—beyond the kissing and the abs. But while asking direct questions from the people who knew her well might seem like the fastest way to get answers, she sensed that in the microcosm of the courthouse, her queries would get back to Lennox, even if she tried really hard to be circumspect. Skye was experienced at keeping secrets for the people she worked for, but Lennox's personal life didn't fall under attorney-client privilege. She knew it and Skye would know it too.

They spent the balance of the meal discussing random other things—the weather; Skye's daughter, Olivia; her wife, Aimee. Everything but Lennox.

When lunch was over, Wren drove across downtown to Thanksgiving Tower. She'd been trying to reach Diane since before the kiss with Lennox, but the only replies Diane had sent to her were several texts to let her know she was working late nights at the office and she'd try to make time soon for them to get together. Wren didn't want to "get together"—at least not in the way Diane usually meant, but she did want to break things off, and if Diane wouldn't come to her, then she was determined to find her and make it happen. It was the right thing to do even if there was to be no more kissing with Lennox. She hoped there would be more kissing.

Wren walked through the halls of the bustling offices of Dunley Thornton, wondering if she was invisible. Hardly anyone looked up from their work, and those that did called out unenthusiastic hellos or gave her nonchalant waves like they hadn't seen her in a few days rather than the last couple of months. She considered stopping by Emma's office to see if she was in, but decided she was simply stalling.

When she reached Diane's door, it was closed. Maybe she wasn't in today. Maybe she was at a deposition. *Maybe you're being a coward.* She leaned her ear against the door and, hearing sounds of movement, she rapped sharply on the frame before she could change her mind.

"Just a minute. I'm finishing up a call."

It was Diane's voice, but Wren thought she heard giggling as well. Diane didn't giggle. She barely even laughed unless it was at her own jokes. If she was giggling, now might be the perfect time for a "Hey, let's call this whole thing off" spiel. She knocked on the door again. "Diane, it's Wren. I was hoping we could talk." She tried the door handle, but it was locked. She was still holding the handle when the knob started to turn. She backed up, thinking Diane was opening the door to let her in, but seconds later, the door flew open and the person standing in front of her was not Diane but Eloise, a first year who'd been assigned to Diane a few weeks before Wren had started at the PD's office.

"Hey, Wren," Eloise said as she walked out of the office. "How's it going?"

"It's going great." Wren pointed at Eloise's mouth where a distinctive red lipstick had smeared. "You missed a spot."

Eloise's hand flew to her face, and Wren took advantage of her surprise by side-stepping her, ducking into Diane's office, and shutting the door behind her.

Diane was sitting behind her desk, acting like nothing was wrong. Wren knew she should be annoyed, but she was mostly relieved.

"Hey, Wren. Did I know you were coming by today?"

Wren blew past Diane's feigned surprise and dove right in. "I'm thinking no or you wouldn't have been mugging a subordinate in your office. You two should coordinate lipstick colors and then it might be less obvious. Oh, and the locked door and the giggling? Dead giveaway something is going on."

"You're angry."

"I'm not." She wasn't. "But I think you know we're through, right?"

"Oh, honey, we've been through," Diane said. "I don't even know who you are anymore. Since you've been slumming it down at the courthouse, we don't have anything in common anymore."

Kissing coworkers, Wren wanted to say. That's about all we have in common. Instead, she suppressed a laugh and decided the right thing to do was to let Diane off the hook, especially since she'd been engaged in side-kissing of her own. "You know, you're right. We don't have anything in common. And that's okay."

Diane looked visibly relieved. "Really?"

"Really. You do you. No hard feelings." Wren waved awkwardly from the doorway and backed out of the room. Easiest breakup ever. She didn't feel a single lingering doubt or regret, only a strong sense of peace. And an even stronger desire to go find Lennox and... What? Tell her, "Hey, I broke things off with this woman I was seeing casually. Want to hook up?"

No, she wanted to find Lennox and finish their kissing session, not just because she was unencumbered, but because it was all she'd thought about since Friday night. Determined to track Lennox down and tell her how she felt, she walked briskly through the law firm toward the lobby. She was about to push through the double doors when she heard a familiar voice.

"Wren, it's good to see you."

Carl Solomon, former Baylor basketball player now partner at Dunley Thornton, loomed over her. His smile said he was happy to see her, but his eyes reflected a tinge of anxiety. Something was up.

"Good to see you too, Carl. I stopped by to pick up a couple of things," she said, not wanting to allude to her encounter with Diane. "Looks like everything is rocking along without me."

"About that. Do you have a minute?"

She glanced toward the elevator doors. If she made a break for it, she might be able to squeeze through the opening before it closed completely. Carl was watching her intently, and she decided flight wasn't the best way to handle whatever he was about to tell her. "Sure."

She followed him back into the belly of the firm to his corner office with a gorgeous view of downtown. He motioned for her to have a seat while she cursed her decision to come speak to Diane in person. She should've broken up in a text and made it easier for all of them. "I'm really enjoying the lawyer-on-loan program. I've had the opportunity to work on a ton of cases—all kinds. And I'm working directly with the chief public defender on an arson case that's probably going to trial. It might even go before I leave the program."

"We need you to leave the program."

The echo of her own words confused her. "What did you say?"

"We need you to come back to work. We've taken on a bunch of additional work from Aspen Jones."

"I heard about the merger."

"More like a gutting. We only brought in a quarter of their team, but all of their work. We need butts in seats, billing their clients, or they're going to think no one is taking care of them."

Wren sat, stunned, unable to formulate a response since she was still digesting the "we need you to leave the program" while listening to him drone on about a merger. When he finally stopped to take a breath, she broke to say, "I can't leave the program. I've established trust with these people. They're my clients."

"They're not your clients," Carl said, his tone lightly scolding. "They're the clients of the PD's office and you are only a visitor. Besides, I'm sure there are plenty of people to cover your work there. You were only there on loan—it was never supposed to be permanent. We're simply cutting the loan short, and I've already notified the county commissioners. We need you back in a week— that should give you plenty of time to hand things off and get up to speed on some of the new matters we have coming in."

Wren's entire body seized up at the idea of dumping Jared's case and all of the others she was handling on the other PDs and coming back here to paper push a bunch of commercial transactions and argue about who owed who for what. This couldn't be happening. Not right now with Jared's trial date looming. Not while she was trying to sort through whatever was going on between her and Lennox. She could hear the mean girls snickering behind her back when they heard the news, but more importantly, she wondered what Lennox would think and she didn't even bother pretending her concern was for professional reasons.

"No." The word was out of her mouth before she could filter her response.

"No?"

"No." The more times she said it, the better it felt. She replayed his words and grew madder with each pass. He'd already notified the county commissioners they were pulling her, but he hadn't bothered to notify her. What if she hadn't stopped by today to see Diane? Was he going to let her know in an email? This about-face wasn't just an affront to the understaffed, underfunded PD's office, it was a slap in the face to her. She'd given every waking moment to this firm over the course of the last four years and what did she have to show for it? A few years from now, if she played by all the rules, she'd become a partner which meant she would be expected to use the money she'd worked for to buy in, but even then she'd only have junior status and very little say about how things were done. Senior partners could make program ending decisions and she'd still be as powerless as she was now to do anything about it.

By contrast, Ford had allowed her to take point on a big case and given her complete autonomy over the other cases she was handling. No, she didn't have a fancy office and a secretary and a coffee bar at the PD's office, but she did have dignity and a strong sense she was actually making a difference. Plus, there was her parents' offer to consider. She'd still be pushing paper if she worked for Bishop Enterprises, but as general counsel, she could affect policy and she wouldn't have people like Carl deciding what was best.

Decision made, she reinforced it with another no. "I'm in the middle of several pretty sensitive matters at the PD's office and they do not have the personnel to handle the files they have on hand— that was the entire purpose of the lawyer-on-loan program. So no, I'm not leaving there yet." How ironic that she'd been considering asking to stay longer and here they were trying to get her to cut her stay short. She took a deep breath and decided to go all in. "In fact, I need to stay even longer, until the Jared Allen trial is complete. If reporting back to this office next week is a condition of my employment here, consider this my notice."

Carl looked stunned, but Wren knew he was a skilled enough litigator he would recover any moment and start listing off reasons she was making a big mistake. He'd sound perfectly rational, and she didn't need his voice in her head while her brain churned through ideas about how to make this work. Bottom-line, she had choices. She could afford to support herself for quite a while or she could take Ford up on his offer to have her come on board permanently or she could finish up Jared's case and then take the position with her parents' development company. Satisfied she would land well no matter what happened next, she edged her way toward the elevator. "I'm late for a hearing," she lied. "I look forward to your response."

She walked out of the office, but he was right behind her, asking her to wait. She knew if she stuck around, he would try to placate her, mostly because he worried about losing her parents' business and not because he gave a damn about the program. Like a sign from the universe, when she reached the elevator, the doors opened, and she stepped into the car. The last thing she saw as the doors closed was the surprised expression on his face. Would Lennox be as surprised when she told her what she'd done? She couldn't wait to find out.

Chapter Fourteen

L ennox reread the police report on her desk for the fifth time without retaining a single word. She tossed the papers to the side and leaned back in her chair and closed her eyes, wishing she could give in to the exhaustion that had consumed her for the past few days. Since Friday night. Since she'd kissed Wren.

She kissed *you.*

Every time she flashed on the memory, she fought this mental battle, but it was pointless. Who initiated the kiss was of no consequence. The kissing was the thing and it had been amazing and all-consuming, and she'd been able to think of little else since. Which was a problem.

Or was it?

Wren was scheduled to leave the PD's office in less than two months. She'd be back in her plush office—she imagined it was plush—at Dunley Thornton and someone else would try the Allen case with Ford. Her departure would mean no conflicts, no workplace romance, no reason left not to explore the intense attraction between them. What would be the harm if they started a little early?

Right. She needed an intervention. She picked up her cell and fired off a text to Nina. *Need a ruling. Are you in?*

Waiting on a jury. Would love the company.

That settled it. Lennox closed the file on her desk and locked her office. Nina's courtroom was two doors down, and she took the back hallway for easy access to her chambers and to avoid the main hallway where defense attorneys lurked with their clients. She told herself she was avoiding them all, but really there was only the one, and it wasn't like she meant to avoid her, she just wasn't sure what to say to Wren after having run out of her apartment Friday night following the best kiss she'd ever had. "Hey, sorry, it's not you, it's me. I always kiss and run."

But that wasn't true. Despite her reputation, she wasn't a Casanova. If Wren weren't a defense attorney, if she weren't here at the courthouse every day, there was a strong likelihood, she'd push past the other stuff, like income disparity and the fact when she wasn't at the PD's office, Wren worked at the same firm as Gloria, and give in to the lure of their attraction. But the mix of it all paralyzed her, which was why she'd rudely ignored Wren's calls and texts since Friday night. God knows what Wren thought of her now, and surprisingly, she cared what Wren thought of her. Enter the need for her best friend's advice.

Nina's door was propped open, and she was sitting behind her desk, still in her robe, eating an unusually large piece of cake. She looked up at Lennox's approach and waved. "Come in. Please help me eat some of this cake before it sends me into a food coma." She rummaged in her desk and produced a plastic fork and handed it her way.

"I don't know," Lennox said. "That looks next level sugary."

"It is and you will eat it with me because you are my friend and when a cake is shared with friends it is less likely to cause me to have to go up a size." She shook the fork to emphasize her point. "Don't make me order you to do it."

Lennox laughed. "You're cute when you're being all judge-like. Fine," she said, taking the fork. "If it will make you feel better." She took a small bite and immediately regretted her hesitation. "Oh my God, that's amazing."

"Right? Reggie made it for Judge Larabee's birthday. You should've dated her and then we could have this cake all the time." Nina took another bite and groaned. "It's not too late." She waved her fork at Lennox. "Go, now, ask her to marry you."

Normally, Lennox would join in with the teasing, but considering she'd come to Nina to talk to her about her dating life, the comments hit a little close to home. "Are you done, because I need your advice, and not about cake."

"Fine. Don't marry her, but be warned I may. What's on your mind?"

She started to make a joke about Nina marrying Reggie and pretend like she'd forgotten why she'd originally come by, but avoiding the subject wouldn't make it go away. The problem was figuring out how to bring it up. Normally, if she'd been attracted to someone, she would've already discussed it with Nina, which left her feeling weird about not mentioning it before now. Weird or not, she was either going to have to think of some other excuse for why she'd needed to talk or plunge right in.

"I kissed Wren."

The simple statement was like ripping off a Band-Aid, but instead of taking a moment to assess how it felt, she stood, started pacing, and kept talking. "Or she kissed me. I don't really remember because it was kind of a blur. We were at her place and we'd been talking, and I told her about Daniel. Well, not everything, but enough, and then I told her about Gloria, but I'm pretty sure I didn't mention her by name. She was sweet and kind and sexy, and she was standing right in front of me and we kissed."

She shut her mouth, fully aware she'd blurted out way more information than she'd planned to share. More than she'd even realized she'd been bottling up inside. Nina's eyes were wide, but she hadn't said anything yet, which probably meant she was thinking of ways to have her committed. But she was a judge—she'd have plenty of ways. Lennox took a deep breath as her thoughts started to careen out of control again. "For God's sake, say something."

"Is she a good kisser? She looks like she'd be a good kisser."

"Nina! Focus. This isn't about the kissing."

"Sure it is. Sit down, you're making me dizzy."

Lennox sank into the chair across from Nina's desk and jabbed her fork into the cake. She shoved the huge bite into her mouth and slowly chewed, savoring the rich, sweet frosting and dense cake. Maybe it was because she was already really hopped up, but the sugar flooding her bloodstream seemed to calm her mood. She pointed at the plate with her fork. "That's really good."

"I know. You want some more?"

"I do."

Lennox leaned forward to grab another bite, but Nina snatched the plate away. "Then talk. Like a rational person. How was the kiss?"

Lennox sighed. Nina wasn't going to let her get away with half a story, and she'd known this going in. "Incredible. I melted, my head exploded—all those things."

"What happened next?"

"There was no next. I left."

"Your head exploded, and you melted at the mere touch of her lips, and you were all like 'thanks, but I have to go now'?"

"Well, when you put it like that, I kind of sound like a jerk." Lennox slouched into the chair, bracing for more scolding. She didn't have to wait long.

"I'm glad you were able to reach that conclusion on your own."

"Thanks. You know, I didn't come here to be heckled."

"No, you came for my advice. You ready for it?"

"Probably not, but that's never stopped you."

"True." Nina set her fork down and pushed the still massive piece of cake to the side. "Go find Wren and get back to the kissing. She's cute and smart and she challenges you. She's exactly what you need in a girlfriend and you better not let her get away. It's time to let go of your dumb rules."

"I have my rules for a reason."

"You spend all of your time here. It's only natural that the person you fall for is going to be here too. Besides, she's not here for much longer, right? Maybe you can admit your feelings and simmer on them for a while until she's back at Dunley Thornton, but at least let the woman know how you feel if you want a chance at something more. Wren isn't Gloria, and Jared Allen isn't your brother. What bad thing do you think is going to happen if you decide to admit you have feelings for Wren?"

She didn't have an answer, but could it really be that easy? She wanted to believe it, but Gloria's betrayal loomed large. "I guess I have trust issues."

"You think?"

"Look, I get I'm being a little irrational, but I hired Gloria to represent Daniel and she sold him out without even discussing it with me."

"Is the issue that she was a defense attorney or that she wasn't a good one?"

"The issue is my judgment was clouded because I was in a relationship with her. I come from a family of fuckups and I know that, but he didn't even remember what had happened. She didn't hire any experts. She didn't even hire an investigator before she convinced Daniel he was better off going to the pen for twenty years. He should've gone to trial."

"Do you hear yourself? Either Daniel was railroaded into taking a plea or he was guilty in the first place. You spend your time vacillating between being mad at Gloria for doing her job and being mad at your brother for committing the crime. It affects everything you do. You prejudge every case—why should your love life be any different."

"That's my job."

"No," Nina said. "Your first job is to be a checkpoint in the system. The cops don't always get it right and you shouldn't even take those cases. When there is a trial, it's your job to fight like hell to win, but most cases need to be resolved without a trial and that's part of your job too. Maybe it's time to admit Daniel was in a much better position to know if a guilty plea was the right way to go. He made that decision, and it's time for you to make peace with it. And as far as Gloria Leland goes, I know you cared about her, but she simply is not a good person. It has nothing to do with the fact she's a defense attorney."

She was partly right. Gloria wasn't a nice person, but the conflict of a relationship with someone on the other side was more than she was willing to take on again. Less than two months. She could tell Wren how she felt, see if she would wait. The time would trudge by, but in the scheme of things, two months was nothing. Wren would be back at Dunley Thornton and they could go on a real date. With dinner and conversation and after dinner back and forth about whose house they'd be spending the night at. She could almost see it playing out. She tried on the feelings of satisfaction and contentment and she liked the way they felt.

She rushed to her feet. "I have to go."

Nina's smile was big and broad. She made a shooing motion. "Yes. Go. Now. Before you change your mind."

Lennox raced up the stairs to the ninth floor. Sally, as usual, was on the phone chatting about the latest episode of *The Bachelor* instead of anything work related. She reached over the counter, grabbed a pen and paper, and scrawled *Is Wren here?* And held the note under her nose.

Sally huffed and told whoever was on the other line to hold. "She left for lunch and never came back."

"Is she in court?"

"Dunno." Sally pointed at the board to her left where the individual PDs signed in and out. Wren had signed out for lunch at twelve thirty. "Far as I know, she's still at lunch."

It was after four. Not many courts held hearings this late in the afternoon, and if Wren was in trial, then Sally, incompetent as she was, would at least know that. She thanked Sally and took off back to the stairwell, but before she entered, she stopped to send Wren a text. When she pulled out her phone, she saw Wren had beat her to it.

I don't know what's going on with you, but I have some good news I'd like share. Can we talk?

She reread the text several times. She'd definitely been a jerk to ignore Wren and it was time to make it right. *Sorry I've been AWOL. Yes, I want to talk. Can I see you?*

The seconds she spent waiting for a response seemed like hours, but the time stamp for Wren's response showed she answered right away. *Yes. I'd like that. My place?*

Only if you tell the burly doorman you're expecting me. She added a smiling emoji.

Done. See you soon.

She started to type a reply but realized they could keep the back and forth going all evening, when all she really wanted was to see Wren before she could change her mind about sharing how she felt. She sent Johnny a text to let him know she was leaving for the day and shoved her phone in her pocket before he could reply with astonishment.

The actual distance from the courthouse to Wren's apartment building was only a few miles, but in early afternoon traffic gridlock, it took her forty-five minutes to make the drive. By the time she found nearby parking and checked in with the doorman, she was keyed up and starting to question whether this was a good idea, but the minute Wren swung open her door, she knew she was exactly where she was supposed to be.

Wren stood inside the door, her expression expectant, but guarded. She'd known it wouldn't be easy to show up on Wren's doorstep as if there hadn't been days of silence between them, but now she wished she'd slowed down a little and thought of what she would say when she got here.

"Are you here to talk about the case?" Wren asked.

"No."

"Do you want to tell me why you've been ignoring me since Friday night?"

"Not really."

Wren took a step back. "Why are you here, Lennox?"

"You said you wanted to talk."

"And you said you did too. Do I have to pry whatever it is out of you?"

Lennox stared into Wren's kind eyes and all her filters faded away. "I'm sorry I ignored you. I'm sorry I ran out of here." She stepped toward Wren and now they were only inches apart. "But most of all, I'm sorry I didn't get to do more of this." She reached for Wren and pulled her close. Wren looked up into her eyes, and like on Friday, her lips were parted and kissable, but she had to be sure. She bent closer, until they were almost touching. "Is this okay?"

Wren let out a breath and wet her lips with the tip of her tongue. "It's perfect."

CHAPTER FIFTEEN

Wren had no idea how long she and Lennox had been standing in her foyer. Kissing and touching and kissing some more. Her T-shirt and Lennox's suit jacket were on the floor, and all she could think about was why they were still wearing any clothes at all as the flames of arousal licked her skin.

When they both stopped to breathe, she whispered in Lennox's ear. "I could kiss you all night."

"Yes. Me too."

"Let's test that premise." She leaned back just enough to see Lennox's hooded, sultry eyes. "Okay?"

"A hundred percent, yes."

She took Lennox's hand in hers and led them down the hall. She had no recollection of the condition of her room, and she didn't care. She'd gladly wade through dirty clothes and half empty coffee mugs for the chance to get Lennox naked and in bed. She only hoped Lennox would feel the same. They'd barely crossed the doorway when Lennox made it clear she wasn't interested in anything but her.

Lennox ran a finger along the edge of her bra. "This is sexy, but can we take it off now?"

"I don't know," Wren teased her, looking down at the very plain black silk bra. "It's the most comfortable one I own."

"Comfort is overrated. For instance, you know you're killing me right now, don't you?"

Wren tugged Lennox's shirt from her waistband. "Said the woman who was wearing the most clothes. How about we both lose all of these clothes so we're on an even playing field." She reached for the buttons and slowly and deliberating started unfastening them. Lennox's breathing grew more labored as she worked. When the last button came loose, she pushed the shirt off Lennox's shoulders, unfastened her bra, and let both drop to the floor while Lennox melted against her touch. The power was intoxicating, especially since she sensed Lennox didn't often cede control. She pointed toward the bed. "Take off your pants and go lie down. I'll be right there."

Lennox hesitated for a moment, her gaze trained on Wren's breasts. She leaned down and delivered a searing kiss, and then, while Wren struggled to catch her breath, she whispered, "Don't take too long."

Wren stood in place and watched. If she'd had to guess, she would've predicted Lennox would be the type of person who stopped to neatly fold her clothes before beginning a perfectly timed and choreographed session of intimacy. She would've been wrong.

Lennox faced her with a sultry stare as she toed off her shoes, slowly unfastened her pants, and let them drop to the floor. She stepped out of them and kicked the pile of clothes to the side. She placed one hand behind her neck and the other along the waistband of her incredibly sexy boxer briefs, teasingly drawing them partway down.

"You said to take off my pants." She pointed to the pile on the floor, and then back up to her briefs. "These too?" she asked with the hint of a grin.

"I'm a little torn about whether they should go." Wren licked her lips. "You look really delicious right now."

"Then I'll let you decide when you're ready."

Lennox turned and walked to the bed, giving Wren a perfect view of her tight ass, and it took every ounce of self-control Wren had to watch her go. When Lennox was settled against the pillows, hands behind her head, looking completely relaxed, Wren slowly started to undress, wishing she'd had the foresight to put on something sexy before Lennox showed up at her door. She followed Lennox's lead and took her time shedding the rest of her clothes while Lennox watched. She'd never had a lover who was so focused and intense, content to wait for pleasure instead of rushing right in, which led her to wonder if Lennox was a cuddler or a leave in the middle of the night lover.

"Everything okay?"

Wren met Lennox's hooded gaze. She needed to stop wondering, and get into bed with this sexy woman right freaking now. "Everything is perfect." She walked to the bed and nudged Lennox over slightly before climbing on top. She looked down at perfect breasts, those delicious abs, and Lennox's shy smile, and she knew perfect was the exact right word. "You are so sexy."

Lennox traced the curve of her hip. "You are."

Wren stretched out over Lennox, electrified when their skin touched. She traced her tongue along her lips and down her neck to her chest, trading time between each breast—licking, sucking, and savoring the way Lennox groaned and arched beneath her.

"Feels so good," Lennox said, her breath labored.

"Yes, yes it does." Wren slid her hand down and ran her fingers lightly along the inside of Lennox's thigh and along the soft cloth of her briefs. "As much as I love these, it's time for them to go." She sat up and pulled on them while Lennox lifted her butt to help her along. Wren sucked in a breath when Lennox was fully nude. Her body was athletic and strong, but lying naked in her bed, she was also vulnerable in a way that Wren found incredibly endearing and undeniably sexy. "You're gorgeous."

Lennox blushed a warm red at the compliment which only highlighted her allure. Wren tenderly kissed the inside of her thighs before settling between her legs. She breathed in the scent of Lennox's arousal and let it fuel her own. Praying there would be time in the future to go slow, she gave in to her desire to bury herself in the taste and smell and sight of Lennox, and hungrily began to explore her sex with her tongue. Long slow strokes at first, dipping inside and out, then drawing a path around her clit. Steady and measured, she embraced the journey as Lennox began to rock beneath her, growing increasingly wet, her escalating moans begging for more.

While she explored with her tongue, Wren entered Lennox with one finger followed by another, cupping them back toward her until Lennox cried out with pleasure, signaling she'd found the exact right spot. She flattened her tongue against her clit, dipping it into her folds, harder and faster, and Lennox tensed beneath her, rising up to meet her touch until they were fused together in a bond of ecstasy. Wren gripped Lennox's ass with her other hand, pulling them closer than she'd thought possible, and Lennox began to buck and thrash against her as the orgasm tore through her body. Wren held her close determined not to let go until every last wave of pleasure receded. And even after because she sensed Lennox might be a cuddler after all.

Soft skin pressed firmly against the back of her thigh. Lennox felt the touch before she opened her eyes. Normally, the idea of someone burrowed into her personal space would be disconcerting, but when she turned to see Wren's sleepy eyes staring back at her, contentment settled over her. Was this a dream or was she really lying naked in bed with Wren Bishop's head tucked against her shoulder?

"Good morning."

Wren wriggled closer. "It is a good morning, isn't it?"

Lennox grinned. "The best."

Wren reached up and placed a finger on her lips. "You have the best smile. I never get tired of seeing it."

"Most people tell me I don't smile enough."

"Most people need to keep their opinions to themselves. You smile when you want. Whenever you're happy." Wren kissed her tenderly and murmured against her lips. "Does this make you happy?"

Lennox could feel her smile stretch wider. "It absolutely does." She shifted so she was leaning over Wren. "You know what else would make me happy?" She slid a hand down, under the sheet, and parted Wren's legs to find her wet and ready. She breathed deep. "Do you always wake up looking so sexy?"

"Eye of the beholder."

"Nope. I'm certain any objective observers would agree. You are undeniably hot." She dipped her fingers into Wren's sex and delivered light strokes from her folds to her inner thighs and back again. Wren's eyes fluttered shut and she began to writhe in the sheets, emitting moans of pleasure that ramped up Lennox's own arousal. All night they'd traded turns, giving and receiving pleasure. By now, Lennox knew exactly where to touch Wren to make her come, and she purposefully avoided all of those places until she teased her to the perfect climax.

When Wren collapsed, spent, in her arms, she reflected back, trying to remember the last time she'd felt so sated, happy, hopeful even. No memory surfaced. Somewhere along the way, she'd decided she wasn't the kind of person destined for a happily ever after, but right now? Right now, it seemed like anything was possible.

Wren rolled over and stretched both arms over her head. The second she pulled away, the space between them was vast and Lennox desperately craved their closeness again. In the courtroom she wasn't shy about asking for anything, but here in Wren's bed, after an entire evening of the best sex of her life, she hesitated to test the boundaries. For all she knew Wren had a strict morning routine and she was mucking it up by staying over. Rays of sun were starting to poke through the blinds. She should probably get up, go home, shower and get to the office, but right now her own routine seemed boring and bland, and she wanted to break free of it. *What have you done to me?*

"Where did you go just now?" Wren asked, reaching for her hand.

Lennox took her hand and squeezed it lightly. "I was thinking I should probably go and give you your space."

Wren answered by snuggling up against her side. "Do I look like I want space?" She kissed Lennox's neck. "I wish we didn't have to work today."

"Me too." Lennox couldn't remember ever wishing she didn't have to go to work—the job was her rock, but right now being with Wren felt more real and solid than the world she'd carved out at the courthouse. "I don't have any hearings this morning." She watched Wren's face for any sign she was thinking along the same lines.

Wren scrunched her brow. "If you're offering what I think you're offering, I'm wishing right now that I'd never filed a motion to suppress on the Lawson case. I also played hooky yesterday afternoon and if I don't show my face, the PD posse will probably rat me out to Ford." She shot upright. "Hey! I totally forgot to tell you. I mean, I didn't forget, but I was distracted by all of the kissing and the sex."

Lennox stared, amazed at how Wren could go from perfectly calm to hyped up in mere seconds. "I have no idea what you're talking about right now."

"Sorry. Of course you don't because I haven't had a chance to tell you the good news. I think I quit my job."

Lennox tried to imagine a scenario where quitting her job was good news. Maybe if she was going to run for a bench—never going to happen—or was offered a job at the US Attorney's office—something she'd considered but wasn't sure it would be the right fit. Wait, did Wren mean she was no longer going to be working at the PD's office? If so, that was news she wanted to celebrate right freaking now. "You *think* you quit? Does Ford know?"

"I haven't had a chance to tell him yet, but I don't think he'll care. I mean he basically offered me the job, so I doubt he'll mind if I stay on. I don't know if it will be permanent. I still have my parents' offer to consider. Did I mention they asked me to come on board as general counsel?"

Too many words. Lennox spent her career standing in the well of a courthouse, handling whatever testimony from witnesses and arguments from opposing counsel that were thrown her way, but in her post-sex haze, she couldn't compute what Wren was trying to tell her. She grabbed her hand. "I so want to understand what you're trying to tell me, but I'm high from last night and this morning and I haven't had coffee, so take it from the beginning. Slowly."

Wren smiled. "Sorry. I have a tendency to get ramped up when I'm excited." She let out a breath. "I had to go by Dunley Thornton yesterday and I ran into Carl, the litigation partner who manages my section there. Basically, he told me that the firm is cutting off the lawyer-on-loan program and they expect me back at the office next week."

Lennox pushed herself upright, her interest piqued. If Wren was going back to her old job right away, then there was nothing standing between them and more nights like the one they'd just shared. "So, you're quitting the PD's office early."

"No. I'm staying longer. I told Carl that if they couldn't keep their promise to the PD's office, and me, to work my full term there, then I would give my notice. Which isn't exactly quitting, but the more I've thought about it, the more I realize I don't want to work for a firm that doesn't keep their promises. I have options."

"Wait a minute." Lennox pinched her nose while she tried to focus. "Your boss told you he needs you back at your job. The one that pays your salary and that let you work for free at the PD's office. And you told him no?"

"I know, right? I admit it was kind of nervy, but my parents talked to me about coming to work for them and Ford said I have a job there if I want, so it's not like I don't have options. In the meantime, I can keep working for the PD's office as part of the loan program, I just need to restructure a few financial matters. The good news is I'll get to see the Allen case all the way through trial. What do you think?"

"Are you serious right now?"

Wren looked shocked at the question. "What's happening?"

"You want to know what's happening? I'll tell you what's happening." Lennox's stomach roiled at Wren's cavalier attitude. "You didn't even think about the consequences of your decision, did you?"

"What are you talking about?"

"Can the PD's office even afford to hire you?"

"I'm not sure it's a permanent solution. I have other options, but for now I'm staying here to see this case through."

Lennox wanted to ask if that was the only reason, but she wasn't about to allude to it if Wren wasn't. "Very practical. What are you going to do for money?"

"I have investments, and my grandparents left me a trust fund."

"Of course you have a trust fund."

"I'm going to pretend you didn't say that, because it's rude, and you're not a rude person."

Wren reached out to her, but she couldn't shake off her agitation that easily. "Well, I suppose that just goes to show how little you know about me. Turns out neither one of us is very good at predicting how the other will act. I didn't think a grown woman would quit her job on a whim."

"Lennox, why do you care if I quit my job? It's not like I'm asking you to support me."

Lennox braced a hand against the headboard of the bed. The bed where she'd just made love to Wren. Where she'd silently proclaimed she'd felt the happiest she'd ever felt. All because she'd listened to Nina's talk about how Wren was cute and smart and sexy and she'd be a fool to let her go. But she'd only given in to her feelings because she though the conflict that kept her from acting on her feelings in the first place would be gone soon. Wren would go back to her law firm, she'd try the Allen case against Ford, and she and Wren could explore their feelings for each other unencumbered by plea discussions and wrangling over motions and working at opposite purposes. In the dreamworld she'd created, they'd discuss each other's very different work over morning coffee, and all would be well. But no, Wren had to bust her expectations to pieces and the kicker was Wren was ecstatic about the prospect of facing off with her.

She pulled away from Wren and stood by the side of the bed. "I have to go."

"No, Lennox, you don't. You can stay and talk to me. Help me understand what's going on here."

"This was a mistake."

"No, it wasn't."

"How's your client going to feel when he finds out you're sleeping with the prosecutor on his case?"

Wren grinned. "Hopeful?"

Lennox pointed at her face. "See. That right there is why we can't date."

"I was kidding."

"I know, but there's truth behind it. You and me? We'll never see things the same way, and if you're working at the courthouse, especially if you're trying this case, we can't be involved. I told you I don't date defense attorneys and I told you why."

"You didn't actually. You offered some scant details about your brother's case and the woman who represented him, but as for your bright-line rule about not dating defense attorneys? Were you for real with that? Attorneys are on opposite sides all of the time. That doesn't mean they can't have personal lives."

"My work is my personal life." Lennox knew the declaration wasn't going to win her any points here, but it needed to be said. "Anyone I date should understand that. It's a bright-line rule for a reason."

"Are you giving me an ultimatum?"

She heard the challenge in Wren's voice. She had no right to issue ultimatums, even after the night they'd shared, but if she did, would Wren side with her? She was almost afraid to find out. Almost. "What if I was?"

"I'm not going to be in a relationship with you based on a threat, but just to be perfectly clear, are you saying that if I don't quit the PD's office before the Allen trial, we're done?"

It was a valid question, and now Lennox felt the frustration of being pushed in a corner and giving in seemed like she was selling off a piece of herself. A quiet voice in her head echoed Nina's speech to her, saying it wasn't rational for her to judge everything in her life as good or bad with no room for in-between. But a much louder voice told her she was better off alone than with someone who didn't—couldn't—see the world the way she did.

"I know it may not seem fair to you, but that's how it has to be." She waited a second, but she could tell by the firm set of Wren's jaw, she wasn't giving in.

Gathering her clothes took longer than she would've liked, and the fact they were scattered was a testament to the fact that last night she'd been out of her head, oblivious to order and acting on a whim. That had been a mistake, and it was one she wouldn't make again.

CHAPTER SIXTEEN

Three months later...

Wren stood in front of the tiny closet next to Ford's office and rummaged through the contents, her frustration rising with each pass.

"I'm sure there's something there that will fit Jared," Ford said.

"Oh, I'm not worried about fit," she replied. "I'm worried about him looking like he walked off the set of *The Mod Squad*."

Ford laughed. "You're a little young to know that show."

"So are you, and so is everyone who isn't in a nursing home. I think you get my point."

"I do, and it's well taken. I know these suits are dated, but they're all donations. If you think the county allocates funds so defendants can dress out for trial, you would be wrong."

"Y'all need to find different donors." The minute she spoke the words, she had a flash of brilliance. She whipped out her phone and sent a quick text. "I'll deal with the clothing issue later. I made a trial notebook for you with all of the pretrial motions, draft jury instructions, and witness statements. I included an outline of key points to cover and a bio for each witness. Is there any other prep you'd like me to do?"

"Yes, tell me you'll stick around when this trial is over. I'm feeling spoiled."

Discomfort twinged in the pit of her stomach—partly because of the upcoming trial and partly because of what would happen after. For the entire summer, she'd managed to avoid direct contact with Lennox, but when Jared's trial started on Monday, they'd be spending twelve-hour days in the same room, less than six feet apart. She held out no hope the closeness would thaw the freeze between them, but what about when the trial was over?

Ford had been nudging her to stay. He'd even gone as far as getting budget approval from the commissioner's court for the position. Carl had called several times to tell her he'd been hasty. That even if the managing partners didn't approve continuing the lawyer-on-loan program this year, he'd lobby for it in next year's budget. His attempt to placate her came from desperation. He needed attorneys in seats at the firm in order to keep all of the new clients they'd brought in from the merger with Aspen Jones happy, and she knew it. And then there were her parents who were trying to give her space to make her decisions, but she could feel the weight of their expectations every time they talked on the phone about unrelated subjects.

The problem was she couldn't give any of them an answer because she hadn't made up her mind. Lennox's over-the-top reaction to her impulsivity had thrown her, and a tiny seed of doubt had burrowed its way into her brain telling her she didn't know what she was doing and paralyzing her ability to move forward.

All she could do now was focus on this case. Jared's trial started on Monday and she had less than a week to finish trial prep. Ford would be first chair on the case, but they'd divided up the witnesses and she'd handle jury selection and give their opening statement.

"Seriously, there is one thing you can do. Lennox left a message that she had some additional discovery. Can you go by her office and pick it up and get her take on the initial set of jury instructions? I know we'll wind up fighting about the lesser included charges, but if we can agree on the rest, it'll save us a lot of time later."

He listed off a couple of other things she could ask Lennox, but she'd stopped listening in order to focus all of her brain power on figuring out how to duck out of this task.

TRIAL BY FIRE

"Did you get all of that?"

Nothing. She had nothing when it came to excuses for why she couldn't do her job when it came to Lennox. Nothing she wanted to admit out loud and not at all to her boss. "Yes. I got it. I'll go see her today." May as well get it over with.

She trudged back to her office and broke out her mini coffee bar. She needed some kind of fortification if she was going to have to talk to Lennox, and since it was the middle of the day, caffeine would have to do. The kettle had just started whistling when she heard a knock on her door. "Come in," she called out.

"The rumor is true."

She turned to see Skye standing in her doorway. She waved her in. "Have a seat. And what rumor is that?"

"The basic rumor is that you bring your own coffee, but there are variations."

"Is that so?" She motioned for Skye to keep talking. "Let's hear them."

"You have special dietary needs. You're too snobby to drink grocery store coffee. You spend more on your accessories than most people who work down here make in a month. But my personal favorite is that you're a coffee heiress." When Wren laughed, Skye held up a hand. "Wait, there's more to it. Your parents own a coffee plantation in Columbia, and they may or may not be connected to one of the major cartels."

"That's ridiculous."

"True, but you don't fit the mold around here, and when people are different, the rest need to make up a reason why so it isn't about them."

"How did you get to be so wise?"

"Lots of experience, much of it from mistakes in my past I learned how to avoid in the future."

Wren nodded. "Tell me how you take your coffee and then tell me why you stopped by."

"Black, and I have a few things I'd like to go over."

"Great." Wren pulled another mug out of her file drawer, pressed the coffee, and poured them each a cup. She handed Skye's

• 197 •

to her and took pleasure from the moan she emitted after taking one sip. "See, it's better than any other coffee in the building."

"It's the best. I don't care if your parents are connected to a cartel."

"Tell me what's up."

Skye opened a folder and pulled out several sheets of notes. "I've been trying to get someone to talk to me about Lisa's boyfriend, Chet Evans. His employer wouldn't talk, probably something to do with the reason he no longer works there, and he was a salesman with his own route, so he didn't have any coworkers he interacted with on a regular basis. The shops on his route have mixed things to say, but most of it neutral. He wasn't good about being on time, often made promises he couldn't keep, but he was a nice enough guy."

"That and the fact he doesn't have a criminal history doesn't bode well for a theory that casts him as organized enough to pull off an arson and set up Jared in the process."

"True, but there's something else. Most of his neighbors were happy to talk to me about how he doesn't mow his lawn on a regular basis, but everyone I talked to had nothing else to add. Until this morning. His next-door neighbors, nice young couple, have been up north for most of the summer and returned last week. They were in town when the arson happened and for a few weeks after."

"And?" Wren prayed they had something, anything to point suspicion in another direction.

"They don't know much about the guy, but they mentioned he had a frequent visitor. A woman."

"That makes sense. It was Lisa, right?"

Skye shook her head. "I showed them a photo, and they said it was definitely not her. Also, the same woman was there on several occasions after Lisa died in the fire. And there's something else."

She hesitated like she was still trying to determine how significant the something else was, but Wren sensed whatever it was, it was something big and she couldn't wait. "Skye, you're killing me here."

"Sorry. I've been trying to sort out what they told me. Eyewitnesses are notoriously unreliable, but this couple was certain the woman visiting him wasn't Lisa, but they were also certain that whoever she was, she looks a lot like Lisa."

"Her sister?"

"I didn't have a picture to show them, but I'm going back this afternoon. I'll let you know if they say it was her."

Wren leaned back in her chair while her mind whirred with possibilities. "I can kind of understand why she might be at his place after Lisa died. She could've been picking up some of Lisa's things or commiserating about her death, but why would she be there before? Once or twice maybe, but a frequent visitor? On her own. You know where my mind's going."

"Same place mine went," Skye said. "It's not the simplest explanation for her visits to his house, but if we could prove they were having an affair before Lisa was killed, it could toss some reasonable doubt into the mix." Skye pulled out another piece of paper and set it on her desk. "This might not mean anything, but I dug it up after I talked to the neighbor."

Wren reached for the paper and saw it was a court order, awarding temporary custody of Jared and Lisa's kids to Denise Sloan, Lisa's sister. "Aren't family court records like this typically sealed?"

"Typically. Don't ask me to tell you where I got it, but my source says Denise is poised to file a motion for permanent guardianship if Jared is convicted."

Wren picked up a pen and started jotting down notes. *Affair? But why kill? And why arson? Insurance money.* She underlined that twice. "It's still a stretch to cast Evans and Denise as suspects. Lisa wasn't married to the guy. If he wanted to sleep with her sister, there was nothing stopping them except common decency—not a big motive to kill. But if we can tie the insurance proceeds to a motive on their part, we might have rock-solid reasonable doubt. We need to explore this. Can you find out if anyone has contacted the insurance company to start the claim procedure? And I'd like to go with you when you meet with the neighbors."

"Sure, no problem." Skye stood. "Want me to pick you up?"

"That would be great. I have to go meet with Lennox in a few, but it shouldn't take long—" She stopped abruptly while an idea formed. "Besides getting your hands on a picture of Denise, are you doing anything else right now?"

"I was going to check downstairs to see if any of our subpoenas are ready, but I suspect you have other plans."

"Come with me to see Lennox. She's got some additional discovery. We can pick it up, ask her any questions, and go over it on the ride to Evans's house."

Skye's eyes narrowed like she suspected there was more to the request, but after a moment, she said, "Yeah, I can do that."

"Great. I need ten minutes to wrap a few things up and I'll meet you downstairs."

Skye left her office and Wren took a moment to stare at the closed door. She didn't have anything to wrap up, but she did need the few minutes to brace for facing Lennox one-on-one. Or two-on-one since she was too chicken to take a meeting alone with her. What was she so afraid of? She wasn't the one who'd walked away from an intense attraction, loaded with possibilities for the future. Lennox was the one who should be dreading any confrontation. She'd been the irrational one, willing to forgo a chance at something meaningful because of the fake construct of their roles in the system. The more she'd thought about it over the past few months, the angrier she'd gotten, and she'd turned that anger into energy, taking to the internet to find out everything she could about what had happened with Lennox's brother that had left her so jaded about getting involved with anyone who worked the other side.

What she found left her with more questions than answers. The first nugget was that Gloria Leland had been Daniel's attorney, which meant Lennox had been in a relationship with Gloria. Now she understood Lennox's reaction when she saw her talking to Gloria. But everything after that was a mystery. Daniel had been found unconscious in a drug house with a dead junkie in the next room and a gun with his fingerprints on it lying on the floor beside him. Daniel had a record, mostly lower-level drug arrests, but nothing violent. He'd been charged with murder, but twenty years was no great deal for an agreed plea. No wonder Lennox had been pissed. But ultimately, the decision to plead guilty had been Daniel's. Had he followed his conscience, or had he felt trapped by circumstance?

With everything she'd learned, Wren's anger had faded, but her frustration remained. Lennox Roy may have been a thoughtful, tender lover, but the best way to get through the meeting today and the trial next week, was to remember she was also a stubborn, impossible woman who'd walked away and never looked back. She was better off without her.

Then why was she torn between feeling anxious and excited about talking to her? Why did she feel anything at all?

CHAPTER SEVENTEEN

Lennox looked up at the knock on her door to see Skye Keaton standing in the doorframe. She'd heard Skye had been hired to work on Jared Allen's case, and she figured she was here to collect the additional discovery for Ford. "Hey, Skye, come on in."

When Skye stepped aside to reveal Wren standing beside her, everything else in the room receded, and it was just the two of them standing there, three-dimensional figures floating in midair. She stared into Wren's eyes, trying to read something, anything from her expression, but other than a flicker of pain in her eyes, her features were firmly fixed in a neutral, professional looking smile. At least it was a smile.

Wren deserved more than the cold silence she'd given her after walking out of her apartment, and she knew it, but one week had passed and then another, and the more days that went by, the harder it became to find a way back to her. She'd seen her plenty of times since that night, but always in a crowded space and never close enough to whisper an apology, to try to make amends. Besides, what would she say? Sorry I left in a huff, but nothing's changed. Wren was still at the PD's office and word was she planned to try the Allen case with Ford. She'd known she'd have to talk to her at some point, and now here she was standing in front of her. The very least she could do would be to chip away at the barrier between them.

"Hi."

"Hi," Wren replied. "Is this a good time?"

Such a loaded question. Would there ever be a good time to smooth things over and pretend nothing had happened between them while they discussed the battle they were about to begin? *Just talk to her. Quit acting like every interaction you have with her is monumental. She brought Skye with her which means she's here to discuss the case, not your personal life.* "Of course." She shoved aside the files on her desk and invited them to sit in the cramped office. "I guess you're here to pick up the discovery?"

Wren stared at her for a moment, but she couldn't read her expression. She reached for the packet she'd prepared and slid it across the desk, keeping her fingers on the edge of the envelope. "It's not much—a few extra photos of the crime scene that weren't included in the initial production. Most of them are duplicates, but I wanted to make sure you have everything."

Wren reached for the packet, and for a moment they were both holding it, the only connection they'd shared this summer and Lennox was reluctant to let go until she spotted Skye watching them with a curious expression. She released her grip and Wren handed the envelope to Skye without giving it a second glance.

The moments of silence that followed lasted forever. Lennox wanted a moment alone with Wren, to clear the air, though she had no idea what she would say given the opportunity. She'd almost mustered the courage to ask Skye to leave, when Wren spoke.

"Did you or the police ever run phone records for Lisa Allen's family or Chet Evans?"

Not the intimate conversation she'd envisioned, but if it kept Wren here in her office, she'd gladly engage. "No. Why?"

"It's no secret that one of our theories is that the police jumped to the conclusion Jared killed Lisa. The less they did to investigate other possible suspects, the more plausible that theory is."

Rarely were defense attorneys this frank about how they planned to try their case, and Lennox appreciated the insight. Was Wren trying to show her she didn't fit the mold? "I'll double-check with Detective Braxton, but he assured me those photos were the only items that hadn't been produced."

"I'm asking Judge Larabee to grant a subpoena for Evans's phone records. It'd be a lot easier and faster if you'd get Braxton to get them for us."

She opened her mouth to give the same response she'd give any other defense attorney who asked her for the same information, which was "It's not my job to do your work for you," but she stopped short. It wasn't her job, but that didn't mean it was the right thing to do. She thought about Daniel's case. Had Gloria dug deep enough to find answers? Had the prosecutor on that case refused to cooperate with straightforward requests?

She mentally reviewed the contents of her file. Braxton had focused on Jared Allen right from the start. Nothing wrong with that—a high percentage of murders were committed by family members, and estranged husbands topped the list. She had asked him to look deeper into Chet and Braxton assured her he had. She had Lisa Allen's phone records and could see how many times she and Chet had exchanged calls, but she knew for a fact Braxton had never given her Chet's phone records, and now she doubted he'd requested them. Sometimes cops didn't dig because if they found exculpatory evidence, the state was duty bound to hand it over to defense counsel, but she suspected in this case it was more about taking a shortcut than malice. Braxton and the fire marshal were convinced Jared Allen was the guilty party and they had arrested him and moved on. She heard the echo of Nina's words. Your first job is to be a checkpoint in the system. She hadn't been a checkpoint. She'd been a rubber stamp. Yes, she'd asked Braxton to dig deeper, but she hadn't followed up to make sure he did.

Lennox picked up the phone and dialed Braxton's cell. He answered on the first ring.

"Whatcha need?" he asked.

"Did you subpoena Chet Evans's cell phone records?"

"Uh, no. He has an alibi, remember?"

His indignant tone got under her skin, but she kept her cool because Wren and Skye were in the room. "Go ahead and get the records and put a rush on it. Larabee's on the bench today. Hand carry the subpoena to him and tell him both sides want it." She placed her hand over the phone and asked Wren, "Anything else?"

Wren exchanged a look with Skye who nodded. Lennox felt a flicker of jealousy at their easy, nonverbal communication, but she knew she had only herself to blame that her connection to Wren had been severed.

"I was planning to ask for a subpoena for Denise's records too," Wren said.

Lennox didn't bother trying to mask her surprise. She told Braxton she'd call him back in a minute and hung up the phone. She met Wren's intense gaze, willing her to read her mind. Wren turned to Skye and asked her to give them a minute. When they were alone, she didn't hold back. "Look, I get investigating the boyfriend, but now you want me to help you investigate one of the victims in this case?"

"Victim?" Wren raised her eyebrows. "You mean because she was Lisa's sister?" At Lennox's nod, she kept going. "What if she's not the victim? Who's the beneficiary on the life insurance if Jared can't collect?"

"The kids, but you know that already. What am I missing?" She threw up her hands and looked at Wren who stared at her intently like she was willing her to figure out a puzzle, which was impossible because she didn't have all of the pieces. "Help me out here."

"It's only a theory at this point," Wren said. "I'm not in the habit of sharing theories with my adversaries."

"But you are in the habit of asking them for favors?"

"Touché." Wren tapped her fingers on her desk and bit her bottom lip in that super cute way that signaled she was deep in thought. "Assure me you'll keep an open mind and I'll tell you what I'm thinking."

Lennox hesitated for a moment. She was used to preparing her case, presenting it, and then waiting until exactly the right moment to poke holes in whatever defense strategy was presented, if there was one, but she rarely got a look at it before it was presented to the jury, *Perry Mason* style. She could think of only one reason Wren would share her ideas with her now. "Are you looking for a new plea offer?"

"No. A dismissal would be nice, but I'm not holding my breath."

"Fine." Wren's approach of sharing her strategy upfront, albeit mere days before trial was foreign to her, and it was natural for her to anticipate pitfalls, but she was inclined to hear her out. Was she doing it because of how she felt about Wren or because it was the right thing to do? Damn. She could analyze her motives to death, or she could act like a person, talking to another person attempting to resolve a mutual problem. "No promises, except I'll listen to what you have to say." At Wren's raised eyebrow, she added, "With an open mind."

"Thank you."

Wren held her gaze for a moment. They'd entered into a silent truce. It wasn't as exhilarating as their interactions had been in the beginning—with the push and pull of attraction—but it was comfortable, and considering how uncomfortable the last few months had been avoiding each other, she'd take it. Maybe they could even be friends. The thought left her with a sinking feeling, but she didn't have the bandwidth to examine it right now. "Let's hear your theory."

"The kids get the insurance money and any other assets Lisa owned. Denise has filed for custody of Lisa's kids. As their guardian, she'll have control over their finances. We have reason to believe Denise was having an affair with Chet, who was supposed to be Lisa's boyfriend—I can get you witness statements as soon as we confirm."

Wren paused and took a deep breath before she continued on. "What if Chet's relationship with Lisa was a farce, designed to get him close enough to her to be able to arrange her death and pin it on Jared so he and Denise could ride off into the sunset with a ready-made family and a bundle of cash?"

"Whoa, that's a lot." Lennox rubbed her temples while she tried to digest Wren's rapid-fire summary. It sounded like something she'd hear on an episode of *Dateline* and she said so.

"That's different than saying it sounds crazy," Wren said. "Look, I know the simplest answer is usually the right one, but like I said before, Jared didn't have much to gain by killing Lisa. He's lost his business, his kids, and he's probably never going to see a dime of that insurance money without years of litigation and only if he's acquitted."

"I don't know, Wren. I mean, I hear what you're saying, but what about all the fights he and Lisa had? It could be the answer is he went to talk to her, they got in a fight. He hit her, she died, he panicked and set the fire to cover it up."

"Which doesn't fit with your 'he bought the gas before he got to the house' theory. The trial's on Monday. You're going to have to settle on a strategy at some point. Am I really going to have to wait until opening statements to learn what it is?"

Lennox sighed. Wren was right and she knew it. And Wren had laid out her entire strategy without her promising anything in return. If Wren was wrong and Denise and Chet weren't involved in Lisa's death, didn't it make more sense to disprove the theory before it ever had a chance of being presented at trial? Convinced she was making the decision based on purely professional reasons, she picked up her phone and hit redial. When Braxton answered, she told him to add Denise's cell phone records to the subpoena, and when he started to push back, she told him to just do it and hung up.

"Satisfied?"

"I will never be satisfied," Wren said with a grin.

"Ah, a *Hamilton* reference. I'm impressed."

"You should be. I've been waiting to find a good use for one since the day we met. You were all surly and mean because I walked into the courtroom during your performance."

"I remember. And I was not surly or mean." Lennox replayed the entire scene. She'd been in the middle of her closing argument in the Shante Carter case when Wren had barged into the courtroom. She'd been momentarily distracted by Wren's striking presence. Who wouldn't? But she'd continued with her closing, fully focused. Being able to set aside her personal feelings for professional prowess was her trademark, but as she'd gotten to know Wren, her skill had become dull. Would cutting Wren out of her life completely bring it back or was her sharpness gone forever?

"You'll let me know when you have the records?" Wren asked, wresting her from her musings.

"I will."

"Great."

Wren stood and walked to the door. So that was it? They kicked Skye out of the room and all they were going to talk about was work? No mention of the kissing and the sex and the argument? Was all of it behind them or merely off to the side, waiting to rear its head some other time?

Wren's hand was on the doorknob. She had only seconds to capture this moment. "Wait. Please."

She watched as Wren slowly turned, her eyes questioning, and she summoned every ounce of courage she could muster. "I'm sorry for walking out on you. For not calling. For not returning your calls, your messages. I would like it if we could be friends."

Wren smiled, but again it wasn't the big, perky smile Lennox had grown to love, it was a smile twisted with pain and regret. "Thank you," she said. "For the apology. I appreciate it."

Lennox's shoulders sagged with relief. She should've apologized much sooner. It wasn't that hard, and of course Wren forgave her. She was too nice a person not to. "Thank you. Friends?"

"About that part, respectfully? No." Wren shook her head. "I have plenty of friends. In you, I saw the potential for so much more. I was falling for you, Lennox Roy, and I'm sure there's a part of me that still is. I'm not Gloria Leland—not even remotely, and if you don't know that by now, I guess you'll never really know me. So, no, we can't be friends, because frankly, it would be too painful to hang out with you, knowing you don't want me the same way that I want you. But I really do appreciate you clearing the air between us."

She put her hand on the knob, opened the door, and in seconds she was gone, leaving Lennox wondering what the hell had just happened and what she was going to do next.

CHAPTER EIGHTEEN

Monday morning, Wren sat at her desk and reviewed her
notes one last time before packing her files into the large
leather file case her aunt and uncle had given her when she graduated
from law school. She hadn't had much chance to use it while she
was at Dunley Thornton, since a team of paralegals was tasked
with making sure all of the witness and exhibit files made it to the
courtroom, but there was something very satisfying about packing
her own bag and making sure she had everything she needed for the
start of trial.

The last files she put in the file case were the ones bearing
Denise Sloan's and Chet Evan's names, and she took a moment to
glance through them one more time. She hadn't planned to disclose
so much of her defense strategy to Lennox last week, but she'd
made the right decision. Detective Braxton had hand-delivered
Chet's and Denise's cell phone records to her last night and she and
Ford and Skye had scoured every entry. There was definitely more
than a friendly amount of calls and text messages between Chet and
Denise, and the contact had only escalated a month before Lisa died.

Skye had subpoenaed Chet's next-door neighbors who would
testify they'd seen Denise at Chet's house on numerous occasions in
the days leading up to the fire. They still didn't have a legitimately
acquired copy of the temporary guardianship request, but Ford told
her she should ask Denise about it when she was on the stand, and
if Denise denied she'd filed for custody, they could ask Larabee

to review the copy of the order they had in chambers and rule on whether it could be admitted.

She'd provided a copy of the order to Lennox who assured her she'd look into it, and that was all she could do. Jury selection started in less than two hours and they were as ready as they could be. For the trial anyway. She wasn't entirely sure she was ready to sit across the room from Lennox and pretend like nothing had ever happened between them.

She heard a knock on her door and looked up to see Skye leaning against the doorframe. She waved her in. "What's up?"

"I figured you'd want me to get a change of clothes over to Sam before things get started. Do you want to pick a suit?"

"Right." She'd almost forgotten. She definitely did want Skye to take a suit for Jared to the bailiff, but something had been on her mind all weekend and she needed to clear her head if she was going to be able to concentrate in trial today. "Before we do that though, may I talk to you for a minute?"

Skye walked in, shut the door behind her, and sat down. Wren liked that Skye could read her mind after only a few months of working together. She was going to miss their easy camaraderie after this case was over, and she hoped what she was about to ask wasn't going to blow it. "I need a favor."

"A case-related favor or a personal favor?" Skye asked.

"Case-related, but not this case."

"Sounds intriguing."

"I want you to take a fresh look at Daniel Roy's case. It's a Tarrant County case from five years ago."

"I know the case." Skye shifted in her seat. "Lennox Roy's brother."

"That's the one. You have a comment?"

"Not my job."

"Come on, spill."

"Sometimes old wounds are best left alone."

"True, but if they aren't healing, it's best to get a second opinion." Wren smiled. "See, I can come up with little truisms too."

"Fair enough. Is this on your dime too?"

"Yes. No limit. If at all possible, I want to know what happened in that drug house and I trust you to tell me if there's nothing to learn."

"Fine. I'll start right after the trial." She took out a notebook and scrawled a few notes. "I have one question."

"Shoot."

"Does Lennox know you're looking into her brother's case?"

"No, and I'd like to keep it that way."

Skye mimed zipping her lips and throwing away the key. Wren had half expected her to ask more questions and was relieved she hadn't since she wasn't sure she'd be able to answer. All she knew was finding answers about Daniel's case was key to understanding Lennox's view of the world and stopping the nagging voice in her head that said she hadn't tried hard enough to be on Lennox's side. It might be too late for that to matter, but she wasn't ready to write it off completely. Not yet.

In the meantime, she needed to go beat the stuffing out of Lennox at trial. "Let's go pick out that suit."

She led the way to the closet by Ford's office, opened the door, and reached inside. She handed a navy-blue Ralph Lauren suit, a crisp white shirt, and a pair of plain black oxfords to Skye. "I think he'll look good in these. Conservative, but well-cut. Makes him look less like a desperado and more like a guy who doesn't need to kill his soon-to-be ex because he can handle any difficulty life throws his way."

Skye grinned. "You're kind of funny."

She returned the grin. "I doubt the rumor mill would agree with you."

"I'm not big on listening to rumors." Skye pointed at the full closet. "I can't say that I've ever seen clients of the PD's office dressed out in anything remotely resembling these fine suits before."

"Ford said they have to rely on donations, and we have some new donors." Emma had responded to her text about the clothes by sending out an interoffice email to all of the lawyers at Dunley Thornton asking for donations, and she'd delivered the haul the day before. Wren had imagined she'd show up with three or four choices, but they'd had to make three trips from her car to carry in all of the clothes, and what they couldn't fit in the closet was stashed behind the door in her office.

"Are you responsible for this?"

She turned toward the sound of the familiar voice to see Jill standing behind her, staring into the closet. Wondering what secret protocol she'd broken now, Wren decided to own it. "I didn't buy these clothes if that's what you're asking. Even rich girls like me have budgets. Some of the lawyers from Dunley Thornton donated to the cause."

Jill stepped closer and touched the sleeve of one of the suits. "Some of them? Looks like they all emptied their closets." She faced Wren, and for the first time since they'd met, her expression conveyed respect. "This is incredible. You have no idea what a difference decent clothes can make."

"Believe it or not, I do." She wanted to melt at the overture of acceptance, but she'd been bullied by Jill and her pals for months and she knew better than to immediately back down. "I may not have been involved in as many criminal trials as you, but I've handled a lot of cases and many of the same principles apply. If a client looks good, they'll appear more confident and less culpable—that's a universal tenet. Appearances aren't always what they seem, but that doesn't make them any less important."

She stopped talking and watched her words sink in. Jill lowered her eyes and bit her bottom lip. It wasn't an outright apology, but Wren got the clear signal she was contrite. No need to hammer the point home. "The clothes are for anyone who needs to use them. Feel free to spread the word. I was thinking we could ask some of the other big downtown law firms to donate as well."

"That's a great idea," Jill said. "My husband owns a moving business. I could get him to do the pickups."

"Perfect. Let's make a plan after this trial."

"Deal." Jill stuck out her hand. "Good luck today."

"Thanks." Wren noted the strong grip and decided they'd moved far enough past their differences for her to forgive and forget. They'd probably never be fast friends, but at least they'd have a non-acrimonious working relationship, like the one she seemed to have settled into with Lennox. The comparison made her sad. Was professional level friendly all she'd ever have with Lennox? After she'd told her they couldn't even be friends, she could hardly expect more.

But she did. She expected a lot more. She'd wanted Lennox to protest when she'd said they couldn't be friends, to say she didn't want to be just friends either, that she wanted to finish exploring the intimacy they'd shared, both in bed and out, and she'd been deflated when it hadn't happened, but was she being fair when she'd never truly tried to see life from Lennox's point of view?

Lennox challenged her, and her life was all about challenges right now, from the big picture of her career to day-to-day interactions like the one she'd just had with Jill. She hadn't thought so before, but she'd lived her life in a bubble, protected by wealth and privilege. It was easy to walk away from her job at the firm because she had plenty of options, but for someone like Lennox who'd grown up without, her choices would be defined more by survival than pleasure.

She was clearer now about how her own circumstances had framed her experience, and while she still remained idealistic, she could see how it wasn't as easy for someone from a different background to buy into her world view. She should be willing to meet Lennox halfway if she wanted a relationship with her, rather than expecting her to do all of the work. When this trial was over, she'd go to Lennox and tell her exactly that and ask if they could start again. If they ended up only friends, she'd live with that, but she hoped they could have more. Much more. Because she'd fallen in love with Lennox and no amount of ultimatums was going to erase how she felt.

"Are you ready?" Ford asked, startling her out of her reverie.

She knew he was talking about the trial, but when she answered, she was referring to her entire life, and most of all the woman who was waiting in a courtroom downstairs. "Absolutely."

❖

Lennox looked up to see Braxton stick his head in her office door. "Are they all here?" she asked.

"Yes," he said. "I've got the parents waiting upstairs and Chet and Denise together in a room on this floor. Johnny is set up in the room next door. How do you want to handle this?"

Good question and she wished she had an answer. Larabee had ordered a jury panel and the potential jurors were all standing in the hall, filling out questionnaires. In a few minutes, Larabee would take the bench and hear any last-minute pretrial motions, and then start voir dire. "Are Ford and Wren here yet?"

"They were walking into the courtroom when I came in here. I spotted Rivera talking to the judge. Think she's checking up on you?"

"Very funny." Mia often showed up whenever there was a big trial starting, partly to show any press who might be present that she was taking a personal interest in the cases her prosecutors were trying, but also to show support for her team. Lennox rarely reached out for help this close to opening statements, but she could use some advice right now and she'd been about to ask for Nina's help, but Mia would be the better choice. "Ask her if she can come talk to me and tell Lisa's parents I'll be by to talk to them soon."

"What about the other two?"

"Let them stew a bit. Did you tell them the room was soundproofed like we discussed?"

"You know it. I imagine they're in there talking up a storm."

"Great. Johnny will let us know if we need to make a move. I'll check in with you as soon as I talk to Mia."

"On it."

She watched him leave and contemplated her options. Wren had been right about the phone records. Chet and Denise called and texted with each other at four times the rate Chet had communicated with Lisa before the fire, and afterward that rate nearly doubled. At her direction, Braxton had delivered a copy of the phone records to Wren last night, but she hadn't had a chance to share several pieces of information she'd obtained this morning. According to Lisa Allen's life insurance company, Denise had been badgering them about releasing the full benefit to a trust that had been set up for Lisa and Jared's kids. Ostensibly, Denise was a concerned aunt, making sure that her niece and nephew were cared for, but Lennox had made a few calls to a clerk she knew at the civil courthouse and learned that the trust paperwork had been filed by Denise herself and she was listed as the trustee. Finally, they'd run Denise's credit report and found she was tens of thousands of dollars in debt with no discernible way of paying it off.

None of this was definitive proof of anything, but Lennox's gut told her that once Braxton did more digging, all signs would indicate Jared Allen was either a victim of circumstance or conspiracy, and that Denise and Chet were the real killers. Which is why she'd arranged to have them put in the same room with Johnny listening in next door ready to text her and Braxton if he heard anything suspicious. Her best chance of making a case against them was a confession, voluntary or accidental—she didn't care which.

When she heard the knock on her door, she called out for Mia to come in, but when the door opened it was Wren on the other side instead.

"Can we talk for a minute?"

Lennox willed Mia to take her time talking to Larabee and motioned for Wren to have a seat. "Sure." She motioned to the papers on her desk. "I've got some more discovery for you. I haven't had a chance to finish going through it, but I'll have it ready for you before we get started." *If we get started.*

Wren barely glanced at the stack of papers. "Believe it or not, I didn't come to talk to you about this case."

Lennox sat up in her chair. They were less than an hour before starting trial and she was trying to figure out if her entire case was about to blow up in her face. But none of that mattered with Wren standing in front of her, looking gorgeous in a fitted black suit and an expectant look on her face. Who had she become? She didn't know but she leaned into this hopeful version of herself. "Have a seat?"

"This is more of a standing kind of declaration."

"Oh, a declaration." Lennox smiled. "You should've led with that."

Wren smiled back at her. "I should've done a lot of things, including giving you the benefit of the doubt. From the moment we met, I thought you were judging me—for my lack of experience, for my privilege, but it turns out I was the one who made assumptions. I assumed you were short-sighted because you're so focused on your side of the equation. But that's what you're supposed to do, and I'm supposed to advocate for the other side, and justice is somewhere in the middle."

Lennox held up a hand to stop her. "I did judge you—"

Wren cut her off. "Sorry, but I really need to get through this. I was going to wait until after the trial was over to tell you all of this, but I thought you might need to hear it now. You're an excellent advocate and if I ever need someone in my corner, I'd want it to be you. If friendship is all you have to offer, I'll take it. Gladly."

Another knock sounded at her door, and Lennox barely resisted groaning at the interruption. All she wanted to do right now was digest what Wren had just said, but with a jury in the hall and trial about to start, her choices were limited. "Come in," she said, and a moment later, Mia was standing in her office. She looked back and forth between them as if she could sense something weighty was happening, and then she stuck her hand out at Wren who clasped it in her own. "Mia Rivera. I'm the district attorney."

Wren shook her hand. "Wren Bishop. Nice to meet you."

Mia turned to face Lennox. "Does she know what's going on?"

"I was about to tell her." *I was about to tell her a lot of things.* Lennox forced herself to focus on the case. She pointed at the stack of papers on her desk and, conscious Mia was paying close attention, delivered her lines. "As I mentioned, I have a few more pieces of exculpatory evidence to share with you. In addition to the phone records, we've just learned that Denise set up a trust for the kids and made herself the trustee. She's also made numerous calls to Lisa's life insurance company trying to collect on the funds. She's in major debt and it's possible she sees the insurance money as a windfall. Obviously, none of these things prove she was involved in Lisa's death, but you're entitled to this information along with the phone records that were provided to you yesterday."

Wren stared at her for a moment, looking puzzled, probably at the sudden return to formality, but with Mia in the room, Lennox regressed into her role as zealous advocate.

"We may need to ask for a continuance based on this new discovery," Mia said to Wren. "I assume you'll agree."

Wren looked at Lennox like she was trying to get a telepathic message about what was happening before she answered, but Lennox offered only a subtle shake of her head.

"No, we won't. Jared's been in jail for months and he's ready for his day in court. Any new discovery you have was likely prompted by my investigator's legwork, but the state has had ample opportunity and resources to learn everything you need to know well in advance of trial."

"Will your client take anything at this point?" Mia asked, ever the cynic. Lennox recognized the approach because it was often her own. Or at least it had been. Exculpatory evidence wasn't a hundred percent conclusive, and it was hard to admit the case you'd worked up didn't prove what you thought it did. Besides, it was a prosecutor's nightmare to dismiss a case and later find out they'd let a guilty man off the hook.

"What's your best offer?" Wren directed the question at both of them, making a point to look Lennox in the eye.

Mia took the lead. "Didn't you offer five before?"

"Wait." Lennox practically shouted the word. Wren and Mia both looked at her like she was crazy, but she pressed on. "Wren, don't say anything." She held up the papers. "I have a stack of reasonable doubt right here."

"Lennox," Mia said with definite tone. "Wren, can you step outside for a minute?"

"No," Lennox said. "Stay." Satisfied Wren wasn't going anywhere, she turned her attention to Mia. "We can dismiss the case now and have a chance to refile it later if it turns out none of this," she pointed at the discovery, "implicates Denise and Chet. But if we start this trial and jeopardy attaches, a dismissal will be permanent.

You know Larabee, he's not going to let us try Allen again if we dismiss after the jury's sworn in." She was placating her boss with words designed to convince her a dismissal was all about strategy, but deep in her heart she knew she was wavering out of an instinct for justice. She met Wren's eyes. They were brimming with compassion and confidence. Wren had said she was an excellent advocate, and if she was going to live up to that declaration, she needed to own her belief about this case and do it right out in the open.

She summoned all the fortitude she'd been saving for the trial and breathed deep. "I don't think Jared killed Lisa, and I can't in good conscience pursue this prosecution or take a plea from him under the circumstances."

The look on Mia's face told her her bid for super chief had just ended and she might be looking for another job altogether, but she didn't have time to consider the consequences because her phone started blowing up with a series of incoming texts from Johnny.

Putting these two together was genius. They're talking about what they're going to do with the insurance money. She thinks the ins co will release it after the trial.

He wants to split 50/50, but she said she should get more since she has the kids.

He won't budge. Says she's been spending that money for months and there probably won't be anything left, but he wants his fair share.

She's pissed. Thinks he almost blew it by showing up at the courthouse with the family so often. "I did the dirty work and have to raise these kids. What exactly have you done?"

"What is it?" Wren asked. "Is everything okay?"

Before she could answer, her phone pinged again with another text from Johnny.

"Holy shit, L, I think they're waling on each other. Get Braxton down here. Now!

Wren ran down the hallway determined to catch up to Lennox and not giving a damn about all of the eyes trained on them or where they were headed. Lennox was shouting into her phone but without context, she couldn't make out who she was talking to or what she hoped to accomplish. All she knew was Lennox sensed trouble and she wanted to be with her for whatever was going down. As they passed the crowd outside of Larabee's courtroom, she had a fleeting thought that he'd have to caution the jury to disregard the fact counsel for both sides had been racing through the halls before the trial started.

If the trial started. Lennox had been adamant that she didn't think this prosecution was justified. Mia could yank her off the case, but it was a little late now that she'd been present for their discussion. The question was why, after all of this time, Lennox had risked her job to argue for the other side.

They were almost at the elevator bank when Lennox turned to the right toward a set of doors that led to the hallway used by the judges and courtroom staff. Wren saw her reach for the handle just as the door flew open and into her side. Lennox staggered and Chet Evans shoved her to the ground and kept running in a straight line, directly in her path. She looked around for someone in a uniform to come to the rescue, but all she saw were potential jurors who'd paused from filling out their questionnaires to watch the show. She planted her feet firmly on the floor directly in Chet's path and crouched down. He was so intent on getting past Lennox, he barreled right into her, knocking her to the ground. He barely lost his balance and started to resume his flight, but Wren reached out, grabbed his ankle, and yanked it to the side. He toppled hard and lay still for a moment as the crowd gasped around them.

"That's him!"

Wren saw Lennox's number two, Johnny, running toward them with several bailiffs in tow. Chet rolled over and was halfway up when the trio of bailiffs converged and pushed him back to the ground. Once Chet was in cuffs, Johnny walked over and reached out his hand and pulled her to her feet.

"Are you okay?" he asked, pointing at her head. "You're bleeding."

She touched her forehead and checked her hand. Red splotches. Definitely blood. She looked down at her very dusty Prada suit and the busted heel on her Jimmy Choo's. "I'm good. Where's Lennox?" He didn't answer right away, and she pushed past him, determined to make it to where she'd last seen Lennox. It was hard walking in the broken shoe and her head was throbbing, but she had to get to Lennox and make sure she was okay.

"Ms. Bishop," Johnny called out after her. "I think you should sit down."

She ignored him and kept walking. It felt like she was in a fun house on one of those optical illusion walkways that appears to expand and recede, threatening to throw you off balance, but she trudged forward and finally she spotted Lennox, sitting, propped against the wall. She reached down and pulled off her shoes and ran toward her, again not caring who saw. A few minutes ago, she didn't know why she was running except to find out what had Lennox stirred up, but now she knew exactly why she was in a rush, and when she finally reached Lennox, she knelt down beside her and took both her hands in hers.

"Are you okay? Tell me you're okay."

The grin appeared. The one she'd missed so very much. She reached up and brushed away Lennox's hair and checked her for cuts and bruises. She had a gash on her forehead from the impact with the door, but otherwise she seemed okay and the wave of relief that flooded her senses brought tears to her eyes. And in that moment, she knew beyond a shadow of a doubt that she had to have Lennox in her life, even if all Lennox could offer was friendship. Lennox was honorable and smart and kind. She challenged her to be a better lawyer, a better person, to consider other perspectives. But most of all, despite her tough veneer, she was tender-hearted and sweet, and Wren knew what a privilege it was that Lennox had let her inside. She opened her mouth to ask if the offer of friendship was still open, but the words that tumbled out had nothing to do with friendship.

"I love you."

Lennox's grin morphed into a big fat smile. "Because I led you on a wild chase through the courthouse?"

"That and a bunch of other reasons." Wren held up her shoe. "I must love you because I really loved these shoes and look."

"Say it again."

"That I love these shoes?" Wren knew what Lennox meant, but she needed to hear the words.

"Tell me you love me."

She leaned close and whispered in Lennox's ear. "I love you. If friendship is all you want, I understand, but—"

Lennox reached for her hand and laced their fingers together. "I want more. Of course, I want more. I love you too."

Wren melted at the words and, completely oblivious to her surroundings, she started to kiss Lennox when the sound of a throat clearing startled her back to reality. Reality where she was barefoot, bruised, and bloody, sitting on the floor in the hall at the courthouse surrounded by a crowd of coworkers.

Ford was the first to speak. "You two okay?"

Wren looked down at their clasped hands. There wasn't much sense pretending they hadn't been about to kiss. Despite her battered condition, she was better than okay. She was over the moon because Lennox loved her, and nothing that happened next could take away from the exhilaration of that feeling. But when it came to answering Ford's question, she let Lennox take the lead.

"We're perfect," Lennox said, squeezing Wren's hand as she spoke. "Absolutely perfect."

CHAPTER NINETEEN

A week later…

Lennox stood in the middle of the massive kitchen and tried to envision where Wren kept her griddle. She had to have a griddle because, judging by the contents of the kitchen, she owned one of everything in stock at Bed Bath & Beyond, and Lennox imagined they carried griddles in all shapes and sizes.

"What are you up to?"

Wren reached around from behind and slid her arms around her waist. Lennox leaned back into the touch. She could feel Wren's bare legs against hers and the sensation was simultaneously sexy and homey. "Jared Allen's case gets officially dismissed today." The dismissal was a formality since Judge Larabee had released Jared on his own recognizance at her request, immediately after Chet was arrested and Denise went on the run. "I was thinking pancakes to celebrate, but I might be overstimulated by your kitchen."

"*I'm* overstimulated by my kitchen. I love housewares but hate to cook."

"You're in luck. I detest shopping for housewares, but I enjoy cooking."

"And this is why opposites attract." Wren kissed her, quick and light, and then started opening cabinet doors, finally pointing to one of the top shelves. "Behold, the griddle. Good thing you're tall.

Did I mention I love pancakes? And I love that you're helping me celebrate a dismissal."

Lennox pulled Wren into her arms. "Let's make a rule. We will always celebrate each other's victories, no matter what. And if they happen to be mutual victories, like this one, pancakes must be part of the celebration."

"I like this rule."

"Good, because I plan to celebrate with you for many years to come." She started mixing the pancake batter. "Braxton called while you were sleeping. They have a lead on Denise. Looks like she rented a car in Phoenix. The family had a cabin near Tucson, and they think she waited to let things settle down before heading that way. Probably ditched her own car on the way."

"I still can't believe she made it out of the courthouse without being caught. You'd think a grown woman running through the hall would draw attention. Oh, wait!"

Wren burst into laughter and Lennox joined her. She couldn't remember laughing this much before she'd met Wren and if she had no other reason to be grateful for their relationship, this would be enough. But there was so much more.

"Lennox."

"Yes?"

"There's something I need to tell you, and I'm a little worried you might get mad, so I've been putting it off."

Lennox paused, spatula in hand, bracing for whatever it was Wren had to say. "You better spill it. I'm not good at long buildups."

"Right. Okay." Wren took a breath and her next words poured out in a rush. "I hired Skye to investigate your brother's case."

Lennox froze at the mention of Daniel's case. She managed to set down the spatula and slowly turn to face Wren. "Why did you do that?"

"I started looking at his case because of you. To try to understand more about you, but then it turned into a passion project. To make up for Gloria's sloppy work and see if we could get some answers. Fun fact about me—I don't do well leaving unsolved puzzles alone."

"I hadn't noticed." Lennox leaned against the counter while her mind flooded with memories of fighting with Gloria who'd refused to discuss her brother's case with her and fighting with her brother who insisted Gloria knew best. She'd been cut out of the process entirely and the memory still stung. "I have one question. Why didn't you tell me?"

"You weren't speaking to me at the time. Not about anything personal. And with everything that's happened this week, I completely forgot to bring it up. Skye texted this morning to let me know she's got some leads and she'll report in when she runs them down." She reached up and wrapped her arms around Lennox's neck. "Skye's doing the leg work, but as far as review and analysis of whatever she brings in, I feel like this is something we should do together. You with your sharp prosecutorial mind and me with the insightful interrogation skills of a public defender. What do you say?"

Lennox turned the idea over in her mind, examining it from all angles. Wren had officially accepted the position at the PD's office after they'd had several long conversations about how to make it work with their burgeoning relationship. She was at peace with the decision, but was opening up and examining old wounds like her brother's case going to bring them together or drive them apart?

She flashed a recent memory of Wren standing in her office doorway, telling her she wasn't Gloria. That statement couldn't be more accurate, and it was time for her to set aside the comparisons and embrace Wren's kind, compassionate nature. Wren was smart and tough and fierce, and she couldn't ask for a better partner.

"Okay."

"Okay?"

"Okay, we'll review Daniel's case together. Top to bottom. I promise I'll be at peace with whatever we find."

Wren reached for her hand and held it tight. "We can do anything together."

"Is that our motto? Because I like it." She nodded a few times while she replayed it in her head, sounding out the perfect addition. "I'd like to make one slight change."

"Revise away."

"How about this—We can do anything. Together forever." Lennox braced for Wren's reaction, hoping she hadn't gone too far too soon, but Wren was quick to respond.

"I love it. Especially the forever part."

And they sealed the deal with a searing kiss.

THE END

About the Author

Carsen Taite's goal as an author is to spin tales with plot lines as interesting as the cases she encountered in her career as a criminal defense lawyer. She is the award-winning author of over two dozen novels of romance and romantic intrigue, including the Luca Bennett Bounty Hunter series, the Lone Star Law series, the Legal Affairs romances, and the Courting Danger series.

Books Available from Bold Strokes Books

Bury Me in Shadows by Greg Herren. College student Jake Chapman is forced to spend the summer at his dying grandmother's home and soon finds danger from long-buried family secrets. (978-1-63555-993-4)

Can't Leave Love by Kimberly Cooper Griffin. Sophia and Pru have no intention of falling in love, but sometimes love happens when and where you least expect it. (978-1-636790041-1)

Free Fall at Angel Creek by Julie Tizard. Detective Dee Rawlings and aircraft accident investigator Dr. River Dawson use conflicting methods to find answers when a plane goes missing, while overcoming surprising threats, and discovering an unlikely chance at love. (978-1-63555-884-5)

Love's Compromise by Cass Sellars. For Piper Holthaus and Brook Myers, will professional dreams and past baggage stop two hearts from realizing they are meant for each other? (978-1-63555-942-2)

Not All a Dream by Sophia Kell Hagin. Hester has lost the woman she loved and the world has descended into relentless dark and cold. But giving up will have to wait when she stumbles upon people who help her survive. (978-1-63679-067-1)

Protecting the Lady by Amanda Radley. If Eve Webb had known she'd be protecting royalty, she'd never have taken the job as bodyguard, but as the threat to Lady Katherine's life draws closer, she'll do whatever it takes to save her, and may just lose her heart in the process. (978-1-63679-003-9)

The Secrets of Willowra by Kadyan. A family saga of three women, their homestead called Willowra in the Australian outback, and the secrets that link them all. (978-1-63679-064-0)

Trial by Fire by Carsen Taite. When prosecutor Lennox Roy and public defender Wren Bishop become fierce adversaries in a headline-grabbing arson case, their attraction ignites a passion that leads them both to question their assumptions about the law, the truth, and each other. (978-1-63555-860-9)

Turbulent Waves by Ali Vali. Kai Merlin and Vivien Palmer plan their future together as hostile forces make their own plans to destroy what they have, as well as all those they love. (978-1-63679-011-4)

Unbreakable by Cari Hunter. When Dr. Grace Kendal is forced at gunpoint to help an injured woman, she is dragged into a nightmare where nothing is quite as it seems, and their lives aren't the only ones on the line. (978-1-63555-961-3)

Veterinary Surgeon by Nancy Wheelton. When dangerous drugs are stolen from the veterinary clinic, Mitch investigates and Kay becomes a suspect. As pride and professions clash, love seems impossible. (978-1-63679-043-5)

A Different Man by Andrew L. Huerta. This diverse collection of stories chronicling the challenges of gay life at various ages shines a light on the progress made and the progress still to come. (978-1-63555-977-4)

All That Remains by Sheri Lewis Wohl. Johnnie and Shantel might have to risk their lives—and their love—to stop a werewolf intent on killing. (978-1-63555-949-1)

Beginner's Bet by Fiona Riley. Phenom luxury Realtor Ellison Gamble has everything, except a family to share it with, so when a mix-up brings youthful Katie Crawford into her life, she bets the house on love. (978-1-63555-733-6)

Dangerous Without You by Lexus Grey. Throughout their senior year in high school, Aspen, Remington, Denna, and Raleigh face challenges in life and romance that they never expect. (978-1-63555-947-7)

Desiring More by Raven Sky. In this collection of steamy stories, a rich variety of lovers find themselves desiring more, more from a lover, more from themselves, and more from life. (978-1-63679-037-4)

Jordan's Kiss by Nanisi Barrett D'Arnuck. After losing everything in a fire Jordan Phelps joins a small lounge band and meets pianist Morgan Sparks, who lights another blaze, this time in Jordan's heart. (978-1-63555-980-4)

Late City Summer by Jeanette Bears. Forced together for her wedding, Emily Stanton and Kate Alessi navigate their lingering passion for one another against the backdrop of New York City and World War II, and a summer romance they left behind. (978-1-63555-968-2)

Love and Lotus Blossoms by Anne Shade. On her path to self-acceptance and true passion, Janesse will risk everything—and possibly everyone—she loves. (978-1-63555-985-9)

Love in the Limelight by Ashley Moore. Marion Hargreaves, the finest actress of her generation, and Jessica Carmichael, the world's biggest pop star, rediscover each other twenty years after an ill-fated affair. (978-1-63679-051-0)

Suspecting Her by Mary P. Burns. Complications ensue when Erin O'Connor falls for top real estate saleswoman Catherine Williams while investigating racism in the real estate industry; the fallout could end their chance at happiness. (978-1-63555-960-6)

Two Winters by Lauren Emily Whalen. A modern YA retelling of Shakespeare's *The Winter's Tale* about birth, death, Catholic school, improv comedy, and the healing nature of time. (978-1-63679-019-0)

Busy Ain't the Half of It by Frederick Smith and Chaz Lamar Cruz. Elijah and Justin seek happily-ever-afters in LA, but are they too busy to notice happiness when it's there? (978-1-63555-944-6)

Calumet by Ali Vali. Jaxon Lavigne and Iris Long had a forbidden small-town romance that didn't last, and the consequences of that love will be uncovered fifteen years later at their high school reunion. (978-1-63555-900-2)

Her Countess to Cherish by Jane Walsh. London Society's material girl realizes there is more to life than diamonds when she falls in love with a nonbinary bluestocking. (978-1-63555-902-6)

Hot Days, Heated Nights by Renee Roman. When Cole and Lee meet, instant attraction quickly flares into uncontrollable passion, but their connection might be short lived as Lee's identity is tied to her life in the city. (978-1-63555-888-3)

Never Be the Same by MA Binfield. Casey meets Olivia and sparks fly in this opposites attract romance that proves love can be found in the unlikeliest places. (978-1-63555-938-5)

Quiet Village by Eden Darry. Something not quite human is stalking Collie and her niece, and she'll be forced to work with undercover reporter Emily Lassiter if they want to get out of Hyam alive. (978-1-63555-898-2)

Shaken or Stirred by Georgia Beers. Bar owner Julia Martini and home health aide Savannah McNally attempt to weather the storms brought on by a mysterious blogger trashing the bar, family feuds they knew nothing about, and way too much advice from way too many relatives. (978-1-63555-928-6)

The Fiend in the Fog by Jess Faraday. Can four people on different trajectories work together to save the vulnerable residents of East London from the terrifying fiend in the fog before it's too late? (978-1-63555-514-1)

The Marriage Masquerade by Toni Logan. A no strings attached marriage scheme to inherit a Maui B&B uncovers unexpected attractions and a dark family secret. (978-1-63555-914-9)

Flight SQA016 by Amanda Radley. Fastidious airline passenger Olivia Lewis is used to things being a certain way. When her routine is changed by a new, attractive member of the staff, sparks fly. (978-1-63679-045-9)

Home Is Where the Heart Is by Jenny Frame. Can Archie make the countryside her home and give Ash the fairytale romance she desires? Or will the countryside and small village life all be too much for her? (978-1-63555-922-4)

Moving Forward by PJ Trebelhorn. The last person Shelby Ryan expects to be attracted to is Iris Calhoun, the sister of the man who killed her wife four years and three thousand miles ago. (978-1-63555-953-8)

Poison Pen by Jean Copeland. Debut author Kendra Blake is finally living her best life until a nasty book review and exposed secrets threaten her promising new romance with aspiring journalist Alison Chatterley. (978-1-63555-849-4)

Seasons for Change by KC Richardson. Love, laughter, and trust develop for Shawn and Morgan throughout the changing seasons of Lake Tahoe. (978-1-63555-882-1)

Summer Lovin' by Julie Cannon. Three different women, three exotic locations, one unforgettable summer. What do you think will happen? (978-1-63555-920-0)

Unbridled by D. Jackson Leigh. A visit to a local stable turns into more than riding lessons between a novel writer and an equestrian with a taste for power play. (978-1-63555-847-0)

VIP by Jackie D. In a town where relationships are forged and shattered by perception, sometimes even love can't change who you really are. (978-1-63555-908-8)

Yearning by Gun Brooke. The sleepy town of Dennamore has an irresistible pull on those who've moved away. The mystery Darian Benson and Samantha Pike uncover will change them forever, but the love they find along the way just might be the key to saving themselves. (978-1-63555-757-2)

A Turn of Fate by Ronica Black. Will Nev and Kinsley finally face their painful past and relent to their powerful, forbidden attraction? Or will facing their past be too much to fight through? (978-1-63555-930-9)

Desires After Dark by MJ Williamz. When her human lover falls deathly ill, Alex, a vampire, must decide which is worse, letting her go or condemning her to everlasting life. (978-1-63555-940-8)

Her Consigliere by Carsen Taite. FBI agent Royal Scott swore an oath to uphold the law, and criminal defense attorney Siobhan Collins pledged her loyalty to the only family she's ever known, but will their love be stronger than the bonds they've vowed to others, or will their competing allegiances tear them apart? (978-1-63555-924-8)

In Our Words: Queer Stories from Black, Indigenous, and People of Color Writers. Stories selected by Anne Shade and edited by Victoria Villaseñor. Comprising both the renowned and emerging voices of Black, Indigenous, and People of Color authors, this thoughtfully curated collection of short stories explores the intersection of racial and queer identity. (978-1-63555-936-1)

Measure of Devotion by CF Frizzell. Disguised as her late twin brother, Catherine Samson enters the Civil War to defend the Constitution as a Union soldier, never expecting her life to be altered by a Gettysburg farmer's daughter. (978-1-63555-951-4)

Not Guilty by Brit Ryder. Claire Weaver and Emery Pearson's day jobs clash, even as their desire for each other burns, and a discreet sex-only arrangement is the only option. (978-1-63555-896-8)

Opposites Attract: Butch/Femme Romances by Meghan O'Brien, Aurora Rey, Angie Williams. Sometimes opposites really do attract. Fall in love with these butch/femme romance novellas. (978-1-63555-784-8)

Swift Vengeance by Jean Copeland, Jackie D, Erin Zak. A journalist becomes the subject of her own investigation when sudden strange, violent visions summon her to a summer retreat and into the arms of a killer's possible next victim. (978-1-63555-880-7)

Under Her Influence by Amanda Radley. On their path to #truelove, will Beth and Jemma discover that reality is even better than illusion? (978-1-63555-963-7)

Wasteland by Kristin Keppler & Allisa Bahney. Danielle Clark is fighting against the National Armed Forces and finds peace as a scavenger, until the NAF general's daughter, Katelyn Turner, shows up on her doorstep and brings the fight right back to her. (978-1-63555-935-4)

When in Doubt by VK Powell. Police officer Jeri Wylder thinks she committed a crime in the line of duty but can't remember, until details emerge pointing to a cover-up by those close to her. (978-1-63555-955-2)